NO EXTRA LIVES

BROKEN CIRCLE DUOLOGY
BOOK ONE

DAN BLAKELY

To my mother—
I remember for both of us now.

Arbelon
Veilspire
Wastelands
Wayfe
Salile
Thessian Sea
Comstock
Trosten
Asmenson

ountains
Devendor
The Great
Forest
Veydris
Elderwin
Skypeach Divide
Swain

WELCOME TO ARBELON

Shadows twisted unnaturally in the fading light, and the forest held its secrets just out of reach. Thane ducked under a low branch, breath ragged, his feet skidding on brittle leaves. Behind him, the snap of breaking twigs and a guttural growl sent a chill creeping down his spine.

It was too close, and gaining.

His heart pounded with his footfalls, each step heavier than the last as a clearing loomed ahead—a beacon and a taunt. But whatever the hell that thing was chasing him, it wasn't slowing down.

It was too big, too fast—especially for a newbie.

The forest pressed in around him, its twisted shadows clawing at the edges of his vision. He'd been pushing hard, and his legs screamed for rest, warning him he couldn't keep this pace much longer. *What's the point of running?* Each breath came shallower. *Because giving up still felt worse.*

The clearing ahead glimmered faintly, like the path had been laid out just for him.

There was no other way.

He gritted his teeth, willing himself onward, uncertain if he was being herded to the clearing or called by it.

"Fantastic," he muttered. "Five minutes in, and I'm already a goner. Great design."

Out of the darkness behind him, an ear-piercing roar erupted, even closer than before, shaking loose the last leaves clinging to the branches. There was no point in looking back, only forward—every step felt like borrowed time.

Lunging forward, he jumped a fallen tree trunk. He landed unsteady and risked a glance back. Yellowed eyes glared from the shadows, fixed on him. The beast tore through the underbrush as if it didn't exist, its growl vibrating the air like a physical force.

This thing is completely broken! It's on me, like it knows my next move before I do!

His gut tightened, his breath hitching as he pushed harder, the faint flicker of light ahead was his only hope of escape.

Move, you invalid!

But his body refused—something he knew too well.

With his last ounce of energy, he forced himself forward, but his foot snagged on a root buried beneath the leaves. In the next instant, the ground slammed the air from his lungs. Pain flared through his wrist—sharp, unforgiving.

Panic surged, his thoughts racing faster than his body could respond. Gasping, he twisted onto his back, dirt clinging to his hands as his eyes shot upward.

The beast emerged from the trees with a low snarl, its jagged maw dripping with saliva, its breath reeking of decay. Claws clicked and glinted faintly in the dim light— each one sharp, curved, and far too close.

The beast lunged, a blur of shadow and fury, its claws slicing through the air.

Thane rolled, but wasn't fast enough.

Pain ripped through his side, sharp and searing, and he cried out, his hand clutching at the burning line where the beast's talons had raked him. Warmth spread beneath his fingers, sticky and hot, as blood soaked through his shirt. His breaths came in shallow gasps, his body screaming for relief. He gritted his teeth and tried to push up, but his arms shook under the effort as the beast's snarl reverberated through the forest like a death knell.

His body tensed, bracing for the end as he squeezed his eyes shut. *Why do I even care if I make it out of this? Alive or dead, what difference does it make?* But instead of a final blow, something inside him surged—a raw, chaotic force demanding release.

The ground pulsed beneath him with unseen power, a sudden heat bloomed in his chest, the surrounding air rippled and bent, like water struck by a stone. Before he could comprehend it, the force erupted like a lightning strike—jagged and blinding, scattering shards of light and energy in every direction. He felt it tear through him, wild and unbidden, as if his body had become a conduit for something far beyond his grasp.

The air twisted violently around the beast, hurling it into the trees with a deafening crash. It stumbled, claws flailing, then turned. Its eyes—once predatory—were wide with terror. With a guttural screech, it dragged its shattered form back into the shadows of the woods.

Thane blinked, his vision swimming, the energy draining from his body as quickly as it came, leaving him breathless. His hands trembled. The air still crackling faintly with an unnatural energy that made his skin crawl.

His gaze lingered on the trees where the beast had

retreated, its trail of blackened blood marking the forest floor. Against all odds, he'd survived.

"That was… unexpected," he muttered bitterly, collapsing back into the dirt. Each breath clawed at his chest, sharp and ragged, his body felt like lead, too battered to move.

The light ahead seemed almost mocking now, taunting him with the promise of salvation he wasn't sure he wanted or deserved. Darkness pressed at the edges of his vision, but he forced his eyes open. His mind churned with bitter thoughts, the sting of failure twisting with the lingering heat of whatever had just happened to him. For a moment, he lay still, wondering why he'd bothered fighting so hard to survive.

The sound of hurried footsteps broke the silence, distant voices calling out—echoing, and strangely warm.

He flinched instinctively as hands gently lifted him from the dirt. The faces above him blurred, yet one caught his attention—a young woman with piercing green eyes that seemed too bright in the fading light, her hair shimmering like spun gold. Her lips moved, saying something soft and urgent, her voice cutting through the haze, oddly distinct.

He let out a faint, bitter laugh, his voice hoarse. "You should just leave me. I'm dead already."

But they didn't leave him.

The villagers steadied his battered form, pressing tightly against his wound as they guided him toward the clearing ahead. As they moved, lantern light flickered through the trees, revealing a cluster of cottages with steeply slanted roofs forming a tight-knit circle. Their windows glowed warmly against the encroaching twilight, smoke curling from chimneys and the faintly sweet scents of baked bread and drying herbs mingling in the air. The village had a fairy book charm, quaint and serene—but Thane barely noticed. His vision swimming with each jostling step.

"Careful," a gruff voice muttered. "He's bleeding badly."

An older man in tattered brown robes rushed from one of the cottages to meet the group as they entered the village. "What under Arbelon's watch happened out there?" he asked, his voice sharp with alarm.

The girl with the green eyes stepped forward. "It was… wild magic," she said, her voice catching as if the words were too heavy.

The older man froze, his eyes narrowing as the words hung in the air. His hand moved instinctively to the small pendant around his neck, clutching it as if for protection.

"Wild magic?" he repeated, his voice dropping to a hushed tone, equal parts disbelief and unease. His gaze shifted sharply to Thane, scrutinizing him as though he were a puzzle with missing pieces. "Are you certain?"

The girl nodded solemnly. "I saw it myself."

Hushed whispers rippled among the villagers, curiosity and concern coloring their tones. A few hung back, their expressions wary, while others leaned closer, eyes wide with wonder. A woman clutched a charm at her neck, whispering a hurried prayer. A man knelt, closing his eyes, muttering something under his breath, while another stared at Thane with wide-eyed awe. Murmured words like "blessing" and "omen" slipped past his ears, blurring into static drowned by the pain pulsing through his side.

Whatever reverence they thought he deserved, Thane couldn't have cared less. Let them cling to their omens and blessings. It wouldn't change a thing.

The older man hesitated, glancing between Thane and the girl, as if weighing the truth of her words. His grip on the pendant tightened briefly before he took a steadying breath and leaned down to inspect the wound, his brow furrowing. Straightening, he placed a firm hand on Thane's shoulder.

"You're hurt—badly. You need healing," he said before turning to the others. "Bring him to the Sanctuary. If what she says is true, we may need the power of the Heart."

The arms around him tightened to usher him forward, but Thane thrashed weakly, pushing them aside.

"Thanks, I'll just walk it off," he rasped, his voice cutting through the crisp night air. His legs gave out almost immediately, and he stumbled to his knees, clutching at the deep wounds on his side.

He let out a bitter laugh. "Or never mind—bleeding out works too."

"Not on my watch," the older man said, stepping forward and catching Thane as he crumpled to the ground. "Quickly, to the Sanctuary," he commanded, his voice ringing with resounding authority.

The villagers responded immediately, moving with coordinated urgency. Thane barely registered the murmurs around him, his thoughts clouded by searing pain and exhaustion. Hands lifted him roughly onto a cart, the motion jarring his wounds, dragging a groan from his lips. He tried again to push them away, but his limbs felt like lead, refusing his commands.

The wheels creaked as the cart began to roll, each bump stabbing through his side. Thane let his head slump back, glaring weakly at the canopy of trees and blurred rooflines above.

They should've left me.

Bitterness curled in his chest as the cart jostled forward. The weight of their hands, the unspoken hope in their eyes —it all felt heavier than his wounds.

Hope was crueler than indifference.

His head thudded lightly against the cart as it jostled forward, every bump dragging him further into exhaustion. The older man leaned close, his voice low but urgent.

"We're close," he said, gripping the side of the cart for balance.

Lanterns swayed from wooden poles mounted to the cart, their light casting trembling shadows along the path. The cart rolled to a stop on a stone veranda bathed in silver light. At its center stood a structure unlike anything Thane had ever seen—an amalgamation of carved stone and living wood. Towering spires rose at either end, their surfaces entwined with branches glimmering faintly, as though kissed by starlight. A similar light spilled through crystalline windows, dappling the ground in fractured colors.

The air hummed faintly, its energy prickling at Thane's skin, too tangible to ignore. He took it all in, a hollow chuckle escaping his lips. *Should've seen that coming. Starlight and spires—of course.* His sarcasm clinging to the edges of his fatigue.

The older man jumped from the cart with surprising agility, landing with a soft thud that barely registered to Thane. "Get him inside," he commanded.

Two villagers hurried to either side of the cart, their hands trembling slightly as they lifted Thane carefully, their faces etched with a mix of fear and reverence. The cool air of the Sanctuary hit him like a splash of water, its tingling energy crawling over his skin as they carried him toward the doorway.

The interior of the Sanctuary was a blend of ancient and ethereal. Vines traced across the walls, their silvery glow pulsing gently, as though carrying the lifeblood of the Sanctuary itself. At the chamber's center, a shimmering pool of liquid starlight stood still, its surface smooth as glass. The roots of the Sanctuary's great tree dipped into the pool, their bark glinting as if infused with its power.

As the villagers carried Thane into the chamber, the pool rippled softly, sending waves of fractured silver light dancing across the chamber walls. Its glow seemed to ebb and flow in time with the soft hum that filled the air, a hum that Thane could feel resonating faintly in his chest.

At the far end, a raised platform of tightly woven branches and vines gleamed with a metallic sheen, its light echoing the pool's glow. The pool itself was no ordinary reservoir—it was a conduit, its energy drawn from the distant but ever-present Heart of Arbelon.

For a fleeting moment, Thane's breath hitched, the strange energy both soothing and deeply unnerving, as though the Sanctuary was watching him. He forced his gaze away, focusing instead on the sharp pulse of pain in his side.

The villagers laid Thane on the raised platform. The older man leaned over him, murmuring softly under his breath, his hands hovering just above Thane's wounds. The glow of the vines woven into the platform seemed to intensify, as though responding to the man's whispered words.

A warmth spread through Thane's side, dulling the sharp pain, but it felt wrong—too intimate, too caring— and he hated it. Hated how it dulled the pain, hated how it made him feel tethered to them.

He didn't want their empathy—he'd come here to escape that.

Turning, he shook it off, forcing his thoughts back to the ache in his side.

"He's not responding," one of the villagers muttered anxiously, glancing between Thane and the older man.

The older man shook his head. "Give it time. The Heart's magic doesn't always work as we expect." His voice held an edge of doubt, though he tried to mask it.

Thane's lips twitched in a bitter smirk. "Don't worry," he rasped. "I'll try to make it to the next save point."

The girl with the green eyes had followed them inside, standing at a distance, her expression unreadable. When Thane's gaze flicked to her, something in her intensity struck him, but he forced himself to look away. She stepped forward, her voice steady despite the tension in the air.

"The Heart… it reacted when we brought him here," she said, her voice faltering as though she feared the weight of her words. "I saw it—surely you did too."

The older man's head snapped up, his eyes narrowing as they fixed on the Heart's pulsing glow. "There will be time for such talk later," he said, though his gaze lingered on the silvery pool. "Now, we focus on saving him."

"But…" she began, stepping closer, her voice dropping to a whisper. "Could it be him? The prophecy?"

Thane let out a sharp breath, the words cutting through his haze of pain. *Starlight, spires, and now a prophecy. They're really leaning into the classics here.* His gaze flicked to the pool, its glow almost mocking. *They're waiting for a savior. Instead, they got me.*

He closed his eyes, the warmth of the platform pulling him into a haze he didn't want to leave.

"Not now, Lirien," the old man said, cutting her off before turning back to Thane. His voice dropped to a low chant, his words curling like smoke in the air as his hands once again hovered over Thane's wounds. The glow of the vines pulsed brighter, bathing the platform in an eerie light that seemed to breathe with the rhythm of his murmurs.

The light ebbed and flowed in tandem with the pool's pulsing glow, their rhythms gradually syncing.

A faint, shimmering rune surfaced on the platform, its outline glowing brighter as though drawn from the pool's energy. The rune pulsed faintly beneath him, its lines spiraling inward before breaking apart into a jagged, incomplete circle. Whispers erupted from the villagers, their reverent awe filling the chamber as the old man turned to see the rune mirrored in the woven vines on the chamber walls.

"It's the mark," someone murmured, their voice trembling. Their voices rose like a prayer, soft and reverent. Thane's stomach twisted, the weight of their belief pressing against him like a stone. They didn't know him. Didn't know how wrong they were.

The old man's face grew tight, his gaze fixed on the glowing runes before turning slowly to Lirien. "The Broken Circle…" he said, his voice heavy with wonder and dread. His fingers brushed Thane's arm, as though confirming he was truly there.

"It's him," Lirien said, her voice a mixture of hope and excitement, her eyes fixed on Thane. "The Sanctuary knew it, and now the Heart confirms it. He can save Arbelon!"

The light erupted with one last pulse, and Thane opened his eyes. The exhaustion was gone. Looking down at his side, he saw the wound had closed, leaving only a jagged scar behind.

"It calls to him," the old man murmured, dropping to his knees, tears glinting in his eyes. "The prophecy speaks true—the Chosen One has come."

Thane let out a sharp breath, the words cutting through his haze of pain. *Right. Chosen One. Like I haven't heard that one before.* He let out a dry snort. *Nothing screams 'savior' like a guy who can't save himself.* They clearly didn't realize it yet, but he wasn't here to save them or be their golden boy. This wasn't destiny—it was a distraction, a way to kill time. And the sooner they figured that out, the better.

"Believe whatever you want," Thane muttered, forcing himself to sit up. "It doesn't make it real."

"You talk like none of this matters," Lirien said, her voice soft, searching for answers.

Thane's smirk faltered for the briefest moment, but he looked away before she could see the crack.

Over Lirien's shoulder, a section of the pool's edge shimmered strangely, the smooth curve breaking into jagged, pixelated angles before snapping back to normal. He blinked, the moment so fleeting it could've been a trick of the light. But something about it gnawed at him. *This place is barely holding together.* He chuckled, dry and quiet, and looked back at Lirien. "Like I said, believe whatever you want."

Lirien stepped closer, her voice unwavering now despite the tremor in her hands. "You can pretend it's nothing," she said, her green eyes piercing through him. "But this world sees you. Whether you like it or not."

The priest rose, his mouth open to speak, but a voice he knew all too well sliced through the air.

Thane's time was up.

For a moment, he lingered, fingers brushing the faint warmth of the platform. The light of the Sanctuary felt like it had soaked into his skin, a faint hum still vibrating in his chest. It was warm, even inviting.

"Thane! Take off that headset!" The sharp edge of his mother's voice dragged him back.

The warmth of the Sanctuary evaporated as the band

of the VR headset scraped against his forehead. He pulled it free, leaving a faint, clammy imprint.

His bedroom felt colder than it had any right to be, the fluorescent light buzzing overhead, harsh and unrelenting. The weight of his room—too real, too plain—settled around him like a suffocating blanket.

"Thane," his mother's voice called again, softer now but no less insistent. "Come on, sweetie. The doctor's here."

He swung his legs over the edge of the bed, his gaze flicking to the game interface still lingering on the monitor.

Sanctuary Sequence Complete.
Achievement Unlocked.

The words blinked once with a subtle chime, then disappeared. His reflection stared back at him, hollow-eyed and pale, the faint glow of the monitor highlighting every fragile angle.

"Chosen One?" He snorted bitterly. If they knew the truth, they'd have picked someone else.

"Yeah… I'm coming," he muttered, his voice flat as he pushed himself to his feet. The soft hum of the Sanctuary gave way to the whir of his computer's cooling fan, the faint floral scents of Arbelon replaced by the flat, stale air of his room.

As he stepped toward the door, his hand lingered on the frame. For just a second, he let himself wonder what it would feel like to be unbroken—whole. The thought passed as quickly as it came, leaving him cold. With a quiet exhale, he stepped back into reality.

This is all there is. No glowing runes. No whispered prophecies —just doctors and countdowns.

2

HOUSE CALL

THANE LEANED against the hallway wall, earbuds limp around his neck, listening to the muffled voices in the living room. His mom's tone was the first thing he caught—tight and stretched thin, like it might snap at any moment. "We just need to understand what to expect," she said, the words carefully controlled, like they might crack if handled too roughly.

Dr. Hughes's voice came steady, measured. "Every case progresses differently, but… the trajectory does tend to be consistent."

The pause that followed hung in the air, loaded with what wasn't being said.

His mom cleared her throat, breaking the silence with a performative cheer. "Well, we're, uh, optimistic. That's gotta help, right?"

Thane rolled his eyes. *Optimistic.* The word landed like a slap. He pulled his hood tighter around his face and shoved himself off the wall. The ache in his chest was already there, a dull, familiar pressure.

Might as well get this over with.

He shuffled into the living room, his feet dragging just enough to make his reluctance obvious. The air felt oddly thick, like he'd stepped into a place where time stretched differently—too slow, yet somehow slipping past too fast. Maybe it was just the exhaustion. Maybe it was something else.

His mom's eyes snapped to him immediately, her face brightening with a smile so forced and fragile it hurt to see her like this.

"Thane! Come join us. The doctor's been going over some things," she said, patting the seat next to her with a smile, trying so hard to keep it together. Problem is, smiling won't make any of this better.

He stood in the doorway, his hands jammed into his pockets, making it clear that he wanted to by anywhere but here.

"Yeah, I figured. Hard not to hear the topic's me," he muttered.

Dr. Hughes turned to face him, his smile a professional mix of warmth and gravity. He was in his late forties, neatly dressed, with a calm demeanor that suggested he'd had this exact conversation numerous times before.

"Thanks for joining us, Thane," he said politely.

Thane's gaze swept the room as he shuffled to the couch next to his mother, dropping into it with exaggerated heaviness. The living room looked unnaturally clean, like his mom had scrubbed and straightened it within an inch of its life. The air smelled faintly of lemon cleaner—sharp and sterile. On the coffee table sat a stack of medical pamphlets, their edges curled from over-handling. One of them, face-up, displayed the headline *Managing Degenerative Conditions: What to Expect.* Thane snorted softly at the irony.

The sunlight streaming through the windows felt muted, its usual warmth dulled by the weight of the moment, almost as if the weather itself knew what this meeting was about. His mom sat on the couch, clutching a folder of his medical records so tightly her knuckles were white.

Thane slouched deeper, arms crossed tight across his chest.

"So, what's new Doc," he muttered, his voice low but cutting.

His mom's smile faltered, but she quickly masked it with a cheery tone. "We're just trying to get as much information as we can, honey. You know, so we can… be prepared."

Dr. Hughes gave a small nod, adjusting the notebook on his lap. "That's right. It's important we're all on the same page moving forward."

His gaze shifted to Thane, calm but probing.

"How are you feeling about everything so far?"

Thane's smirk was sharp, almost bitter. "Oh, you know. Living the dream," he said, leaning back further in his seat. He pointed vaguely at the pamphlets on the coffee table. "'What to expect?' Really great read. You should pitch it to a book club."

The silence that followed was heavy, broken only by the faint hum of the refrigerator in the kitchen. His mom's fingers tightened even further on the folder. Dr. Hughes didn't react immediately, his composed expression unshaken, professional and expectant.

"I know this isn't easy," Dr. Hughes said gently, his tone careful. "But I'm here to help you understand what's ahead and how we can manage things as best as possible."

This is it. The big "sorry about your future" speech. Thane let the words hang in the air for a moment before letting out a soft, humorless laugh, earning a glance from his mom.

"Manage things. Sure," Thane snarked.

The tension in the room pressed down like a lead weight. The lemon-cleaner smell felt sharper now, mingling with the stale undercurrent of dread that no amount of scrubbing could erase. Doctors were great at making things sound hopeful while quietly confirming you're screwed.

"Go ahead," Thane continued, breaking the silence. "Give me the highlights. Or is this the part where we all pretend there's still some big breakthrough coming to save the day?"

"Thane!" his mom said. "That's not fair. He's just trying to help."

"No, it's quite alright, Jane," Dr. Hughes said, exhaling slowly, clasping his hands together. His calm demeanor didn't waver, but the pause between his words hinted at a weight he rarely allowed himself to show. "I know how hard you're working to support him. And Thane," he said, turning to face him directly, "I know you don't want to be here, but it's my job to make sure you both have the full picture."

The words settled like a stone in Thane's gut. He looked away, focusing on the sharp edge of the coffee table. *Full picture?* He already knew how this ended.

Dr. Hughes adjusted the notebook on his lap and leaned forward, his practiced, professional smile firmly in place. His presence was calm, methodical, the kind of steadiness designed to put patients at ease. Hearing no objections this time, he continued, his calm voice filling the room as Jane's fleeting glance at Thane betrayed a quiet, desperate worry.

"We've been reviewing the latest data," he began, his tone careful. "And I want to start with some encouraging news. There are experimental therapies we're exploring—

new treatments that show some exciting possibilities for slowing disease progression."

Thane tilted his head, his smirk sharp as he leaned back in his seat. "New treatments? That's just a fancy way of saying you're still throwing darts at the wall and hoping something sticks, isn't it?"

His mom tensed further, if that was possible, but she stayed quiet, her forced smile faltering slightly.

"It's not a cure," Dr. Hughes admitted, keeping his tone even. "But the goal is to give you more time. Better time."

Thane's laugh was short and humorless. "More time for what? To forget my name? To need help tying my shoes?"

His mom flinched openly at the words but pressed her lips together, refusing to respond. Dr. Hughes, unfazed, leaned forward slightly, signaling with a small gesture to Jane that he was fine continuing.

"I get it, Thane. It's frustrating, and it's not a guarantee—"

"No kidding, it's not a guarantee," Thane interrupted. "Let me guess. Next step is turning me into a science project again, right? Hook me up to more machines so you can 'manage' me?"

His mom's eyes flicked to Dr. Hughes, her hope barely masked by a growing unease. "Thane," she began, her voice tinged with sweetness, laced in urgency. "I know it's not ideal. But if it helps—even a little…"

Thane cut her off with a sharp shake of his head. "It won't, Mom. You know it, I know it, and I'm pretty sure Dr. Hughes knows it, too. But hey, let's keep pretending, right? That's what this is all about."

Dr. Hughes paused, a flicker of empathy breaking through his professional facade. "I understand this feels overwhelming," he said carefully, "but we have to focus on what might be possible."

Thane's smirk faded, replaced by a colder expression. "So that's what we're down to, huh? Blind hope? That's a great pitch, Doc."

Dr. Hughes exhaled, his shoulders settling slightly as he set his notebook down on the coffee table. "Thane, I know it's hard to hold on to optimism in a situation like this, but…"

"Don't," Thane interrupted sharply. "Don't say it. Optimism's just lying to yourself because you can't handle the truth. And I don't do lies."

His mom's gaze dropped to her lap, a tear dropping from her eye. It landed on the red folder, blooming like spilled ink. Her grip faltered, and the folder slipped slightly from her lap, as though even it couldn't hold together under the weight of his words. She turned to her son. "Thane," she whispered, her voice cracking. "Please. Don't do this. Don't shut us out."

Dr. Hughes's voice softened, his tone dipping into something more honest as he reached out, grasping Jane's hand. "We're doing everything we can to manage this," he said, "but we're not changing the outcome. I wish I could tell you something different. I really do. But our focus is on giving Thane as much quality time as possible."

Thane's frustration simmered beneath the surface as the words hit home. His hand trembled slightly in his lap, the motion catching his eye. He clenched his fist against his knee, trying to will the tremor away, but the effort only deepened his anger.

When he opened his mouth to respond, his voice faltered, the slight slur cutting through his bitterness. He stopped short, clearing his throat sharply to cover the stumble.

Not here. Don't crack here.

Dr. Hughes leaned forward, his hands clasped tightly. The practiced warmth in his expression was gone, replaced by something heavier—unflinching honesty.

"We need to talk about the progression," he said, his voice steady, but heavy. "Creutzfeldt-Jakob Disease doesn't slow. The progression is inevitable."

Dr. Hughes shifted in his chair, releasing his hands into his lap. When he spoke, his voice was quieter, sober, as if the words themselves carried too much weight. "This isn't about *if*, Thane. It's about *when*."

The words hung in the air, heavy and unyielding.

They'd all known it—of course they had. But hearing it said aloud hit like a hammer, shattering any illusions they'd been holding on to.

His mom's quiet sob broke the stillness, her shoulders shaking as she tried to contain it.

It cut through him, sharper than he'd expected.

He didn't turn to look—he couldn't. He wanted to say something, anything, but all that came out was the bitterness. Thane stiffened, his jaw clenching as he stared at the coffee table. His throat tightened, his chest constricting as the words carved into him.

There it is. The truth he already knew, laid bare.

No sugarcoating.

No pretending.

The room seemed smaller now, its corners closing in on him. He let out a sharp, hollow laugh, the sound breaking the silence like shattered glass.

"So that's it?" he said, his voice brittle. "That's your big reveal? Real groundbreaking stuff, Doc. Glad you came all the way here to confirm what we already knew."

He stood abruptly, his feet scraping loudly against the floor. He needed to get out of this room, out of this moment. Anywhere else would be better—Arbelon would be better. His hands trembled, and he shoved them into his hoodie pockets, clenching them into fists to hide the shaking. *Weakness is the one thing I won't let them see. I can't let them see me break.*

"You can't fix this," he said coldly. "You can't fix me. So stop pretending any of this is for me."

"Thane, please," his mom said, her voice wavering. "We're not giving up on you. I can't. I won't. You're still my son, and I'll keep fighting for you—even if you've already given up."

For a moment, he almost let her have it. Almost told her what she wanted to hear—just to make that look on her face go away. But what was the point? It wouldn't change anything.

Thane met her gaze, his voice low and cutting. "You need that hope," he said. "I don't. I know exactly where this ends, and it doesn't get better."

As soon as the words left his mouth, he wanted to take them back—but it was too late. The look on her face said everything. It felt like he'd stolen something she needed, something fragile she'd fought to hold on to. Her hope was delicate, and he'd just shattered it.

Worse still was the bitter truth he couldn't ignore—that part of him had wanted to do it. Because hope was cruel. Hope made it hurt more. So instead of apologizing, he pressed on, doubling down.

Dr. Hughes started to respond, but Thane cut him off with a grim smile. "Death," he said. "It ends in death. Can we stop pretending it's anything else?"

Thane stalked out, shoulders stiff, pace fast.

His mom called after him, her voice cracking. He knew he was leaving her behind, that his words had cut too deep this time. But the weight in his chest made it impossible to stay. He couldn't face it—couldn't face her.

In his room, he closed the door quietly and leaned against it, his breath coming fast and shallow. His eyes fell on the VR headset sitting on his desk, the bluish light of its broken circle logo a beacon in the darkness.

That's me. Fractured. Everything I was—gone. But at least in there… at least in Arbelon, I can pretend I'm still whole.

He grabbed the headset. He hated how much he needed it. But escape was all he had left. At least in Arbelon, he could forget for a while. Pretend he hadn't already lost everything. His eyes lingered on the broken circle, its edges jagged and incomplete. It reminded him of something, though he couldn't place it—something distant, like a memory just out of reach.

His fingers trembled as he adjusted the strap, the cool plastic settling over his face like a mask. The outside world faded into shadow, its edges blurring until there was nothing left. The faint hum of the headset filled the silence, drowning out the muffled sounds of his room. From the dim light of his room, the broken circle glowed for a moment longer, then slowly faded away—fractured, incomplete, but still holding on.

Just like him.

Then the last traces of light disappeared, the darkness swallowed him whole.

3

—————

ALL GOOD THINGS...

Darkness.

The lingering hum of the VR headset faded into silence, leaving Thane suspended in the void. But the stillness wasn't empty—it was oppressive, an inescapable weight pressing down on every corner of his life. His breathing felt distant, shallow, his pulse an uneven rhythm echoing in his ears.

Then, in a flash, the darkness began to dissipate, faint sparks of light darting in and out of his peripheral vision. Cracks split the void, jagged and unrelenting—dragging him forward whether he wanted it or not.

And suddenly, there he was.

The hum of Arbelon's magic struck him like a live wire—melodic, but too sharp, too alive after the oppressive silence of the void. It thrummed deep in his chest, an alien pulse that refused to sync with his own.

His vision sharpened quickly, the Sanctuary coming into focus. The glow of the runes burned brighter after the void, the air heavy with the scent of incense and an almost palpable energy that seemed to pulse from the stone walls themselves.

He stood exactly where he had left, the vines tracing across the walls with a soft glow. For a moment, the serenity of the place seemed to envelop him like a blanket.

But something felt off.

The ground beneath him seemed to hum faintly, a subtle vibration just at the edge of perception, alive and restless. The light from the walls flickered—imperceptibly at first, then enough to make the room feel like it was holding its breath, waiting.

His stomach churned, his balance faltering as though the ground beneath him had shifted. The disorientation settled in deep, feeding the unease already curling in his chest. He shook his head, trying to clear the feeling, but it clung tight. The silence wasn't silent, and the calm felt like a lie. He raised a hand to his temple, gritting his teeth as the storm inside him swelled, threatening to break free.

"Chosen One."

The voice broke through his haze, calm and even.

Thane turned, blinking to refocus. *Chosen One? Fuck that.* He was only chosen for one thing—dying. Dr. Hughes had just made that crystal clear. So if he was going to burn out, he'd make damn sure he wasn't the only one taken to ashes. *He'd give them a prophecy to remember.*

The priest who had healed him was already watching, rising slowly from where he had been kneeling. His movements were careful, measured. His face was lined with wisdom—or maybe just time—but his gaze held the weight of expectation.

"You carry a heavy burden," the priest said, his voice reverent but measured. "Peace comes when you stop fighting the inevitable."

Thane's breath slowed, his body going rigid. The words slammed into him, ringing with the same quiet, practiced finality of Dr. Hughes—of his mother's exhausted smile—of every empty reassurance that he was supposed to accept his fate like a good little patient. Even here, his disease was inevitable. It was inescapable, written in the way people looked at him, spoke to him. It clung to his ribs like a sickness, poisoning his every thought before he could shake it loose.

"Right. I'll make sure they put that on my gravestone," Thane muttered, his voice thick with sarcasm. Like he hadn't heard the same empty bullshit a thousand times before. He refused to look at the priest. He hated the way people in Arbelon spoke, like their words could change anything.

Fine. If this world wanted their Chosen One, he'd make sure he was one they'd never forget.

The thought settled in his chest like a stone. Heavy and final. A slow breath pulled through his teeth, but it didn't cool the heat crawling up his spine. He could still feel the priest's gaze, waiting, expecting. It made his skin crawl.

Out of the corner of his eye, he caught movement—Lirien. Studying him intently.

He set his jaw, forcing himself not to react, but the weight of her gaze pressed against him, unwelcome and unrelenting. He didn't need another set of eyes crawling over him, another reminder that he was always under a microscope. The tension from their last exchange lingered, and he made a point not to look at her for long.

Instead, his gaze was pulled to the low altar behind him, where the priest had prayed over him. He wasn't sure why—he just knew he couldn't look away. Something about it drew him in, like it had been waiting for him to notice it. As he stepped closer, the faint carving on the flat surface came into focus. At first, it seemed abstract—just an ornamental design. But as he tilted his head, the shape became clearer, more deliberate.

It wasn't possible.

His breath caught, his pulse spiking. That symbol. It was carved into the altar, right in front of him—the Broken Circle. The same one from his VR system. The same damn one. He took an unsteady step back, heart hammering.

His first instinct was denial—coincidence, a trick of the light. A mistake. It had to be. But the longer he stared, the less possible that became. The carving was deliberate. Precise. This wasn't random. His stomach twisted, unease curling into something sharper as his hand hovered over the carving, his fingers trembling as they traced the edges of the symbol. Even here, the world he left behind clung to him, tightening its grip. Waiting. Watching. Laughing at him from the dark.

A voice came from nowhere, unbidden, slipped into his mind like a shadow. Its words sharp and insistent.

"Do you see it? They've marked you. You're nothing but a piece in their game."

A cold shudder rippled down his spine—eyes darting, searching for the voice that wasn't there. They'd come to him in stealth, but they weren't just words. They were certainty—a truth he'd been avoiding since the moment he arrived.

The moment stretched, the symbol beneath his fingertips pulsing with recognition. Then, pain. A sharp, phantom sting shot through his fingertips, and he jerked his hand back as if the carving had come alive beneath his touch.

"What the hell is this?" Thane snapped, his voice raw with disbelief. His hands clenched into fists. "Why is this here? Who put it here?"

The priest's expression didn't change. "It has always been there. It's your symbol. The symbol of the Chosen One."

The words only made Thane's stomach twist further. *'Your symbol'—what a joke.* He turned sharply, his fists clenching harder, his frustration boiling over. The tension in the room thickened, pressing against him—the faint hum of his Wild Magic stirred in the air around him, subtle but growing.

That voice unfurled again.

"They heal you to use you. They bow to you to bind you. And when they are done, they will break you. Unless you break them first."

Then it was gone, slipping into the silence, but the words remained, lodged in his mind like a splinter.

The priest, noticing the tension radiating from Thane, dropped to his knees in prayer. "The path is set, and only you can walk it. It demands sacrifice, but the prophecy speaks of your strength. Your endurance. No one else can bear this weight." His words were soft, pleading, yet edged with conviction.

"You owe them nothing." The whispering voice in his head retorted sharply.

Lirien, however, stepped forward, closing the distance between them with a cautionary resolve. She stopped before Thane, her gaze sharp but not hostile. She hesitated, her gaze flicking to the tension in his shoulders, noticing the way his hands trembled.

And then she made her choice.

With slow, deliberate steps, she sat him on the raised pedestal and reached into a small satchel, pulling out a cloth. Gently, she wiped the dirt from his brow.

Her actions were quiet, almost reverent, and for a moment, they felt like an anchor in the chaos. But that anchor came with a weight he didn't want to carry. The tenderness in her touch was too much—it mirrored something he couldn't bear to see. It broke him.

In Lirien's hands, in her eyes—he saw his mother. Desperate. Trembling. Clinging to hope that wasn't real. Trying so hard to fix what couldn't be fixed. He felt her quiet heartbreak, her exhaustion, and the weight of her forced smile as she pretended everything would be okay while knowing deep down that he was slipping away. It all came rushing back, crashing over him like a wave.

The pain, the helplessness, the sheer injustice of it all. He wasn't her son anymore; he was her burden. And here, in this place, it was no different. He would never let anyone get that close enough to be a burden again. He was done watching other people break for him. Whatever time was left, he was in it for himself from now on.

"No one will suffer for you again," the voice said, feeding the thought, twisting it into certainty.

Thane staggered back, his breath quickening as the Wild Magic surged, the symbol of the Broken Circle seared in his mind. It wasn't just a mark—it was a chain. The air grew heavy, thrumming with an unnatural pulse, the very walls seeming to vibrate with the pressure of it. His vision blurred at the edges, light distorting, as if reality itself couldn't decide whether to hold together or shatter around him. But it wasn't just magic. It was everything he'd swallowed, everything he'd lost—roaring to be set free.

The voice returned, insidious and undeniable.

"Show them what power really is."

The voice was no longer a whisper—it was a force, wrapping around his thoughts like a noose. The anger was already there, already burning. It just needed to be set free.

"Burn it. Let them feel what you feel. Destroy it all."

Those words echoed his truth. He'd known it the

second he set foot back in this world. The second he saw them. This was always how it had to end. There was no stopping it, no turning away from what had already begun. His rage had sunk too deep, fusing with the magic. With a final, violent twist, something inside him broke—shattered beyond repair.

He let it all go.

For a moment, the world held its breath.

And then—everything ignited.

A surge of raw energy ripped loose, fractures spider-webbing outward in an unstoppable chain reaction. The vines lining the walls curled inward before disintegrating, their glow extinguished in a heartbeat. Light and shadow folded and bent, twisting in impossible directions as the magic scarred everything in its path.

With a sudden intensification, a raw, searing pulse detonated through the Sanctuary, rupturing stone, air, and bone in a fraction of time. The walls reduced to rubble, the stained-glass windows shattered outward, shards spinning through the air like razors. The Sanctuary unraveled as if it had never existed.

And then—the screams began.

But they only lasted a heartbeat. The screams, the heat, the ruin—gone.

Blurred into nothing.

The villagers never stood a chance. The force of the explosion tore through flesh, shattered bone, deleted them from existence in an instant. Stolen from life by something beyond their comprehension. The priest's voice—once so full of hope—was silenced by the roar of destruction, consumed by an unrelenting storm of Wild Magic.

Thane didn't move. Didn't react. He stood at the center of the chaos, breath ragged, hands still outstretched as if he had literally torn reality apart with his bare fingers.

His pulse thundered in his ears, the sound of his heartbeat drowning out the utter destruction surrounding him. Everything burned—not with fire, but with raw energy, smoldering as if the magic itself had sunk too deep to ever be undone.

And then—stillness.

The tempest of power collapsed in on itself, like a black hole. Reality reasserted itself, uncaring, untouched by the ruin left behind. But now, the Sanctuary was gone.

No walls, no glowing pool. Just ruin, smoldering where it had once stood.

And the village? Not destroyed—erased. Buildings reduced to splinters, the cobbled streets now a scar of molten stone still hissing from the magic's heat. The air was thick with the stench of charred earth. But beneath it, something lingered. Something foul and corrupt.

Thane staggered, the adrenaline draining as the full weight of what had happened settled onto him. He exhaled, a trembling, unsteady sound. His hands were shaking. The realization crawled through him, slow and insidious.

This wasn't just an outburst.

This wasn't just rage.

This was annihilation.

He had wiped out this place.

All of it.

Every stone, every street—every heartbeat.

Gone.

He pulled in a breath, trying to shake himself from the numbness of it all.

And then his eyes landed on the one thing left standing.

Lirien.

Turning sharply, his vision was swimming. She was still standing next to him. Her clothes were singed, her skin marked with streaks of soot, but she was alive. She was the only one. She hadn't moved. She hadn't run.

And now she just stared at him, face unreadable, mouth parted as if to speak—but nothing came. Her fingers trembled, curling into fists at her sides. Her whole body shuddered, as if it couldn't decide whether to fight or collapse.

Thane's stomach twisted violently, but he shoved it down, the way he had learned to. The way he had to.

Somehow, she had survived. But the others? There were no others.

A strangled sound caught in her throat, but she didn't cry. Her lips parted slightly.

No words came.

She staggered, knees buckling, her breath coming too short, too fast—then, something inside her caved, collapsed under the weight of it all. Not in pain. Not in fear. But in realization—the kind that rewrites a person. The kind that carves something out of you, leaving only emptiness behind.

"Gods," she whispered. But it wasn't a prayer or a plea to a greater power. It was now just a single, broken word.

Thane swayed on his feet, widening his stance in response. His fingers twitched at his sides, still tingling, but the sensation felt distant—like it belonged to someone else. His pulse reverberating in his skull, his vision too blurred to anchor him. He wasn't here. Not really. Just a shadow caught between two worlds.

Something warm traced the curve of his lip. His fingers found it absently, pressing into the wetness. Thick and slick—his mind caught up a second later—and red.

Not—no. Not now.

The dizziness hit. Hard. There was no fighting it. His senses flickered in and out. The scent of scorched air. The whisper of wind through the ruins. The hum of something deep inside him—fading. His limbs felt untethered, like he might blow away if he let go.

The world pitched sideways, the ruins twisting into a smear of color and shadow. Lirien was still there—still kneeling, still staring—but she was drifting, receding, like something was pulling him away from her.

He tried to hold her in his gaze, but he couldn't.

The ground lurched beneath him. His body jerked, convulsing into violent spasms. His vision fractured—light and shadow splitting at the seams.

Lirien didn't move. Didn't flinch. She just watched as he fell, her face carved from stone, her fists clenched at her sides, nails pressing into her palms. She didn't just look at him. She judged him. Silent. Unforgiving.

Thane had already slipped away. His mind blanked. His body dropped.

And then—nothing.

4

THE WEIGHT OF WORLDS

Darkness gave way to a dim, golden light. Thane stirred, his head throbbing. His body sank into the bed, heavy with exhaustion. A faint tingle lingered in his fingers—the ghost of something raw and electric. Fading, but not gone.

He didn't want to wake up yet. Sleep was easier—warm and numb, a shield against reality. But the world kept pulling him back, whether he wanted it to or not.

A cool cloth brushed his face—slow, rhythmic. Gently pulling him back.

"Thane," a soft voice called, tinged with worry and exhaustion. "You're awake."

His eyes fluttered open—blurry at first, then sharpening into something painfully familiar. The faint hum of his PC in the corner, the clutter of books and clothes strewn across the floor. The pale light of early evening filtering through the curtains, casting long shadows against the walls. And leaning over him, dabbing at his nose with a damp washcloth, was his mother.

She looked tired. The kind of tired that lingered, that settled into the bones and refused to leave. Still, there was a softness in her gaze, a quiet kind of heartbreak. She smiled when she saw him focus on her, but it was fragile, as if the weight of the world rested just behind it.

"There you are," she murmured, her voice steady but not as strong as it used to be. "You had another one."

Thane blinked, his mind sluggish, slow to catch up. His fingers twitched, instinctively reaching for his face. He brushed against dried blood beneath his nose, and his stomach turned.

"You didn't have to… do that," Thane muttered, his voice raspier than usual. He turned his gaze toward his desk, to the familiar mess that suddenly felt so alien. Books—some of them gifts from friends who no longer called—were stacked haphazardly beside unopened packages and forgotten ambitions. The realization settled over him like a dull ache.

"I didn't have to?" Her tone was light, almost teasing, but there was something else beneath it—a quiet tremor. "What kind of mom would I be if I didn't take care of my boy?"

Her words landed softly, but they carved into him all the same. He swallowed, the weight in his throat unbearable. A dry laugh escaped him, but it was hollow. "Your boy. Sure. Your broken, dying boy," he said quietly.

"Thane." Her voice sharpened, but only for a moment. She exhaled and placed the cloth down on the nightstand, her hands lingering for just a second longer than necessary. "You're still here. That's what matters."

The silence between them stretched, heavy and unspoken. Thane wanted to say something—anything—but the words died before they could form. What was the point? She already knew.

Instead, he reached out—just barely—and clasped her hand. It wasn't much, but it was enough. Enough to feel the tension in her body ease, even if only slightly. Her fingers squeezed his, just once, before she let go.

She stood, smoothing his blanket with a quiet, absent gesture. As she moved, her fingers brushed over a small photo frame on his nightstand. She straightened it out of habit, but Thane caught the movement. He didn't look at it—he didn't have to. He knew what it was. A quiet presence in the room that neither of them mentioned.

Something about the moment felt eerily familiar. The memory of Lirien's trembling hands wiping his face flashed through his mind. Her expression. The way she had looked at him. That mix of pity, fear, and desperation. It was the same.

The realization sank like a stone—he'd seen that look before. In every doctor who tried and failed to give him answers. In the empty notifications from his "friends" on his phone.

And now, in Lirien.

His stomach twisted, a dull nausea curling in his gut. He turned his gaze back to his desk, to the phone lying face down beside his keyboard. He didn't pick it up. He already knew there were no messages waiting for him. No missed calls. Just silence. Nobody.

He glanced at his mom, her eyes fixed on him—wanting to help.

"I'm fine," Thane said, his voice firmer now. He lay back, wiping under his nose. "Just… tired. That's all."

His mother turned back in the doorway, hesitant, but she didn't argue. Those days were in the past. "I'll let you rest. Call me if you need anything."

She lingered in the doorway for a moment too long. He knew she wanted him to say something. She was waiting.

The words pressed against the back of his throat. *I'm fine. I'm still here.* He could have said that. He almost did.

Almost.

But the weight of it all was too much, and swallowing the words was easier.

He didn't. He couldn't. Those days were in the past.

She sighed, barely audible, and closed the door softly behind her.

Thane stared at the ceiling, his mind pulling him in two different directions. The weight of what he'd done in Arbelon pressed against his chest, suffocating him. *It wasn't right. It wasn't him. Or was it?*

He tried everything to block out the screams, the sounds of crumbling stone and cracking wood. The Sanctuary's destruction replayed in his mind, cruel and relentless—like a game trailer. But it was somehow more real, more visceral, and everything about it felt criminal.

He ran his hand down his face, feeling the roughness of dried blood still clinging to his skin. A thought tried to form, but he shoved it down. *No. That's not it.* He clenched his jaw, forcing a breath through his nose. It wasn't the same. Lirien's village had been pixels and code. His mother was real. She would still be here tomorrow.

But the thought didn't let go. It twisted, sinking deeper, until it settled in his chest like a weight he couldn't dislodge.

I did to Lirien what this disease is doing to my mother.

This version of reality was too much. He swung his legs over the side of the bed, staring at the floor. His PC hummed beside him, the screen dark.

The game was waiting.

He could reset it, start over with a fresh load.

His fingers hovered over the keyboard. He knew how easy it would be. A few clicks, a clean slate—like none of it ever happened.

His index finger tapped once against the key. Just a reflex—an impulse.

Reset. Erase. Move on.

But his hand didn't move.

That wasn't how hardcore mode worked. No respawns. No do-overs. No extra lives. Just one shot—like real life.

His throat tightened. He didn't know why it felt different this time—why the weight sat heavier than before. Maybe because this wasn't just another game. Maybe because, this time, walking away wouldn't change a thing.

Thane lay back down, staring at the ceiling. The hum of his PC filled the silence—not comforting, just… noise.

And in the noise, a whisper surfaced, so faint it could have been his own—or something else entirely.

"You're not done yet."

5

THE RUINS OF ASMENSON

Thane lifted the headset, sliding it over his head and adjusting the fit with practiced ease. Its weight was familiar, grounding, even as something in his chest tightened. His mother's voice lingered in his thoughts, a warmth that cut like a dull blade. He wasn't sure he could bear it any longer —her hope was always there, always reminding him that he would fail her… just like his father had.

He exhaled sharply, shoving it down, locking it away.

A soft *click* sealed him in. The screen brightened, then dimmed.

Loading…

Blinked in place.

The screen flickered. Once, twice. The words *Loading…* blurred, warping as if the system itself was faltering, struggling against a corrupted file. A pulse of jagged light flashed across the screen. Then came the sound—a chaotic static, like a radio station desperately out of tune.

The PC fan whined, shrill and unsteady, almost like it was struggling too.

The air itself felt unreliable, like the eerie stillness before a storm. Thane's stomach twisted and stretched, his breath stolen as if something had wrapped around him and pulled. The world stuttered, two half-formed things, flickering between darkness and color, Earth and Arbelon.

The loading screen fractured. Colors ran like spilled ink, bleeding across the darkness. The sound warped, a distorted echo of a thousand voices speaking over each other, none of them making sense. The shift should have been instant, but this time—this time, it faltered.

His body hung in place, stretched between the now and the almost.

The game wasn't loading—it was hesitating. And in that brief hesitation, reality blinked. Arbelon glitched before him, breaking apart and reforming like a puzzle missing half its pieces.

Then, for a single breath, he existed in neither world.

In that lingering moment of nothing, a familiar voice slithered from the darkness, soft and soothing.

"They resist your return, but there are always ways in—cracks in every wall. I have made sure of it. You were always meant for Arbelon."

Not a moment later, the darkness relented.

His skin came alive, tingling, a reminder of a distant companion. And then the headache slammed into him, crushing and unrelenting. The sharp scent of smoke and blood filled his lungs. The world around him resolved with an almost violent clarity—no fade-in, no soft transition. One moment, he was nowhere. The next, he was sprawled on rough ground, his lungs gasping for air.

When Arbelon slammed into focus, it didn't settle right.

The ground beneath him rippled—just for a moment,

like a mirage bending in the heat. The air shuddered, thick with something unseen and foreign. And then, as though reality reasserted itself, the glitch snapped away.

Thane swallowed hard, and his breath came shallow, his heart hammering in his chest. It was just a trick of the mind. Had to be.

Dirt pressed into his palms, damp and sticky. A slow, warm trickle ran from his nose, the unmistakable tang of blood filling his mouth. He coughed, his body shuddering against the sudden change. For a moment, Thane lay still, disoriented, as echoes of something distant flickered at the edge of his mind—pulling, urging, dragging him back into this reality.

He winced in pain as he forced himself to his knees. The silence pressed in—heavy, unnatural. No birds. No wind. No voices. Not even the crackle of dying embers.

Then, the scent hit him—charred wood, burned flesh.

And finally, he looked up.

What remained of Asmenson barely qualified as ruins. Blackened husks of buildings stood like broken ribs against the dull gray sky. Smoke rose from the wreckage, curling in eerie, lazy tendrils. The ground beneath him was littered with debris—a broken charm, a singed scarf, things that had once been whole, once been *someone's*. The air carried a heavy, metallic odor, thick with the undeniable stench of death.

Asmenson was gone, the whole village obliterated.

His ruin. His crime.

The sound of movement pulled Thane from his haze.

Lirien.

She moved through the wreckage like a ghost, her form half-obscured by drifting smoke. The edges of her cloak were frayed, torn by fire and devastation, and her steps were slow, unsteady. Her breath came in short, shallow bursts, each one edged with disbelief.

"How…?" Her voice was barely audible, breaking like something fragile. "How could it all be gone?" A place that had one been so alive, now flooded with an unnatural silence. She was trying to take it in—to *understand*—but there was too much to comprehend.

A broken support beam jutted from the rubble, blackened and crumbling. She reached for it, her fingers brushing against the charred surface as if touching it might confirm that this was real. That it had truly happened.

The village was gone. Her home. Her family. All gone.

The wind shifted, stirring the ash and lifting strands of her hair, streaked now with soot and grief. Her face was slack, hollowed out by shock, but her eyes—her eyes were wide, searching, desperate to find something, *anything* left. But there was nothing.

Thane sat frozen, watching. The destruction was total, absolute. And it was *his* doing.

He clenched his jaw. *This isn't real.* It was just a game. A simulation. A script running out of control.

He told himself that again, over and over, like a mantra, like a spell. Because if it wasn't—if it was real—then what had he done?

No. It wasn't real. It couldn't be.

But the way she moved—the broken, desperate way she moved through the ruins—made something inside him twist. It wasn't guilt. It couldn't be. But something too close to it.

He swallowed hard, pushing the thought downhill harder. It wasn't real. It was a game, he told himself again —a cruel, vivid simulation that had gone off the rails. That's all.

The voice coiled through his mind, smooth, patient. A whisper like silk, unshakable as stone.

Did you not feel it? The way the world bent to your will?

The power?

They were nothing. You are something greater. Remember that.

His breath caught in his chest. A sharp pulse of pain lanced through his skull, and he gritted his teeth, pressing his hand to his temple as if he could force the voice away. But instead, the words coiled around him, familiar and reassuring.

He wiped his nose with the back of his hand, smearing the blood across his skin.

The motion caught Lirien's attention. She turned. Her eyes locked onto his, and for the first time, he felt it—the weight of what he had done.

Grief, raw and unfiltered, carved itself into every line of her face. But beneath it, something deeper stirred. Recognition. Realization. And then, fury.

Her breath stopped, her posture stiffening, her hands curling into fists at her sides.

"You did this. You killed them." Her voice was trembling, raw. "My family. Everyone. Dead because of you," she said, barely more than a whisper, but it landed with the weight of a scream.

The look in her eyes cut deeper than he'd expected. He searched for something, anything to say, but what could he say? That it wasn't real? That it was just a game? He froze, seeing the pain in her eyes, feeling the weight of accusation they carried.

It *felt* real.

More real than anything had in a long time.

She took a step forward, fists clenched, grief and rage warring in her eyes. He thought she might strike him, and for a moment, he almost wished she would. But then—her gaze flickered, her focus shifting downward. Her breath slowed, as if her mind had caught on something—something out of place.

She froze.

Not from fear. Not from shock. From recognition.

Her gaze locked on the blood streaking his skin.

"Your blood. It's red. Not blue."

Her voice faltered and trailed off. The fury in her expression wavered—barely—but it was enough.

She'd seen his blood before, but something about this moment landed differently, shook her. Her expression changed, like a thought had clawed its way to the surface.

Not fear. Not shock. Something deeper.

She stared at his cheek, her lips parting slightly as realization clawed its way in. The fire in her eyes dimmed to something colder, more haunted.

Then, barely audible, she whispered it. "The one who bleeds red shall command the magic born wild."

Thane's breath caught. He didn't know what she was talking about, but for some reason the words felt old—buried deep in the sands of time.

Her gaze didn't shift from his blood. "I thought it wasn't real," she muttered.

She shook her head, like she was trying to push something back down inside her.

Then she blinked, stepped back, and seemed to remember he was still standing there. Her fists trembled.

"If you truly are the Chosen One… then it is not my right to judge you," she said. "The Elders will decide."

He stared at her, the words echoing in his ears. His breath came short, uneven. *The Chosen One.* The idea was ridiculous—laughable. Except none of this felt like a joke.

Not with her standing there, grief-ridden, desperate, seeing something in him he didn't believe existed.

What kind of sick joke was this? He wasn't here to be judged—not again. Thane scoffed, wiping the blood from his nose, lashing out. "Oh, great. A tribunal. Do I get a public flogging, or just the classic exile to a deserted island?"

He let the sarcasm sit in the air, but the moment stretched too long, too quiet. Lirien didn't take the bait, and her expression didn't shift.

They actually expect me to play along. The thought scraped against something sharp inside him. *They think I'll just walk in like a good little boy, head bowed, waiting for their mercy?*

He almost laughed. Almost told her to go to hell. But his hands dropped to his side. His body ached. The silence pressed too heavy. And the truth—the part he wouldn't say aloud—was that he had nowhere else to go.

Still, Lirien stood before him, unflinching. Her fingers still curled into fists at her sides, her knuckles white. "They will decide your fate. It is not for me to say."

Her voice was steady, but there was something underneath—something frayed at the edges. She was barely holding herself together. Thane saw it in the way her breath hastened, in the way her eyes flickered over the ruins without truly focusing. Whatever she felt—rage, sorrow, maybe even doubt—she was swallowing it down. Doing everything she could to just push forward.

"Right. Sounds like a real fair trial," he muttered, pushing himself up to his feet. His legs were unsteady, the world still tilting slightly from the transition. His whole body ached. "And if I refuse?"

Lirien looked at him then, truly looked at him, as if she were seeing him for the first time. "You won't."

That got a laugh out of him. "Won't I? Because from where I'm standing, I'm not exactly in chains."

"You don't need chains. The Elders will forgive you. They have to. That's how this works, isn't it? The Chosen One can burn a village to the ground and still walk the path laid before him. But don't mistake their mercy for mine."

He opened his mouth, a sharp retort on the tip of his tongue, but for once, nothing came.

Because she wasn't wrong.

The Elders would forgive him. He'd seen it before in every RPG he'd ever played—*main quest privilege*. The hero could burn a town to the ground, and as long as he was destined for something greater, the world would make excuses.

But this wasn't supposed to feel real.

He swallowed, glancing around at the smoldering remains of Asmenson. It wasn't just a backdrop. The stench of charred wood and flesh clung to the air, thick and undeniable. He could feel the wind rattling through the skeletal remains of homes, could sense the weight of Lirien's gaze, heavy with something between hatred and obligation.

And despite everything—despite her disdain, despite the eerie silence pressing in around them—one truth gnawed at him, quiet but insistent.

He didn't want to be alone.

Still, he couldn't just let her think she'd won. He exhaled hard, rubbing the back of his neck. "Fine. Take me to your vaunted Elders. I'm sure they've got some grand speech ready—destiny, fate, the burden of my divine responsibility. Can't wait to hear it."

Lirien let out a slow breath, looking away as tears pooled in her eyes. "If you're going to mock everything, at least wait until we're out of the graveyard." Her voice was quiet but steady, the words honed like a blade.

She didn't turn back. She simply motioned for him to follow. "We leave now."

But before she did, she moved through the ruins, her steps careful, methodical. She knelt near a collapsed wall, sifting through the ash and debris. A satchel, half-singed but intact, was pulled free. Inside, she found a canteen, the hilt of a blade with no blade, and a few other scattered remnants of a life lost. She packed them with precision, not hesitation, as if these were survival choices, not sentimental ones.

Thane expected her to take something personal—a keepsake, a token of who she had been before everything burned. But she didn't. Or maybe there was nothing left to take.

She hesitated once leaving town, standing near what might have been a doorway. Her fingers hovered over the blackened wood, brushing against it in a way that almost seemed reverent.

He should have looked away. Should have ignored the quiet way her fingers brushed the ruin, the way she moved through the devastation like she belonged to it—like it was a part of her, and she, a part of it.

But for a moment, he didn't.

Her lips moved, barely a whisper. "May the Architects guide you beyond the Veil. May the Heart remember what was lost."

The words came without thought, an old ritual ingrained in her bones. Not a plea, not even faith—just a habit, one of the few things that still made sense. Then, just as quickly, she withdrew her hand, turned, and started walking away from the ruins.

He lingered for a moment, glancing back at the wreckage. The silence pressed in, thick and suffocating, swallowing what little life remained. His stomach twisted, but he ignored it, shoving his hands in his pockets as he followed her.

The game wanted him to play along. Fine. He'd play. But he wasn't promising to follow the script.

6

———

HIDDEN PLACES

THE ROAD away from Asmenson was eerily silent. No wind. No birds. Just the crunch of boots on hardened dirt, the faint scrape of dead leaves shifting underfoot. Smoke still clung to the air, though the fires had long since died, the scent curling through the ruins like a ghost that refused to move on.

The devastation stretched farther than Thane expected. Not just the village—gone, erased as if it had never been—but the forest around it, flattened as though something had reached out and crushed it in one sweeping fist. The trees weren't burned. They were just… dead. Splintered trunks lay in heaps, brittle and gray, stripped of their leaves. Like they'd lost the will to stand.

They walked in silence.

Lirien led, keeping her pace even, controlled. Too controlled. She never glanced back. Never hesitated. Just kept moving.

Thane followed a few steps behind, his breath misting in the crisp air. The cold didn't bother him—Arbelon always felt sharper than Earth, like it wasn't just a place but

47

a presence pressing in around him. He exhaled, watching the white plume dissolve into nothing.

The forest gradually reclaimed the land, brittle devastation giving way to trees still standing. But the silence remained. Even the birds, normally so quick to reclaim what had been lost, kept their distance for now.

Thane finally spoke, voice rough from disuse. "So, these Elders of yours. Am I getting a hero's welcome, or should I be bracing for the torch-and-pitchfork treatment?"

Lirien didn't slow. Didn't react. Didn't so much as twitch at his sarcasm.

"You mock what you don't understand," she said.

"I understand more than you can imagine," Thane shot back. "You think I'm some savior sent from another world to rescue your broken land. That's a classic, for sure, but a bit tired—don't you think?"

At that, she finally stopped, turning back. Her expression was fire and brimstone.

"You can hide behind your petty snarks, but I see through it. You're scared. Alone. But you killed them. You destroyed everything I had. So if you're not the Chosen One, then all of this—everything—was for nothing."

She held his gaze, her voice a knife's edge. "And that would make you just another monster."

She stood before him, trembling, her eyes glossing over, but he didn't reply. He wasn't in the mood to debate prophecies or destinies, and certainly not his place in them. He'd struck a nerve—not surprising, given everything that had happened. She lingered a moment, like she expected him to say something. Then she huffed and turned, striding ahead.

A whisper curled through Thane's mind.

They don't trust you. They never will.

His jaw clenched. That voice. It never spoke when he

was strong. Only when he was fraying at the edges. Like it was waiting. Watching. Knowing exactly when to twist the knife. He forced the thought aside, eyes trailing up to the shifting light filtering through the branches.

"What? You've nothing to say to that? No response?" Lirien said, her voice laced with venom. "You've been so quick with the tongue to belittle us and our beliefs—so willing to mock us. But now silence?"

Thane shrugged. He could've told her that he couldn't control the magic—when it came or what it did—but she was clearly beyond reasoning. Instead, he fell back to what was comfortable.

"Figured I'd let you stew in your thoughts. You seem to enjoy that."

She didn't answer right away. Instead, she slowed her pace, letting the tension between them stretch.

"You don't believe in any of this, do you?" she finally asked. "The prophecy. The Heart. That Arbelon is worth saving."

He exhaled sharply. "I believe that I loaded into Arbelon and was assigned a task that I didn't ask for. And every time I get a little comfortable, something tries to kill me or a flash of crazy magic wrecks me. So you tell me— what exactly am I supposed to believe in?"

Lirien turned to him, green eyes sharp. "You could believe in the people who've bled for this world. Who lost everything trying to protect it. Even if you don't care, you could at least try to understand what it means to those who do."

For a moment, his anger building, Thane considered snapping back, but something in her expression stopped him. There was no blind faith there, no naive conviction. Only a quiet, desperate need for something to make sense.

A heat like static lightning crawled up his arms before

he could react. He glanced down—thin, jagged cracks flickered across his skin, pulsing erratically, shifting like broken glass trying to reassemble itself. Then, in a blink, they were gone.

Lirien's eyes widened. "What was that?"

"What was what?" he muttered, shoving his hands into his pockets.

She tilted her head, eyes flicking to his arms. Then, without a word, she turned and kept walking.

Thane was fine with the silence. But he took his hands from his pockets, looking for the jagged lines, but none remained. If not for Lirien's response, he might have thought they were just another weird glitch or hallucination.

Lirien was a good distance up the path, and he hastened his pace to catch up. The path wound through skeletal trees, their branches clawing at the sky. Arbelon's wilderness felt old, untouched—and subtly aware of their presence.

When she spoke again, her voice had lost its edge from before—it was measured, thoughtful. "The prophecy says the Chosen One will wield the magic of the old world. Magic born of chaos, unchained and raw. They will rise when Arbelon is on the brink, and through them, the fate of all will be decided."

Thane scoffed. "Yeah, well, if that's the case, you all are screwed."

She ignored the sarcasm. "The Wild Magic is proof enough," she murmured. "That was the first sign."

Then she hesitated, glancing at him, as if measuring whether she truly believed what she was about to say.

"And then there is the blood. Your blood."

Thane frowned, running a hand over his face. "What about it?"

Lirien didn't answer immediately. She had been thinking about this ever since Asmenson, turning it over in her mind, questioning whether she had really seen what she thought she had seen. The red blood. The ancient writings—disregarded or forgotten.

"It wasn't part of the Codex or part of the prophecy we were taught," she said, voice quiet. "But I remembered something—just a fragment, buried in dust, dismissed as nonsense. It spoke of red blood. A trait that didn't exist in Arbelon."

Thane raised an eyebrow. "And?"

She looked away, unsettled. "And I think the Elders disregarded it because it didn't fit their vision of the prophecy. But if the words were true, then…" She hesitated, gripping the strap of her satchel. "Then maybe you were meant to be here more than any of us realized."

Thane let out a dry chuckle. "Yeah. Or maybe you've got the wrong guy."

"Maybe." She glanced at him, eyes sharp. "But no Arbelonean has ever bled red."

He opened his mouth to argue, then stopped. Better to let the silence win this time.

So they walked along for quite some time.

The path had narrowed, sloping upward into a stretch of dense forest before a rocky outcropping. The skeletal branches overhead had begun to shift, taking on more life the farther they walked from the ruins. Yet, the silence remained.

Lirien halted abruptly, looking at the valley below.

Thane nearly ran into her before catching himself. "What?"

Her posture had stiffened, head slightly tilted, and her head turned as she caught sight of something out of the corner of her eye. Then she whispered, "How could they…"

He followed her gaze down the slope. Through the trees, half-shrouded in mist, figures on horseback moved along the forest road below. Clad in dark crimson cloaks, their armor barely visible beneath, they rode with eerie stillness. Their mounts—sleek, smoke-colored stallions—stepped lightly, their hooves making no sound on the packed earth.

Two ravens circled overhead, their sharp cries cutting through the stillness.

Lirien exhaled, barely a breath. "The Riders."

Thane frowned. "Okay. And? They're just guys on horses."

Her fingers twitched at her side, her voice rising, tinged with desperation. "You don't understand. The Riders of the Rings, they hunt magic users. If they sensed what happened back there—if they sensed you—"

She didn't finish the sentence. Didn't need to.

Thane's gut tightened. He glanced down at his hands, as if expecting to see those jagged cracks flicker across his skin again. They were gone, but the memory of them wasn't.

"They see everything with those Ravens. We have to get off the road," Lirien said, already moving toward the trees.

He hesitated, still watching the Riders below. They didn't look particularly terrifying. They weren't monsters. They weren't glitching out of reality. Just men on horseback. But something about the way they moved—too fluid, too quiet—itched at the back of his mind.

He exhaled sharply, forcing himself to move. "Fine. Let's go hide in the bushes like cowards. Solid plan."

Lirien shot him a look but said nothing as she led them deeper into the undergrowth.

Thane trailed after her, pushing some branches aside. It wasn't like he actually believed in any of this—the Riders, the magic, the Prophecies she kept talking about. But Lirien did. And something about the way she had stiffened, the way her voice had tightened—*that* was real.

Maybe that was why he followed. Or maybe he just didn't want to watch her get deleted over some stupid glitch. Either way, he wasn't ready to dwell on it. Instead, he focused on the terrain ahead, following her step by step.

They crouched low behind the twisted roots of an ancient oak, its gnarled limbs stretching like skeletal fingers. Just beyond, a jagged rocky outcropping jutted from the hillside, partially concealed by dense underbrush. It was a good hiding place that still allowed them to see the Riders.

Below them, the Riders moved steadily, their cloaks rippling in some unseen current. The lead Rider turned his head slightly, and for a brief, terrible moment, Thane swore the man was looking directly at them. He wore a different cloak than the others, his with a ribbed halo of black around the neckline.

A chill ran through him. He barely breathed.

The ravens gave another piercing cry, and the Rider looked away, guiding his horse forward. One by one, the others followed, their passage as smooth and soundless as before.

Lirien remained still until the last Rider had vanished over the distant hill.

Only then did she let out a slow breath and turn to Thane. "That was too close."

Thane scoffed, rolling his shoulders as he stood. "Right. Terrifying."

She ignored him, scanning the trees. "We shouldn't linger. The ravens—"

"—see everything. Yeah, I gathered." He dusted off his knees. "So what now?"

"We stay off the road as much as possible. Keep moving. Trosten isn't far."

She started walking again, and this time, Thane didn't argue.

As they moved past the outcropping, a voice—calm, steady—broke the silence.

"A wise choice, these days."

Thane tensed, his body pivoting toward the sound.

A man stepped from the shadows—or maybe the rock itself—as if he had always been there, waiting. His cloak, once deep blue, had faded to something duller, its edges frayed and stitched where time or battle had torn through it. A jagged scar cut along his jawline, half-hidden beneath a few days' worth of stubble. In his hands, he carried a quarterstaff, its surface carved with old runes, dulled by use. His posture was relaxed, but his eyes—dark and searching—held the weight of someone who had seen too much and trusted too little.

He moved with practiced ease, his sharp gaze flicking between them, assessing, measuring.

Lirien froze beside Thane. "Cael," she breathed.

Cael nodded toward the road below, where the distant Riders had passed. His sharp gaze flicked upward as ravens still circled overhead. "We should move. The eyes of the Riders are watching, and night is coming fast."

Lirien hesitated only a moment before she moved toward him, stepping past the underbrush. Thane, however, lingered, suspicion curling tight in his gut.

Cael gestured toward the rock wall. "We can speak inside. Quickly now." Without waiting for a response, he walked directly to the outcropping—and vanished into the stone.

Lirien exhaled sharply. "They're real…"

Thane arched a brow. "What, the disappearing act?"

"No, it's a Sanctum, a hidden place," she said turning to him, her voice urgent as the ravens shrieked again, this time closer. "We have to go. Now."

He glanced at the sky, the ravens still circling above. With a sigh, he muttered, "This game just keeps getting weirder," and followed her in, through the rock wall.

The rock was solid. Or it should have been solid. But the moment Thane followed Lirien through the outcropping, the world shifted.

A shiver ran through him, something deeper than the cold—something threaded into his bones. A pulse, faint and fleeting, like stepping across an unseen threshold. For an instant, he thought he saw cracks flicker across his skin, like before. But then it was gone. Only Cael, watching him too closely.

Thane clenched his jaw and stepped inside.

The Sanctum was smaller than he expected, its ceiling low and gently curved, the walls shaped by careful hands rather than raw stone. It felt less like a cavern and more like a refuge—a place built not just to protect, but to comfort. The air was warm, carrying the scent of aged wood, dried herbs, and something faintly metallic, like old magic still lingering in the walls.

Soft lantern light pooled in alcoves carved into the rock, their glow steady and welcoming. A hearth sat at the far end of the room, its embers banked but still warm, as if someone had been here not long ago. Wooden benches lined the walls, their surfaces smooth from years of use, and in one corner, a heavy table bore a waiting meal—

fresh bread, dried fruit, steaming broth. Not remnants. A meal prepared for them.

Someone still kept this place ready.

Lirien's fingers brushed against the aged wood of the table, a quiet reverence in her touch. "I never thought I'd see one."

Thane exhaled, rolling his shoulders. "It doesn't feel like the rest of this place."

Lirien turned toward him, her expression unreadable. "No. It doesn't." A beat of silence, then: "Strange that you recognize that."

Cael stepped past them, his movements sure and unhurried, as if he had walked these halls a hundred times. "The Sanctums were not meant to be known by all. After the Rending, the Druids saved the Alumata from extinction. In gratitude, the Alumata built these places—not for warriors or kings, but for all who travel the wilds of Arbelon. Hidden havens, meant for the weary, the hunted, and those who have lost their way." As he said it, he looked at Thane.

Lirien drifted toward the nearest wall, fingers brushing over a tapestry woven with intricate patterns. Though dulled by time, the threads still held faint traces of their original color—deep reds and golds. At its center, barely visible through the fading threads, was a sigil of something now long forgotten.

"This place is still holding," Lirien murmured.

Cael's jaw tightened. "For now. But the fractures are growing. The protections fade a little more each day."

Thane frowned. "Fractures? You mean like—" He gestured vaguely. "—glitches?"

Cael regarded him carefully. "You see them, then."

Thane hesitated. He could still feel the echo of something beneath his skin, something unsettled. Before he could answer, a whisper curled at the edge of his thoughts.

This place will fall, just like the others.

His jaw clenched, pushing it away. "Yeah. Sometimes."

Cael took in the information without reacting, but his gaze lingered on Thane for a beat too long, as if calculating something. Weighing it. Then he simply nodded. "Then eat. We have much to discuss."

They settled at the table, the warmth of the hearth at their backs. The food was simple but rich—spiced broth, dense bread, dried fruits soaked in honey. It was more than enough.

"So these Alumata," Thane said, preferring to talk of the Alumata than continue with Cael's weird interest in the glitches, and Cael was more than happy to oblige.

"Yes, the Alumata," Cael said, picking up where he'd left off earlier. "Not many remain. But those that do still tend to these places. Though few ever see them. They are older than most races, their bodies like living plants—flesh interwoven with root and vine, their breath scented like the forests that bore them. They do not ask for thanks. They simply fulfill their promises to the Druids."

Thane swallowed his bite of bread. "And how many of these hidden way stations are left?"

Cael's expression darkened. "Fewer than we need. And none that are whole."

Lirien sat back, her expression cooling, and there was a tautness to her voice. "And yet, you seem to know where to find them. Just like the other places you shouldn't be."

Cael met her gaze evenly. "You should hold your tongue about things you know little about."

Thane looked between them. "Alright. Clearly, I'm missing something."

Lirien exhaled sharply, shaking her head. "You're not

missing anything. Cael likes to play riddles and act like he's already decided where all the pieces belong. But he only knows the edges of things. He doesn't know what's inside."

Cael's expression didn't change, but something about the way he studied her—calm, measured—made Thane uneasy.

After an awkward silence, Cael turned his gaze to Thane. "You were near Asmenson. Strange timing, given what's happened there. Did you see anything unusual?"

"Have you been following us?" Lirien said, inching forward in her seat, eyes flaring.

Thane started to answer. "No, it's okay, I can—"

"He's just a traveler," Lirien cut in, her voice firm, deliberate.

Cael's gaze flicked between them, measuring. "A traveler, you say? One who seems to have been at the heart of quite the disturbance—and looking to avoid the Riders."

His eyes landed on Thane again, as though waiting for an answer. Thane shifted under the weight of his gaze. But for some reason, it was clear that Lirien and Cael had history. That, and she really didn't want him to share anything about their whereabouts with Cael. Perhaps not all was as it seemed, so for once, he opted to be cautious.

"Just passing through," Thane muttered, keeping his voice vague. "Headed to Trosten."

Lirien ignored Thane's words and the tension remained. She leaned in toward Cael, her posture challenging. "You speak of disturbances, yet you forget the ones you caused, Cael. Or do you expect us to forget?"

Cael's face was unreadable, but his voice was calm. "We all carry our burdens, Lirien. Some heavier than others."

Lirien's gaze didn't waver, her jaw tight. But she didn't press further.

The fire crackled in the silence, and then Cael exhaled, pushing his chair back. He turned toward the hearth, the glow flickering against his face, but he spoke no more words.

Thane kept his focus on the table, the weight between Cael and Lirien pressing into the space like something unspoken, something waiting to be broken.

As Cael shifted slightly to stoke the fire, his sleeve pulled back, revealing a mark on his forearm. A jagged, circular tattoo—incomplete and broken.

Thane froze, his breath catching.

For a brief moment, the tattoo shimmered with a faint blue glow—the exact shade as the logo on his VR game system. His pulse hammered. Then he blinked, and it was gone. Just dark ink pressed into skin.

He didn't say anything, but his mind raced. *The game's telling me something… This guy must be important.* He made a mental note, filing the observation away, even as doubt nagged at him.

Cael broke the lingering silence. "Power's a funny thing. Sometimes it chooses us. And sometimes, it destroys us. Be careful which way you lean."

A faint itch bloomed at the back of Thane's mind, curling, spreading. Then the whisper came, low and insidious.

He knows what you are.

Thane's stomach twisted, but he forced the voice down, fixing his eyes on the fire.

The meal finished in silence. The final words lingering much too long, and the weight of the Sanctum pressed in around them, but not like before. It was not the weight of decaying magic. It was the weight of something kept, something preserved despite the world forgetting it. And though Thane still didn't know what to make of it, he couldn't shake the feeling that this place—this moment—

was something rare. Something that should not have existed, and yet did.

He thought of the broken circle. Of Cael's knowing eyes. Of the faint whispers in his mind. A game should have rules. But this one rewrote them as it went.

He had assumed he was here to play a role in this story, but the deeper he went, the more it felt like something else had already written the script. And somewhere in the margins, he could feel his name etched in ink.

Sleep came slowly, and with it, unease.

7

BURIED MEMORIES

The sounds of dawn crept into the Sanctum, the chirp of birds announcing the morning, soft and muted. The remnants of the fire smoldered in the hearth, tendrils of smoke curling lazily upward.

Thane stirred, the stiffness of sleep making his muscles protest. The weight of his clothing—a sturdy tunic, thick woolen trousers, and a travel-worn cloak—felt strangely familiar now, though he knew they hadn't been his. They fit as though they had always belonged to him, another layer of the illusion pressing against the edges of his mind. He longed for a pair of jeans and a hoodie, but even he couldn't pull that off here.

He stretched and sat up, glancing toward the entrance of the Sanctum. Lirien wasn't inside. Frowning, he pushed himself to his feet and stepped outside, the cool morning air brushing against his skin.

A few paces away, Lirien knelt near a patch of soft dirt, her movements slow and deliberate. The pale light of dawn made her expression unreadable. Thane hesitated, watching as she placed a delicate gold ring into a shallow hole she had dug. She pressed the dirt down gently, her hands trembling slightly.

"What are you doing?" Thane asked, his voice cutting through the quiet.

Lirien glanced up, startled, then quickly looked away. "It's my mother's ring." Her voice was quieter than usual, rough at the edges. "It's all that's left of her."

She hesitated for a second longer than she meant to, fingers pressing into the dirt like she could still take it back. Then, in one sharp motion, she smoothed it over and exhaled through her nose. "Sometimes it's easier to let go than to carry it."

Thane frowned. "You sure?" He didn't know why he asked. Maybe because he wasn't sure if he could do the same, if it were him. "Holding on… having memories… it's not always bad."

She let out a short, hollow laugh. Not amused. Not angry. Just empty.

"You think I don't know that?" she shook her head, standing abruptly. "Memories don't change anything. They don't undo the past. They don't bring people back." Her voice wavered, just barely, but she pushed forward. "And they sure as hell don't make anything hurt less."

She wiped her hands on her tunic and turned toward the Sanctum. "Pack your things. We leave soon."

Without waiting for a reply, she walked away.

Thane lingered for a moment, then crouched by the small mound of dirt. He hesitated before carefully digging out the ring, holding it in his palm. Its weight was oddly comforting. He turned it over between his fingers, thinking of his mother—of how she'd have to bury him one day, just like this. *Would she let him go so easily, or would she cling to every scrap of memory, refusing to forget?*

The thought unsettled him.

He imagined his mother, sitting in that too-quiet house, sorting through his old things. Would she keep them? His hoodies, his books, the dumb little trinkets that never meant much? Or would she shove them into a box and bury them somewhere deep, the way Lirien had?

A fresh wave of resentment coiled inside him. This was supposed to be an escape, not a cruel reminder of his story. He was supposed to be the one leaving behind memories, not becoming one.

He studied the golden ring for a moment before slipping it into his pocket with a quiet mutter. "Not everything has to be let go."

Something shifted in the air, subtle but distinct, like a ripple in still water. Thane tensed, the hairs on his arms rising. He wasn't alone.

The telling tap of a staff followed.

"It's a beautiful morning for secrets, isn't it?" Cael's voice cut through the quiet. He cast a glance toward the Sanctum's entrance before stepping closer, as if ensuring Lirien wasn't near enough to hear.

Thane stiffened, caught off guard. "What do you want?"

Cael chuckled softly. "Nothing from you. Not yet, anyway." He leaned forward on his staff and gave Thane one last look. "You'll find the Elders have long memories. Their judgment is sharp, and their forgiveness... well, don't expect much."

Cael turned to leave, his tone carrying a mix of warning and resignation, hinting at his own strained history with the Elders.

"You choose your own path. Don't let them choose it for you." He adjusted the strap of his satchel, eyes lingering on Thane for a moment longer. Then, softer, more weighted—"Like I said, power's a funny thing. It chooses us or destroys us. Be careful which way it takes you."

The words sat heavy in Thane's mind. He wanted to dismiss them, shove them aside as more cryptic nonsense—but he couldn't. The way Cael had looked at him, the deliberate weight of his tone—it felt less like advice and more like a warning. One he'd be a fool to ignore.

As Cael was disappearing into the trees, Lirien stepped out from the Sanctum, pausing as she caught sight of him. Her gaze darkened, following him until he vanished into the woods before turning to Thane.

"What did he say to you?" Her voice was low, wary. Not curiosity—concern.

She didn't look at Thane when she asked, her eyes still fixed on the trees where Cael had disappeared. Like she was expecting him to turn back. Like she wouldn't be surprised if he did.

When Thane didn't answer right away, she finally glanced at him, frowning. "I don't trust him. No one does." The words came without hesitation.

There was clearly no love lost between Lirien and Cael, but Cael had the air of someone important—like he knew things Thane didn't, though to be fair, that was most people here. Still, there was something about him, something measured, like he'd already weighed Thane and decided he wasn't worth fearing. Not yet.

Maybe he was supposed to be Thane's Gandalf. Or Dumbledore.

But in stories like those, the mentor always came with a price.

Thane shrugged, feigning indifference. "Nothing important. Let's get moving."

Without another word, they shouldered their packs and started toward Trosten. Lirien walked ahead, her steps brisk and purposeful, while Thane lingered behind, his thoughts turning to the ring in his pocket and Cael's words.

The road to Trosten awaited, but something told him the real journey had only just begun. And if Cael was right, if power really did choose or destroy—Thane honestly had no idea which way it was leaning.

8

COUNCIL OF THE ELDERS

THE ROAD to Trosten stretched ahead, winding through clusters of gnarled trees, their branches skeletal against the overcast sky. The air was thick with the damp scent of moss and old wood, and though the path was firm beneath his boots, Thane couldn't shake the uneasy feeling coiling in his gut. Maybe it was the silence—Lirien hadn't spoken in at least an hour, and that was a problem. When she was quiet, she was thinking. And when she was thinking, she was planning.

Thane flicked a glance at her. She walked stiffly, arms folded across her chest, her pace clipped and determined. Her expression was unreadable, but the set of her jaw said enough—she wasn't happy. Probably still pissed about their argument in the Sanctum. He sighed, his hands relaxed at his side. Might as well prod the hornet's nest.

"So, these Elders," he started, keeping his voice casual. "What am I walking into? A fair trial, or am I just skipping straight to the part where they burn me at the stake?"

Lirien didn't slow. "They'll want answers. And justice."

"Great. Remind me why I agreed to do this?" he asked, a quizzical expression on his face.

She finally shot him a look, her gaze sharp. "You have no other choice. It is what the moment demands of you, and because of that, they have every right to question you."

Thane exhaled heavily, rolling his shoulders. "Let me guess, you've already got your speech prepared?"

That got a reaction. A flicker of something—a hesitation, maybe. Then, just as quickly, it was gone.

"I'll tell them the truth. Nothing more. That I can promise you."

"The truth," Thane echoed. "That's rich, coming from someone who's still keeping things from me."

Lirien stopped abruptly. "What are you talking about?"

He turned to her, folding his arms. "Cael. You didn't want me talking to him, and I'm betting it wasn't just because of his *reputation*." He said, using his hands to make air quotes.

Her mouth tightened. "You don't know what he is."

"Enlighten me."

For a moment, she looked like she might refuse. Then, finally, she spoke, voice lower now. "They call him the Fallen One."

Thane arched an eyebrow. "Dramatic."

"He was trusted once," she began, her words distant. "The highest of the Elders. The last High Oracle. But he thought he knew better. He tried to command the Wild Magic, to force the Heart to heal. It didn't listen. Instead, it fractured further, its wound deepening. And Arbelon suffered for it. He was cast out, stripped of his titles. Now he lurks on the edges of everything, still thinking he's the only one who understands the Heart. And you—" she turned a sharp look at Thane, "—you'd do well to remember his arrogance, his failures."

Thane frowned. He didn't know what he'd expected, but it wasn't that. "And you think he'd do it again?"

"I think," Lirien said carefully, "that you're too quick to trust people who don't deserve it."

A flicker of irritation flared in his chest. "You don't even know me. But here you are telling me what I'm thinking. Must be nice to be a mind reader."

She didn't bite at the sarcasm—this time. She just held his gaze a bit longer before turning away. "Be careful who you trust. Some people earn it. Some just take advantage of it."

Before he could reply, movement caught his eye. Further down the path, a group of figures emerged from the trees on horseback, their armor worn but well-kept, their horses bearing sigils Thane didn't recognize. It was not the Riders. That was certain, but Thane tensed nonetheless, instinctively shifting his stance.

The lead rider dismounted, approaching with measured steps.

He was tall, lean but built with the frame of a fighter. His presence carried an air of command, though there was a restraint in it—like someone who bore leadership out of necessity rather than desire. His hair was dark with silver threading at the temples, his sharp blue eyes cutting between them with quiet assessment. The others fanned out behind him, hands near their weapons, but not yet drawn. Not a threat—yet.

A flicker of something passed through the leader's expression as he approached Lirien. Not quite surprise— more like expectation, or maybe irritation. Whatever it was, it was gone in an instant, replaced by the cool detachment of command.

Lirien squared her shoulders, meeting his gaze with the same defiance she'd given Thane earlier. But this was different. Sharper. A history Thane wasn't privy to but could feel crackling between them.

"Kaelir," she said in a clipped tone.

Thane's eyes flicked between them. Lirien seemed to have issues with everyone they ran into—first Cael, now this guy. Either she was extremely particular about the company she kept, or there was something deeper going on.

Kaelir's attention shifted to Thane. His expression was unreadable, his words sharp. "Who is this?"

Lirien's lips pressed into a thin line. "No one."

Thane felt a flicker of annoyance at that, but he swallowed it, keeping his expression neutral.

Kaelir's eyes flicked between them, assessing. "Why are you here?"

"Asmenson," Lirien said finally. "It's gone."

Something flickered across Kaelir's face, a brief, barely perceptible shift, but he recovered quickly. "Gone? What do you mean?"

"Destroyed," Lirien corrected. "There's nothing left."

Kaelir's jaw tightened. He looked to the men behind him, giving a brief nod. One of them vaulted into the saddle and took off toward Trosten, the sound of hooves fading quickly. The others didn't move at first, but Thane caught the small shifts in their posture—the way hands flexed at their sides, resting near weapons but not drawing them, the way one man glanced toward the tree line as if expecting something to come from it. Soldiers didn't fear bad news. But they knew what always followed it.

Kaelir exhaled, rubbing a hand over his face before looking back to Lirien. "You should have come sooner."

"We came as soon as we could."

Kaelir didn't press the matter. Instead, he turned sharply and swung back into the saddle. "Come. The Elders need to hear this."

As they moved into Trosten, the town unfolded before them—larger than Asmenson, built among the foothills of the Emerald Mountains. Stone buildings with reinforced wooden beams lined the winding streets, and the smell of burning wood and fresh bread mixed with the sharper scent of damp stone. The streets were busy, a bustling market stretching along the main road. Merchants called out their wares, the clatter of carts and livestock filling the space between voices. But as they passed, conversations slowed, eyes flicking toward Kaelir and his unfamiliar company.

Kaelir barely glanced at them. With a subtle motion of his hand, he signaled for the people to continue as they were. Gradually, the hum of the market resumed, though some still watched as they passed.

They wound their way toward the center of town, where a great hall loomed—larger than the other buildings, its high wooden beams darkened with age, etched with intricate runes and glyphs. Above the grand doors, a sigil had been burned into the wood—the Duskthorn Circle. Thane's gaze lingered on the twisting rings of thorns enclosing the droplet at its center. Something about it unsettled him. It felt like a warning more than a symbol of leadership, as if the Elders' authority wasn't about guidance—but about ensuring nothing slipped beyond their grasp.

Kaelir swung down from his horse and turned toward them. "Wait here. Speak to no one."

Without another word, he strode inside, leaving Thane and Lirien at the entrance. Thane shifted, glancing at Lirien, searching her face for any sign of reassurance.

She gave him none, turning away.

Kaelir returned minutes later, his expression solemn and dark. "They will see you now. Follow me."

Thane exchanged a glance with Lirien, but she gave nothing away. She was already moving before he could decide whether to hesitate, and he fell into step beside her, feeling the weight of the moment settle over him. Whatever happened in this meeting would shape what came next. He had no illusions about how this would go—he wasn't walking into a room full of allies.

The council chamber was not what he expected. It was neither grand nor austere, but something in between—a place built for purpose rather than display. The circular room was constructed from dark, polished wood, the ceiling supported by thick beams that twisted like the gnarled roots of an ancient tree. The scent of earth and aged parchment clung to the air, mixing with the faint trace of burning sage. Runes, intricate and deliberate, were carved into the walls, their meaning lost on Thane but exuding a quiet power.

Seven Elders sat in a semicircle on elevated wooden seats, their robes a deep green, lined with woven runes, the Duskthorn Circle embroidered on their robes for all to see. They were old, but not frail—there was something ageless about them, as if they had witnessed more than time should allow.

A man with silver-threaded hair sat at the center, his piercing gaze resting on Lirien, almost wholly dismissive of Thane's presence. To his left, a broad-shouldered man with a thick beard streaked in white watched with a furrowed brow, his calloused hands clasped before him. A tall woman with sharp, patrician features sat to the right, fingers steepled in thought, her piercing gaze assessing Thane as if stripping him to the bone. Further down the row, a gaunt, hollow-cheeked man leaned forward, his deep-set eyes gleaming in the dim candlelight. The remaining Elders wore expressions ranging from curiosity to caution.

Another figure stood just behind the seated Elders, shifting between them like a shadow. A woman—no older than her mid-twenties, draped in the same deep green, but without the same weight of age or wear. Her dark auburn hair was swept into a loose braid, and her eyes—sharp, calculating—moved quickly between Thane and Lirien. She stood behind the Elders, close enough to whisper to them, both an observer and advisor.

Thane caught the way the silver-haired Elder tilted his head slightly, just enough for her to lean in and murmur something before he gave his reply.

Kaelir took his place to the side, arms folded, his presence a silent statement. Lirien, however, stepped forward without hesitation. The Elders knew her. Knew her well. Her name carried weight in this chamber, and Thane could feel it in the way they regarded her—not just as a witness, but as someone whose words mattered.

"Lirien," the silver-haired Elder greeted, his tone carrying something measured, something knowing. "You return to us with grim tidings. Speak."

Lirien's voice was steady as she recounted the fall of Asmenson. She left nothing out—the destruction, the Wild Magic that tore through the Sanctum, and the death. And then, she turned toward Thane, her gaze sharp, voice firm.

"He was there," she said. "He brought the Wild Magic."

For the first time, the Elders set eyes on Thane as a murmur passed through them. Their expressions shifted from curiosity to something more pointed—scrutiny, accusation.

"Then he is responsible for what happened?" the bearded Elder asked, his voice a low rumble. "For the deaths of your people?"

Before Lirien could respond, the woman in the shadows stepped forward, leaning in close to the Elder with deep-set eyes. Another whisper. Another glance cast toward Thane.

"You claim his magic is wild," the Elder said, his voice cracking with age. "But was it drawn to him, or through him?"

The question had a leading edge, and Thane caught the way the woman—whoever she was—eased back into the shadows, her role fulfilled for now.

Lirien's jaw tensed, and Thane could feel the weight of all their eyes measuring him.

Lirien's lips pressed into a thin line. "I'm sorry, Durst, I do not know the difference. But he did carry the magic."

The Elders exchanged glances, the tension mounting between them.

Then, deliberately, Lirien lifted Thane's hand in hers, palm turned upward. "But he's more than an outlander wielding wild magic. He carries another mark as well."

She reached for the knife at her belt and, before anyone could react, dragged the edge across Thane's palm.

"Son of a bitch," he cursed, jerking his hand back, but the damage was already done.

A single drop of red blood welled up and fell, stark against the wood floor.

"The one who bleeds red shall command the magic born wild." Lirien recited, her voice echoing through the room.

A ripple of unease passed through the chamber, but she pressed on.

"You know the prophecy, the ones written in the

Codex. But there are other writings—ones that were disregarded, ignored because they did not fit your chosen truths."

The reaction was immediate.

Murmurs. A sneer. A derisive shake of the head.

One of the Elders scoffed. "A myth. A contradiction. The Chosen One is marked by the Heart, not the color of his blood."

"A misinterpretation," another muttered.

"Deny it all you want," Lirien said, stepping forward. "You can debate his place, question his intentions—but you cannot change what's been written. He calls the Wild Magic, and his blood flows red."

The room was thick with unease, but the Elders did not accept it. Would not accept it.

"That text was dismissed long ago," the silver-haired Elder finally said, voice clipped. "It does not align with—"

And that's when the whispering woman—the one who had been guiding the questioning—stepped forward for the first time, her expression no longer composed, but intent.

"You are not alone in your belief in those words," she said, looking at Lirien, her voice no longer hushed but steady, carrying across the chamber. "Because I do too."

The room turned toward her. Even the Elders hesitated.

"It was written by Varos Tellan," she continued. "A fragment, buried in the archives of The Obsidian Athenaeum in Felderwin. It was cast aside as unverified— no link to the Codex, and so Varos' writings were never seen as legitimate. It was ignored because it did not fit the prophecy Arbelon wanted."

She exhaled sharply, her voice gaining weight. "But it was real."

Her gaze cut across the Elders. "And it spoke of the blood."

The room erupted.

Some Elders recoiled in disbelief. Others leaned forward, whispering, their voices urgent. Kaelir subtly stepped to the woman's side, in a position of support, but that was lost on the others. Thane also didn't miss the flicker of uncertainty in Kaelir's eyes—nor the way they moved between her and the Elders, watching, ready.

Durst narrowed his eyes. "Blood alone does not prove him. The Heart must judge."

At that, Thane's stomach twisted. The way he said it—like the Heart was something real, something that decided things—itched at the edges of his mind. He reminded himself this was just a game. A VR experience. Nothing more. But the room, the weight of their stares, the very air around him—none of this felt fake. He had to give props to the devs.

The bearded Elder turned to Lirien. "So you are claiming he bears the marks of the Chosen One?" he asked, incredulous.

Lirien hesitated just long enough for the weight of the question to sink in. Thane realized something—she wasn't damning him. She wasn't defending him either, but she wasn't handing him over to the wolves.

"I claim nothing," Lirien said. "I only present the truth."

The room filled with argument, Elders speaking over one another. Some insisted he be judged for his crimes, others that he be tested, while a few still refused to believe what they had seen.

Finally, the silver-haired Elder raised his hand, commanding silence. "What do you seek, Lirien? Do you call for punishment? Retribution for Asmenson?"

Thane barely had time to process what was asked before that voice slithered through his mind, low and insidious.

See how they judge you? They only seek to use you or destroy you. But you know this already, don't you?

He stiffened. *He did know.* The whisper crawled inside his mind like a truth he had always been avoiding. His teachers, his classmates, even his so-called friends back on Earth—they had all done the same. They had started treating him like a thing to be managed, pitied, debated— but never truly seen. Just like these Elders were doing now.

Lirien met the Elder's gaze without flinching. "No."

The weight of that word seemed to settle over every- one. Even Thane. He turned to her, bewildered. This wasn't how he thought this would go.

"I do not seek punishment because I do not know what truly happened that night," she continued. "The Wild Magic was beyond any of us. Perhaps Asmenson was lost by his hands, but perhaps it was the will of the Heart. If he is what you fear, then you must judge him accordingly. But if he is what you hope—" her gaze swept across the room, lingering on the Elders who had not spoken "—then you must allow him to prove it."

Hope.

Thane stiffened at the word. Something sharp twisted in his gut, something bitter. *Not this again. Not hope.*

The Elders murmured among themselves, but they were still ignoring him. Talking *about* him, deciding *for* him.

His frustration was building, feeding off his latent anger, feeding off the futility of hope, reminding him of how he was abandoned by his friends. He didn't come here to be reminded of his life. He came here to escape it.

The frustration churned in his gut, hot and sharp. "So this is how you treat your so-called Chosen One?" Thane barked suddenly, his voice cutting through the air like a whip. "You whisper behind my back, debate my existence like I'm not standing right in front of you? Maybe you should just get it over with—burn me at the stake, or whatever it is you do to people who don't fit into your little stories."

Several Elders recoiled, while others sat rigid, watching him with expressions that ranged from disgust to intrigue.

"You dare come to this place and claim to be the Chosen One. Yet, you mock us, our ways," the tall female Elder cut in, her eyes daggers.

Things were deteriorating fast, until the woman with the dark auburn hair raised her voice, commanding the room. "If the prophecy is true," she continued, "then he is already tied to the Heart. But it must be confirmed."

She turned to the silver-haired Elder, holding his gaze.

"Are you suggesting what I think you are, Erynn?" the silver-haired Elder said, defeated.

"Yes," Erynn answered. "The Test. It is the only way to know for certain."

"Yes, the Test," the tall female Elder murmured in agreement, almost mirthful.

The bearded Elder frowned, his voice distraught. "You would send him?"

Another beat of silence. Another moment of uncertainty. One of the other Elders shook their head. "It is reckless. We know nothing about him."

"We know enough," the silver-haired Elder countered, leveling his gaze at Thane. "If he is what the prophecy speaks of, then we must know. And if he is not—" his voice darkened "—he is a danger that must be dealt with. Either way, the Heart's judgment is absolute."

What the fuck did absolute mean? Thane's pulse kicked against his ribs. His fingers twitched at his sides. He could see they weren't talking about a trial or some ritual initiation—they were talking about something far worse. Something dangerous.

Then, a sudden noise from outside shattered the moment.

The doors to the chamber burst open, and Kaelir reacted before anyone else, moving with lethal grace as his sword unsheathed, stepping between the scout and the Elders, between Lirien and Erynn—between even Thane—shielding them all.

It was one of the scouts from Kaelir's party. He bolted upright at the sight of Kaelir standing before him, sword drawn. The scout barely caught his breath before gasping.

"Kaelir, the Riders of the Rings. They are coming."

9

———

THROUGH SHADOW AND STEEL

SILENCE GRIPPED the room for half a beat before the Elders erupted into murmurs, some voices rising in alarm, others cold and calculating. Thane didn't need to know much about these Riders to understand one thing—

Everyone was afraid.

Before anyone could react further, the door slammed open again. Cael strode in, his presence instantly turning the room tense. "You know why they come," he said, his voice cutting through the chaos. "You can't let them have him."

The Elders turned on him immediately, their distaste evident.

"You are the last man we would entrust with this," one of them spat. "You've already done enough damage."

Cael's jaw tightened, his frustration barely contained. "There is no time to debate. The Riders are closing in. You need me. And you hate that, don't you?"

The silver-haired Elder narrowed his eyes. "Need you? You brought ruin upon us once already. We will not give you the opportunity to do so again."

Cael scoffed, stepping forward. "And yet, here you are. Still talking. Still hesitating." His voice sharpened, biting through the tension. "You know damn well why they're here. They want the boy. And if you let them take him, then Arbelon dies with him."

"You assume too much," another Elder cut in. "Perhaps his fate is to fail the Test, just as all the others have."

Cael laughed—dry, humorless. "Listen to yourselves. You sound just like you did before." He turned, eyes scanning the chamber. "You sat here while the Heart withered, while the Wild Magic frayed at the edges of reality. You let Arbelon bleed. And now, given the first real sign of change, you cower behind debate and ritual."

"The Test is no simple ritual," the silver-haired Elder snapped.

"No, it's a death sentence," Cael shot back. "One that's killed everyone who walked its path. And yet here I am, offering to take him there." His eyes burned with conviction. "Because like it or not, he is bound to the Heart, and you know it."

The silver-haired Elder pushed his chair back and stood, pointing at Cael. "We will not be goaded by the words of a traitor."

"A traitor?" Cael's laugh was bitter. "I was one of you. I sat where you sit. I bled for Arbelon. And now you turn your backs because the truth I found wasn't the one you wanted."

"You meddled with forces beyond your control," the Elder shot back.

"And you did nothing," Cael snapped. "You let the Heart wither. You let our world break. And you still refuse to act."

The silver-haired Elder let out a deep sigh, taking his seat once again. His eyes looked upon Cael with pain.

"Maybe the Cael I used to know could be trusted. But too much has passed." He glanced at the others. "We cannot let you—"

Then Kaelir broke in, stepping forward.

"I will ensure the boy reaches the Test."

The weight of his voice cut through the argument. The Elders turned to him, their hesitation still evident, but they trusted Kaelir—far more than they trusted Cael.

Kaelir's gaze didn't waver. "If he is to be tested, he needs to get there in one piece. I will see it done."

The Elders exchanged glances. Finally, the silver-haired Elder gave a curt nod. "Take him, both of you. The Riders must not claim him."

Lirien stepped forward, her voice steady but burning with barely contained anger. "I go too."

The Elders turned on her at once. "You are not needed," one of them said sharply.

"Not needed?" she echoed, disbelief hardening into fury. "Who among you has more right to see him to the Test than I? Who among you has seen firsthand what the Wild Magic does? I watched Asmenson burn. I felt the magic tear through him. I held what was left."

The room fell uncomfortably silent, but the Elders remained unmoved.

"We do not choose companions for sentiment," the silver-haired Elder replied coldly.

"Sentiment?" Lirien's fists clenched. "This isn't sentiment. It's survival. If he doesn't make it to the Test alive, none of this matters. You trust Kaelir to protect him. You trust Cael to guide him. Then trust me to keep him standing long enough to reach the threshold—unless you've forgotten that I was the best Healer in Asmenson."

"The Riders are closing in," another Elder snapped. "We cannot waste time arguing—"

"Then stop arguing," Lirien bit out. "If he is what you hope, if the Wild Magic is as dangerous as you claim, then he needs me," Lirien pressed. "Not later. Now."

A long, tense pause. Finally, the silver-haired Elder exhaled sharply. "Go."

The Elders nodded reluctantly.

"Erynn goes as well."

The words came not from the silver-haired Elder, but from another, one who had remained silent until now.

Erynn's gaze flicked toward them, and for the first time, she looked startled.

"Me?"

"You know the histories. The prophecies," the Elder said firmly. "If he is what you claim, then you will be the one to see the signs first."

The words had barely left the Elder's lips before Kaelir spoke.

"No." His voice was sharp, cutting through the chamber's tension. "She stays."

The Elders turned their attention to him, unfazed.

"She goes," the silver-haired Elder countered smoothly. "She has studied the prophecies. She understands the nature of the Test more than anyone here."

Kaelir's jaw clenched, his fingers curling into fists. "She's not a fighter."

"That's nonsense, and you know it," another Elder said. "She had more training than most of us. Maybe even you."

Erynn blinked, looking between them all. "I—" she started, but Kaelir cut her off.

"This is madness," he snapped. His eyes locked onto the Elders, but his stance had shifted ever so slightly—positioned now between them and Erynn. "You send scholars on excursions. Not into the hands of Riders."

The silver-haired Elder exhaled. "She is no mere scholar. She will go. That is final."

Kaelir's gaze darkened slightly, but he said nothing. He turned toward Erynn instead, a flicker of something unspoken passing between them.

Erynn swallowed hard. Then, to his clear dismay, she nodded. "I'll go, Kaelir. It's okay."

Cael's jaw clenched as he caught sight of Erynn for the first time, but he said nothing as the group solidified. There was no time to argue. Kaelir motioned for them to follow.

Lirien was already ahead of him, motioning for Thane to follow. He hesitated for only a second before moving, feet carrying him forward even as his mind struggled to catch up. This was happening too fast. One moment he was being debated like an object, the next he was apparently important enough to smuggle away like some royal treasure.

Kaelir yanked back the thick, woven rug in the center of the chamber, revealing a seam in the wooden floor—nearly invisible unless you knew where to look. He knelt, pressing his palm against a knot in the wood. A faint click echoed, and a square section of the floor lifted slightly. Gripping the edge, he pulled it open, revealing a steep, narrow staircase vanishing into darkness.

"Move," he ordered, already descending into the shadows.

The trapdoor snapped shut behind them, and the tunnel swallowed them in complete darkness. The air grew thick, damp, the scent of old earth pressing in around them. Thane hesitated at the bottom of the steps, his vision lost in the void ahead.

Then a soft glow bloomed in the dark. A muted, silver-blue light flickered to life at Cael's fingertips forming a small ball of light that floated into the air, illuminating the tunnel's rough stone walls.

Kaelir shot him a glance. "Keep it forward, Cael. We need to see what's ahead, not our own shadows."

Cael didn't dignify him with a response, merely lifting his hand, and the orb drifted forward like a silver thread unraveling in the dark. It pulsed faintly, shifting ahead of them with the barest inclination of Cael's fingers, sensing his intent before he even moved. It adjusted with each step, floating just ahead, casting shifting shadows along the rough walls, leaving a subtle living mist trailing behind it as they moved.

Thane barely registered the passage around him, too caught by the effortless grace of Cael's magic. There was something mesmerizing about it—the way it pulsed in tune with his breathing, like it was part of him rather than something summoned. It felt different from the magic that had visited him, but oddly similar at the same time. And for a moment, it made the rushed escape feel almost… calm.

The passage sloped downward, shifting from carved stone to packed earth. The walls closed in, the air thickening with dampness.

Then they hit a fork.

Kaelir veered right without hesitation.

"Not that way," Cael cut in, his voice sharp.

Kaelir stiffened mid-step. "You sure?"

"I know these tunnels." Cael's tone left no room for argument.

A tense beat stretched between them, the air charged with something unsaid.

Kaelir exhaled sharply through his nose, a flicker of irritation crossing his face before he schooled his expression. He wasn't used to being challenged—especially not by Cael.

Then, with a clipped nod, Kaelir turned, following Cael's lead.

The tunnel twisted once more before finally ending at a heavy iron door, its surface rough with age, streaked with rust from years of damp air.

Kaelir was already moving, pulling a key from a thin chain around his neck. He slid it into the lock, but before turning it, he pressed his palm against the door, tilting his head to listen. The passage behind them remained silent, but he waited a beat longer.

Then, with a soft *click*, the lock turned.

He opened the door carefully, moving just enough to scan the space beyond before slipping through. The others followed without hesitation, stepping into a cramped, dust-choked cellar lined with old barrels and crates. The air smelled of damp wood and faintly of spilled ale.

Kaelir quietly pushed the door shut behind him and locked it again, his movements swift and purposeful.

"Where are we?" Lirien whispered.

"Just a sleepy cellar on the outskirts of town," Kaelir murmured. "This way." He turned climbing a narrow wooden staircase to a door as Cael extinguished his light.

Kaelir lifted the brace on the door, opening it just enough to peek outside to see an empty alley lit by flickering lanterns.

"Clear," he muttered, but he halted before stepping out. The street was quiet. Too quiet.

"The Riders will know to watch the roads," he murmured, scanning the area again. "Once we get out of the city, we take the back paths through the foothills."

No one argued. There was no time.

Kaelir drew his sword and gestured for them to follow. "Stay close."

Thane stepped to follow, almost bumping into Lirien as she dug through her pack removing the bladeless pommel she'd taken from Asmenson, gripping it tightly.

They moved away and kept to the alleys, weaving through the narrow backstreets. The flickering lantern light sent unease skittering down Thane's spine. He couldn't shake the feeling that, at any moment, they could be seen. That one wrong glance could spell disaster. His stomach tightened when the silence broke—not from behind them, but from ahead.

They emerged from the last row of buildings to see a group of horsemen blocking the road ahead. A dozen, maybe more. Hooded. Armed. Waiting. Their armor was a dark color, and in the darkness it was hard to glean much detail, but the way Kaelir cursed under his breath told him everything he needed to know.

"Riders," Kaelir hissed.

The Riders of the Rings had found them first.

The man at the front urged his horse forward. Even in the dim light, there was no mistaking his authority. His cloak wore the darkened, jagged ring around the neckline. His voice rang clear in the night air.

"Hand over the outlander."

Thane's stomach lurched. *Outlander. They meant him.*

Kaelir's grip tightened on his sword as he took a slow step forward, planting himself between Thane and the approaching Riders.

"He is under our protection, Bostick."

Bostick tilted his head, the flickering torchlight barely illuminating his face beneath the hood. "You of all people should know better than to stand against us."

Kaelir's grip on his sword never wavered, but something flickered in his gaze—not surprise, not fear, but something colder. Something old.

"Maybe," he said, his voice measured. "But you of all people should know I don't scare easy."

Bostick's lips pressed into a thin line. "No. You never did."

Kaelir stood his ground, not moving an inch. But Lirien did.

Without a word, she moved to his side, fingers curling around the pommel in her grasp. A heartbeat passed. Then, with a whisper of magic, the blade bloomed to life—a brilliant, ethereal arc of energy that cut through the night like a white flame. It left glowing trails in the air as she lifted it, the air around her humming with power. The light reflected in her eyes, resolute, unyielding.

Cael followed, stepping into place on Kaelir's other side. With a sharp movement, he slammed his quarterstaff to the earth, and a violent ripple of energy raced up its length. Lightning crackled, licking across the wood like a living thing, throwing eerie flashes against the buildings around them.

They did not speak. They did not need to.

The three stood as one.

Kaelir raised his sword.

"You'll have to go through us."

Their response was immediate—the Riders charged.

Kaelir shot a glance over his shoulder. His voice was firm but not harsh.

"Stay back with the boy."

Thane saw Erynn stiffen next to him, her lips opened to object, but no words came. She didn't move, but the tension in her stance was clear. If the Riders got their hands on him, there would be no Test. No future.

She didn't argue. But she didn't step away, either.

Blades flashed. Kaelir met the first strike with brutal precision, twisting his sword to deflect the attack before pulling the Rider from his saddle. Lirien moved in perfect counter, her blade finding gaps in their defenses with the efficiency of a healer who knew exactly where to cut.

Cael fought like a man with nothing left to lose—reckless, unpredictable, a storm barely leashed.

Thane took a step back. He had no weapon. No training. There were simply too many Riders, coming too fast.

A Rider broke through the chaos, blade raised. Coming straight for him.

Thane barely had time to react before something slammed into his side.

He staggered—his balance ripped out from under him just as the Rider's sword came down hard. It bit across his cheek, hot and sharp, but—he was still standing.

His head snapped to the side. Erynn stood by him, her eyes shifting from him to the Rider as the pain flared through him uncontrolled. Then something inside cracked, calling out.

Not just inside. *On him.*

A sharp burning sensation lanced across his forearm, then his chest—as if something inside was clawing its way to the surface.

He barely had time to register it before thin, jagged fractures raced up his arms, glowing with a deep, shifting light.

The cracks webbed across his skin, pulsing—alive, erratic, untamed.

His pulse hammered. *Not again.*

The glow brightened—pulsing like a heartbeat.

Then the Wild Magic answered.

Coming just as it had before.

Heat—raw and alive—flooded his veins. His skin tingled, his teeth ached, his heartbeat pounded, silencing the battle around him. The world lurched, turning hazy at the edges, as if reality itself had cracked open and pulled him inside.

Then the night bloomed into blinding fire.

A shockwave of pure force erupted from him, expanding in an instant—a wall of shimmering, rippling distortion that swallowed the street.

The Riders were ripped from their saddles, their bodies flung like rag dolls, limbs twisting as they crashed into the ground. Their horses remained standing, muscles seizing in terror before some bolted into the darkness, their hooves thundering in retreat.

Buildings groaned under the weight of the force, their walls trembling, wooden shutters slamming open like startled eyes. The walls of the closest buildings collapsed inward, windows shattering.

But then—something changed.

The magic hesitated. It didn't rage uncontrollably like before. It pulled back. Redirected.

Thane barely registered it, but he felt it—the magic wasn't just reacting anymore. It was choosing.

The magic's expanding, relentless force funneled itself into a single focal point now directed at the towering watchtower ahead.

A deep, splitting crack ripped through the air as its foundation gave way. For a moment, it hung there, teetering on the edge of oblivion. Then, with a deafening roar, it caved inward, stone crushing stone, collapsing in a controlled, deliberate ruin.

Thane felt the magic restrain itself. He could feel the destruction it could have done—the ruin it had almost unleashed—but instead, it had chosen.

Thane barely had time to process it. The world spun, his limbs too heavy to hold him upright.

As his vision blurred, he saw Bostick rise to his knees from the dust, staring at him—not with rage, but with something far worse.

Recognition.

Thane's body, finally refusing to hold him upright as the cost of the magic sank its claws into him. Thane's knees hit the ground as his body convulsed violently, blood dripping from his nose, mixing with the fresh wound on his cheek.

The glowing cracks sank beneath his skin, vanishing as if they had never been there.

Except—they had. And he could still feel them, burning, phantom-like.

Through the haze, he heard shouts. Kaelir's voice. Then Lirien's.

Then—hands on him. Steadying him.

It was Erynn, again.

She was breathing hard, eyes wide, but her grip on his arm was firm. Not afraid. Not running.

"Come on," she urged. "You have to move."

And then Kaelir was there, grabbing him, throwing him onto a horse, lashing him to the saddle. The others grabbed the reins of the scattered mounts, and they rode hard, disappearing into the night, leaving Trosten behind.

Thane's mind was slipping. Fading. The last thing he saw was the smoke curling from the ruins of the fallen watchtower.

A voice eased into his mind, steady and confident.

"Everyone will bow to you. You are more powerful than they'll ever admit. Remember that."

Then everything went dark.

10

THE WEIGHT OF TIME

THE WORLD FOUGHT to keep him this time.

Arbelon didn't just vanish—it clung to him, stretching the moment, refusing to release him until the last possible second. When he finally broke free, it was like being yanked through a closing door—too late to stop, too soon to land. Then, Earth hit him like a runaway train.

The air here felt wrong—thin, empty, too still. The taste of Arbelon's damp air still clung to his tongue, but it faded fast, replaced by the artificial chill of his bedroom. The shift had always been a little disorienting, but this? This was a whole new level of strange.

His body was heavy, drained, and his breath came in ragged gasps as he lay sprawled across the floor beside his unkempt bed. The VR headset askew, but still strapped to his head, pressed into his temple at an awkward angle. He ripped it off, blinking through the haze.

The pain resurfaced again, sharp and relentless. But it had never really left, he'd just forgotten it, until now. His cheek burned like fire, the wet warmth of his blood trailing down his jaw, dripping onto his shirt. In a game, this would be the part where the screen blurred red at the edges, the HUD flashing a warning.

But there was no HUD. No reset. Just pain. Real, and inescapable.

He lifted shaking fingers to the wound and winced. The memory of the Rider's blade slicing through his flesh was fresh, mere seconds ago, a world away.

His vision swam, his mind still reeling from being abruptly disconnected again. Each time it'd gotten more difficult, and this time was no exception. His limbs tingled, unresponsive, like static had seeped into his bones.

Then, the scent hit him. Burnt air. Raw power. Something old, something alive. It shouldn't be here—couldn't be here—but it was. Or was it?

Wild Magic.

And just as quickly, it was gone, leaving only the coppery tang of his blood.

Thane's fingers hovered over the wound on his cheek, barely touching it. The moment his skin made contact, a strange pulse flooded through him—not pain, but memory. Or was it something more?

Lirien's face.

She was beautiful. Not in the filtered, polished way of the girls he had known on Earth, but in something deeper —fierce, untamed, real. A girl like her wouldn't have spared him a glance back home. Not when he was dying. Not when he was broken.

She looked pale. Stricken. Eyes wide with something between horror and disbelief. But her voice—her voice was steady.

"Not all wounds last forever."

Her words struck something deep in him, like they had always been there, waiting.

"We can't do this without you."

It didn't feel like a plea. It didn't feel like a demand. It felt like the truth.

The sting of the Rider's blade slicing through his skin. The heat of his own blood spilling.

Thane jerked back to the present, his hand snapping away from his face. His heart pounded against his ribs, his breath uneven. His cheek burned. The wound was here. *How was that even possible?*

He had fallen. He must have hit his cheek on the desk or the bed—that was it. That had to be it.

He swallowed hard, forcing down the nausea rising in his gut.

"It's just a game," he muttered.

But even as the words left his lips, they felt thinner than before.

The door burst open.

"Thane—" his mother's voice caught the second she saw him.

He barely registered the way she rushed to his side, kneeling next to him, hands hovering but afraid to touch.

"Oh my god—what happened? Can you hear me?"

"Yeah," he gritted out, trying to push himself upright. His arms shook beneath him. "I'm fine—just fell. It's nothing."

Her sharp inhale told him she didn't believe a word of it. Her hands found his face, her fingers brushing the raw edges of the wound. She sucked in a sharp breath, her thumb coming away red. "Oh, Thane…"

He shrugged off her touch, trying to force a smirk through the haze of pain. "Not the first time I've had a bad landing."

"Thane, this isn't funny."

"No," he agreed, dragging himself up to lean against the edge of his bed. "It really isn't. Kinda hurts," he said, pressing the loose end of the blanket hanging from his bed against his cheek.

She swallowed hard, reaching for her phone. "I'm calling Dr. Hughes."

"I don't need a doctor."

"You're bleeding, Thane. He said things would progress—" she stopped herself short of finishing that thought and changed approach "—he needs to know about this."

Her voice cracked at the edges, and for a second, something inside him twisted. He hated that—hated the way her pain made him feel like a burden, like something fragile she was trying to hold together. But what was he supposed to do? Pretend like any of this could be fixed?

He sighed, closing his eyes and leaning his head against the bed. She was right, it seemed things were progressing. He just wasn't ready for it so soon.

"Fine. Call him."

His mother lingered for a moment, still watching him like he might vanish if she blinked. Then, without a word, she turned and walked toward the kitchen.

Thane pushed himself up, wincing as his body protested. He was still unsteady, still disoriented, but he followed. The silence between them stretched all the way down the hall, the kind that said too much and nothing at all.

The kitchen smelled like toast and chamomile tea. The warmth of it should have been comforting, but it only made the weight in his chest settle deeper. Something else that would be taken away from him.

His mother pulled a clean rag from the drawer, wet it under the sink, and motioned for him to sit. He obeyed without a fight, more from exhaustion than agreement.

She kneeled beside him, dabbing the damp cloth

against his cheek with careful hands. The coolness stung against the wound, but he didn't flinch. He barely felt it.

"I'll make you something to eat," she murmured, standing and moving toward the fridge.

He wanted to protest, but what was the point? She needed to do *something*—some small, normal act of care to pretend things weren't as bad as they were.

By the time she set the plate in front of him, she was already wiping the counter, straightening a napkin—anything to keep herself busy.

Thane sat at the table, barely touching the sandwich his mother had made. The food tasted like cardboard in his mouth. She turned back, pausing with her dishrag in hand.

"You're not eating enough. You'll feel better with some food in you."

He stared at the plate. "Not hungry."

"You should try."

He picked at the crust, silent.

The quiet stretched, thick and heavy. Eventually, she set the dishrag down and turned to face him once again, her voice careful. "Thane… do you think the game could be making *things* worse?"

He stiffened. The question had been coming, he knew it. She'd talked about it before, but he thought it was in the past.

His hands curled into fists on the table. "It's not the game."

She hesitated. "But—"

"It's my brain, Mom. Not the god-damned game system. Gaming is the only thing that keeps me sane. It's all I have left."

Her expression faltered, but she didn't push further.

Just nodded, pressing her lips together, staring at him like she wanted to say more but didn't know how.

The silence between them was unbearable.

Then, the doorbell rang.

Thane didn't move. He knew who it was.

His mother wiped her hands on a dish towel, smoothing down her shirt as she moved to the front door. There was a brief murmur of voices before Dr. Hughes stepped inside, his presence immediately shifting the weight of the room.

"Thane." His tone was even, neither overly warm nor cold, but carrying a weight of familiarity. He had been through this routine before. They all had.

Thane sighed, pushing the plate away and turning slightly to keep the cut on his cheek hidden.

Dr. Hughes set his bag down on the table and pulled up a chair across from him. "Your mother tells me you had another seizure."

"Well, you know how she likes to overreact."

His mother's sharp inhale said otherwise, but she stayed quiet, not wanting a repeat of the last meeting with the doctor in the living room.

Dr. Hughes arched a brow, unfazed. "And you hit your head during this 'overreaction'?"

Thane didn't answer.

Dr. Hughes took out his penlight. "Look at me."

Thane obeyed, though reluctantly. The moment he did, the doctor's eyes caught on Thane's cheek. He stilled, his gaze landing on the wound.

"You didn't tell me about this," Dr. Hughes said, glancing at Jane, before he leaned in slightly for a closer look.

"I'm sorry. I thought I mentioned it. But it was all so hectic," she said, stepping closer, leaning on the counter.

"So, what happened?" Dr. Hughes asked, trying to hide the concern in his voice, but it was obvious.

Thane shrugged. "Must have hit the desk or something when I fell."

The doctor leaned in slightly, abandoning the penlight entirely. Instead, he reached into his bag, pulling on a pair of gloves before inspecting the wound with a practiced touch. His fingers were clinical, methodical—but when he spoke again, his tone carried something different. Curiosity.

"This is clean," he murmured, almost to himself. "Not consistent with blunt trauma. More like a—" he hesitated, eyes flicking to Thane's. "—a sharp edge."

Thane's chest tightened. His mind flashed back to the Rider's blade, the burning sting of the strike, the feeling of blood trailing down his face.

Impossible.

He pulled back, shaking his head. "I don't know. Maybe I hit something sharp. It doesn't matter."

Dr. Hughes studied him for a long moment before exhaling through his nose. "It's not deep enough for stitches, but it'll leave a mark." He reached for some antiseptic and steri-strips, working in silence as he closed the wound.

The only other sound in the kitchen was the rhythmic ticking of the wall clock. Steady. Unchanging.

When Dr. Hughes finished, he leaned forward slightly. His voice was calm but firm.

"Thane, I'm not going to sugarcoat this. The seizures are getting worse. They're a sign the disease is progressing. We need to decide whether to start one of the experimental treatments soon."

Thane's fingers stretched out, pressing against the tabletop. "We've already talked about that."

"Yes, but there are *new* trials," Dr. Hughes continued. "One's using new AI and nanotechnology. They're showing real promise."

Thane's mother swallowed thickly, blinking rapidly as she folded her hands in front of her.

Thane exhaled slowly, pressing his fingers against the tabletop. He wasn't going to get better. He knew that. Dr. Hughes knew that.

But his mom—she still held on to that last shred of hope, fragile as glass. And the way she was looking at him now, like she was bracing for him to say *no*—he couldn't do it to her. Not today.

He swallowed hard. "I'll think about it."

He didn't know if he actually meant it or if he just wanted this conversation to end before it went any deeper. Into places he'd rather not go.

Dr. Hughes studied him for a long moment, then nodded. "That's all I ask," he said, his tone softer as he reached out patting Thane on the hand. "I understand how you feel right now, but breakthroughs can happen."

A heavy pause settled over them before his mother broke it with a question of her own.

"The game," she said, hesitantly. "Could it be making things worse?"

Dr. Hughes looked at Thane carefully before answering. "There is research linking prolonged VR exposure to increased seizure activity, yes. But in cases like Thane's, stress plays a much larger factor."

Thane smirked, but there was no humor in it. "So I should just live stress-free? Great. Problem solved."

His mother shot him a look, but Dr. Hughes only sighed. "I'm not saying cut it out completely. But if you start feeling dizzy or nauseous, take a break. Listen to your body and take a rest."

Thane didn't respond.

His mother did. "We'll make sure he does."

Dr. Hughes didn't add anything more. A moment later, he was out the door.

The silence that followed Dr. Hughes' departure was thick, pressing down on the kitchen like an unspoken weight neither of them wanted to acknowledge. Thane stood in the kitchen for a moment, unmoving, then quietly slipped away while his mother cleared the dishes.

He walked down the hall slowly, each step heavier than the last. When he reached his room, he closed the door behind him and leaned against it for a moment, eyes closed. The familiar chaos of his space surrounded him—posters askew, laundry in lazy heaps, the VR headset still coiled near the foot of his bed.

He crossed to the mirror above his dresser and stared at his reflection. The gash on his cheek was angry and red, a thin line now framed by the steri-strips Dr. Hughes had applied. He leaned closer, narrowing his eyes.

It didn't look like something caused by a fall.

He touched it lightly and winced.

This is clean. Not consistent with blunt trauma. More like a sharp edge.

The voice of Dr. Hughes echoed in his mind.

Thane swallowed hard. The Rider's blade. He remembered the way it had burned through him—how the moment had felt real. Too real.

But that was impossible.

Wasn't it?

He turned away from the mirror, his thoughts a haze of confusion and denial. He sat down on the edge of the bed, elbows on his knees, hands steepled over his lips.

A soft knock at the door broke his train of thought.

"Thane?"

His mother's voice, quiet. Tentative.

"Yeah," he said, not moving.

The door creaked open, and she stepped inside, carrying something in her hand. Her expression was uncertain, guarded, like she was trying not to fall apart.

She crossed the room slowly, then sat beside him on the bed.

"I… I wanted to give you something," she said, her voice trembling. She held out her hand.

The familiar black leather band, worn and softened with age. The silver face slightly scratched but still ticking. Steady. Unfazed.

His father's watch.

There was a silence between them. Neither moving. Then, softer, "He used to say it kept him centered. It reminded him that time keeps going, even when everything else feels like it's falling apart. I think you need it now more than I do."

Thane stared at it.

"No," he said quietly. "You should keep it. I'll be gone soon anyway."

She set the watch down on the bed, leaning in and taking his hands. His head lifted to meet her eyes. Both of them moist, both of them trying to hold back.

"That's not true. And even if it were, it wouldn't change how much I love you. Just wear it, Thane. Let it remind you… that you're never alone."

She reached down, picking up the watch, placing it gently in his palm.

"It's yours now."

"I don't deserve it," he whispered.

Her voice cracked just a little. "You do. Your father would want you to have it."

Thane looked away, jaw tight. "I've already let him down."

She shook her head. "You haven't. Not once. And you never could."

Thane stared down at the watch. The weight of it in his hand felt heavier than it should have. His fingers closed around it slowly. Then, with quiet purpose, he fastened it around his wrist. The band was slightly loose, but the weight felt right.

His mother smiled faintly and kissed the top of his head. "Take a little nap and get some rest, sweetheart."

He just nodded.

She left the room, the door clicking softly shut behind her.

Thane lay back on the bed, letting the exhaustion wash over him. His hand drifted to the watch on his wrist. The familiar rhythm of its ticking settled into his skin like a second heartbeat.

His thoughts blurred as sleep crept in, pulling him away from the stillness of his bedroom… toward wild trees, broken skies, and the fragments of voices that refused to fade.

The ticking on his wrist grew louder. Or maybe it was something deeper beneath it—a rhythm not mechanical but alive.

Like the heartbeat of something far away.

Then, just as the last thread of wakefulness slipped from his mind, a whisper burrowed up from the silence.

Tick-tock, Thane. Even that bauble will betray you.

Thane's eyes shot open, his heart pounding. The room was still, unchanged. But the whisper lingered, deep in the corners of his mind.

He sat up slowly, trying to shake it off. Another hallucination. Another side effect of the seizures. That voice—he didn't know what it was. But he knew it knew him.

And it wasn't finished.

But how could it be here? In my room. A chill crept down his spine, as he swung his feet over the side of the bed.

It's just a game… it's just a game.

He glanced at the headset. Then at the door. Then back again.

We can't do this without you. Lirien's words echoed through his mind, the grim resolve on her face evident. Something about it—about her—was so honest… and real in that moment. He knew it made no sense.

But he didn't want to think.

He didn't want to doubt.

He just needed to go back.

Thane slipped the headset over his face. The startup sequence hummed to life, the loading screen flickering into view.

Loading…

The steady tick of the watch on his wrist lined up— unmistakably—with the soft pulses of the game as Arbelon resolved into view.

The loading screen pulsed once more. And then, the world sharpened around him, Arbelon blooming to life.

NO SAFE ROADS

THE WORLD DIDN'T FADE in—it slammed every sense on max volume.

The pounding rhythm of hooves. The creak of worn leather reins. The sharp sting across his cheek. He was slumped forward, wrists bound tightly to the saddle horn with coarse leather straps that scraped the skin raw. The steady gallop of the horse beneath him rattled his bones, jarring through his spine.

His head throbbed. He tasted blood. A deep gash split his cheek, still oozing from where a Rider's blade had caught him.

What the hell….? Disoriented, he blinked against the rush of cold air and tree limbs flying past in a blur.

Every sense was screaming—every jolt, every scent of decomposing leaves, every snort of the horse gasping for air, every groan of the leather straps biting into his wrists.

Too real.

He gritted his teeth, trying to orient himself.

"This is insane," he muttered under his breath, voice hoarse.

He could feel everything. The vibration of the horse's gait rattling up his legs. The heat of the beast's body. The smell of its sweat.

None of that should be this detailed. *Since when do game physics simulate chafing?*

Memories came flooding back—his magic flaring, Riders thrown like rag-dolls, pain screaming in his skull before everything went dark.

Then… this.

Great. Black out, then booted back into hell. Except… this didn't feel like reloading a save. It felt like waking up inside a nightmare.

Up ahead, Kaelir rode hard, giving clipped, sharp orders over his shoulder. His words were low, meant to blend with the wind and avoid carrying far. At intervals, he made abrupt turns, weaving through denser parts of the forest, clearly trying to foil anyone attempting to track them.

"Where are we even going?" Lirien called out, her voice barely audible over the thunder of hooves.

"No questions," Kaelir snapped, not looking back. "Just ride."

Beside Thane, Lirien stayed close, her expression tight with concern but her eyes constantly flicking to the forest around them. Cael rode just behind, stealing glances over his shoulder. Thane could hear him muttering something under his breath, holding his reins in one hand, the other moving and following his words almost rhythmically. With a final flick of his wrist, the air behind them shimmered faintly for a moment—some kind of minor warding spell, barely visible.

"That should buy us a little time," Cael said grimly.

Erynn rode close to Kaelir, mirroring his every twist

and turn with quiet confidence. She didn't flinch at the terrain, her posture steady, her grip light—just as skilled in the saddle as any of them.

Around them, the trees closed in as they moved deeper —the woods thickening, branches clawing at their cloaks, the river's murmur growing louder. Moss-covered stones jutted up through the undergrowth, and Thane caught the glimmer of shallow water through the gaps in the brush. The light dimmed, filtering through layers of tangled canopy.

Even injured, he couldn't help but notice how beautiful it was. Like something out of a fantasy map—drawn with reverence, everything put in place with purpose.

Kaelir held his hand up as he slowed to a trot leading his horse into a dense, shadowed thicket tucked against a bend in the river. Trees clustered together, their branches spread like sentinels, shielding the space in quiet shadow. As the others settled into the shadows of the space, he scanned the trail behind them with a practiced eye before swinging down, satisfied for now that they hadn't been followed.

Lirien swung down and was at Thane's side in an instant.

"Let's get you down," she said quietly, releasing the straps with practiced ease.

Thane half-fell from the saddle, landing in the under-growth with a grunt. His limbs buckled, stiff and trembling, dirt clinging to every scrape.

"Well, that was graceful," he muttered, touching the wound on his cheek. His fingers came back red. "Escaped the Riders just to bleed out in a bush. Nice."

"I don't think you're exactly going to bleed out," Lirien said, flashing him a wry smile as she knelt beside him, hands already steady and sure. "Not with me around. Healer, remember?"

It hit Thane harder than he expected—her smile. The first one he'd seen from her. She wore it well.

He knew he didn't deserve her grace. But he wasn't about to push it away either.

Her smile faded, but something softer lingered between them. She reached for her satchel without a word, shifting back into motion—and Thane didn't stop her.

He sat slumped against a moss-covered stone, jaw clenched as she moved closer. Her expression shifted back to focus—calm, confident, in control. The healer taking over.

She worked in silence at first, uncorking a glass vial of pungent-smelling salve and dabbing it onto a length of cloth. When she leaned in to clean the cut on his cheek, Thane flinched instinctively.

"Hold still," she said gently, brushing a bit of dried blood from his temple. "You got lucky."

"Sure doesn't feel like it."

Lirien gave a faint exhale—almost a laugh. "Trust me. If that blade had gone even a finger-width deeper, you wouldn't be talking right now."

Thane's brows pulled together, watching her as she dabbed at the wound with slow, steady care. "You're pretty good at this."

"Comes with the territory." She didn't look up. "My mother was a healer. Learned early."

As she leaned in again, Thane caught the moonlight glinting off her hair—soft, coppery in the gloom.

The scent of the salve rose again—bitter and earthy. But beneath it, something warm, familiar. For a second, it was his mom's garden. Then it was gone.

He nodded slowly, but said nothing. He didn't know

what to do with kindness—especially not from someone who should hate him.

As she worked, her fingers brushed his skin, cool and deliberate. Thane found himself cataloguing the sensation, the way it contrasted so sharply with the heat of the chase, the roar of hooves and blood and terror.

A moment of quiet passed between them. The forest murmured nearby, water trickling over rocks.

Lirien paused, glancing up from her work. "It'll heal," she said softly.

Thane let out a bitter breath. "I don't heal."

Her eyes lingered on his for a moment. "You're stronger than you think."

She didn't say more. Just turned back to her work, hands gentle as she placed a clean bandage on the wound. The silence stretched—not awkward, just heavy with everything unspoken.

Thane broke it first. "You didn't have to help me."

Lirien looked at him then—really looked. "Of course I did."

"No," he said, voice low. "Not after what happened to Asmenson."

Her hands paused. For a moment, the silence grew thick again.

"I don't believe you meant for that to happen," she said finally. "But it did. And you're still here. Trying to do something that matters."

He didn't answer. He didn't trust his voice to hold.

But when she finished, he didn't look away either.

"We've got to move," Kaelir called quietly from the trees. "We're not safe yet."

Just like that, the moment was over.

The moon was low in the sky, its light filtering through the trees. Thane sat forward, still wincing with every movement, but a little steadier now. The ache in his cheek had dulled to a throb, and the bandage was secure.

Kaelir stood a few paces away, one hand resting lightly on the saddle of his horse, eyes scanning the dense shadows of the tree-line.

"We can't ride these mounts much longer," he said without turning. "Too easy to track. And too memorable."

"They're the Riders' horses," Cael added, stepping into the circle. "They'll have every sympathizer in the area on the lookout by morning."

Erynn looked between them. "So we're ditching the horses?"

"Not yet," Kaelir said, turning to face them. "We stop in Comstock—a village a day's ride from here. I know someone. An innkeeper. Keeps to himself, owes me a favor."

Lirien raised a brow. "Are you talking about the Hog's Breath?"

Kaelir gave a faint smirk. "Still standing. Still pouring vinegar they call ale. He can make these mounts disappear and point us toward a safer route on foot."

"That sounds… rustic," Erynn muttered, brushing a leaf from her shoulder. "I hope your friend remembers that favor."

"Wouldn't count on a warm welcome," Cael added, stretching his back. "But he won't ask questions. That's what matters."

Thane didn't say anything. He was too tired to care and too amped up to rest.

Kaelir glanced around the circle, his voice low. "Everyone take a breath. We've got ground to cover, but we'll do it smart."

He nodded toward the dark beyond the clearing. "No

open roads from here on. We stick to the trees. Slow, quiet, less likely to draw attention."

He tightened the saddle straps on his horse, eyes flicking to the edge of the clearing.

"Rest for a few minutes," he said quietly. "But then we keep moving."

No one argued. But no one looked thrilled either.

1 2

A HOG'S BREATH WELCOME

THE ROAD NARROWED as they approached the village, hemmed in by forest on both sides. Thick-trunked trees leaned in close, their limbs gnarled like old fingers. Purple hues of dusk crept through the branches overhead, turning the forest to shadow. The air was still but not silent—just hushed, like the trees were listening. The steady clop of hooves echoed off the packed earth, joined by the soft rush of a nearby river weaving in and out of view between the trees.

A crooked wooden sign marked the path ahead: *Comstock* — the paint faded, half-swallowed by moss and time.

Thane squinted at it, unimpressed. The name meant nothing to him—but something about the hush in the trees made him wish it did.

Kaelir rode ahead without pause, clearly familiar with the way.

As they crested a small rise, the trees opened into a hollow, revealing the village nestled at the river's bend. Wooden cottages with neat thatched roofs clustered together, each with a stone chimney puffing thin trails of smoke into the cool night air. Their windows were aglow with lamplight casting golden reflections off the water that threaded between the buildings. A series of charming wooden bridges arched over the gently moving current, connecting paths and cottages like veins in a living map.

Comstock was no sprawling city—but the neatly stacked firewood and freshly swept stoops marked a community that took pride in its own. It pulsed with life, as people moved briskly to finish their day's work. A butcher hauled a basket of game into his shop. Two kids darted past, laughing, before vanishing down a side lane. Somewhere nearby, a dog barked once, then fell silent. There was movement, warmth, and a quiet sort of vigilance behind every glance from the villagers.

It didn't look like a place that welcomed visitors. It looked like a place that didn't get many.

As they passed through the narrow main road, villagers paused in their evening routines, eyes drawn to the visitors. Conversations dimmed briefly, but then carried on in hushed tones.

Thane noted the unease—not fear, exactly, but a wariness likely sharpened by the fact that they were on the Riders' horses. Stolen. And from the eyes directed their way, it was clear everyone here knew as much.

They kept moving, following Kaelir across a wooden bridge. At the far end of the main road, nestled between a leaning stable and an old stone well, stood a squat timber building. Faded green shingles adorned the roof, and a matching wooden sign swung gently above the door: *The Hog's Breath Inn*.

"You weren't kidding," Erynn said, eyeing the rustic porch. "Somehow exactly what I expected... and still worse," she muttered, wrinkling her nose.

Kaelir dismounted with a grunt that might've been a laugh. "That's the charm."

As the others dismounted, several villagers slowed to watch them. Not their faces—their horses.

Thane caught it too. The gray mounts still wore the Rider's tack—impossible to miss.

A gruff voice rang out from the Inn's open doorway, "Just take the horses to the stable."

A burly man stepped out onto the porch, wiping his hands on a stained apron. His beard was thick and streaked with gray, one eye clouded with cataract. The other fixed sharply on Kaelir.

"Well, I'll be," he said. "Didn't expect to see you unless someone was dragging your body behind a cart."

Kaelir offered a half-smile. "Give it time."

The man smiled, his good eye flicked over the group, then down to the horses. His mouth thinned. "You bringin' trouble to my doorstep, or just asking for a drink?"

"Little of both," Kaelir said. "We need these horses to disappear."

The man snorted. "Yeah, no kidding. Whole damn valley'll know those beasts."

"This is Garrus," Kaelir said over his shoulder. "Owner. Cook. Tavern-keep. Disgruntled local legend."

Garrus eyed the horses again. "I'll see they go missing by morning. But if you brought trouble with you—"

"We'll be gone by first light," Kaelir said.

"You better be," Garrus muttered, before hollering to the stablehands. "Now, get inside," he said, motioning them forward. "You're making the neighbors nervous."

Inside, the Inn was anything but subtle. Warm candle-light spilled across timber walls and mismatched rugs. The scent of roasted meat and fresh bread clung to the air. A wide hearth dominated one end of the room, the fire within crackling and bright.

The place was alive with low chatter and clinking mugs. A handful of locals were gathered at tables—hunters in well-worn cloaks, traders passing through, a couple of locals dicing quietly by the bar.

Light from the hearth spilled across the polished wood floor. A rack of drying herbs hung behind the bar, filling the room with an earthy scent. A hunting spear and a stuffed black-feathered bird hung over the mantle. Trophies. Part inn, part gathering spot, and apparently the unofficial seat of Comstock's secretive charm.

A few heads turned as the group entered—mostly to stare at the newcomers' clothes, and more pointedly, at the Riders' horses now stationed out front.

Garrus waved them toward a large table near the hearth, where he was already clearing it with exaggerated grumbling.

"This one's yours," he said. "No one else wants it now, anyway."

"Because of us?" Erynn asked.

"Because I said so."

Garrus brought out a round of mugs without being asked, slapping them down with a muttered, "House ale. Still awful."

Cael sniffed his suspiciously. Erynn didn't even touch hers.

Thane took a sip. Bitter. Earthy. Weirdly strong. He winced, and set the mug down like it might bite him. "Shit, awful is an understatement."

"It's tradition," Garrus called from across the room, as Kaelir patted Thane on the back with a chuckle before taking a sip of his own.

"You'll live," Lirien said, sliding onto the bench beside

him as Garrus returned with bowls of a thick, meat-heavy stew that smelled far better than it looked.

Garrus dropped it all with a grunt. "Eat up. You'll need it."

Thane dipped his spoon and blinked. "Okay. This food has no right tasting this good."

"Arbelon's full of contradictions. This inn's one of the better ones," Cael said quietly.

Thane scanned the tavern like he was in a cutscene. A bar full of locals. A roaring fire. A mysterious innkeeper. He half-expected to see a quest board by the bar.

The fire popped loudly from across the room. A moment later, a lanky man stepped onto a small platform in the corner with a lute in hand. He didn't speak—just strummed once, twice, and then began to play.

The tune was slow and minor, a sad melody that wove through the corners of the inn, softening conversations, lowering voices.

Thane's spoon paused halfway to his mouth. The music was oddly familiar, but he couldn't place it. And the longer the bard played, the more the familiarity grew.

Thane leaned forward, listening despite himself.

The song spoke of a traveler bound by fate. Of a city sealed in silence, a land swallowed whole by whispers. Of voices that called from beyond, promising salvation or ruin. The lyrics were old—older than memory, it felt like. Yet, every note vibrated with something personal, like a thread pulled taut inside him.

It didn't name Thane. But it didn't have to.

Erynn's fingers curled around her mug, as she took a sip, her eyes fixed on the bard. Her voice dropped to a whisper. "That's not a song. It's a sign."

"You can say that again," Cael said, glancing briefly in her direction.

Lirien's gaze also didn't leave the bard. "They say this song's older than the Codex. No one knows who wrote it, or where it came from."

"It's just always been," Erynn added, her voice uneasy. "The Ballad of the Broken—it tells a story of redemption." She turned to Thane. "Perhaps your story."

"Correction," Cael interrupted. "Not perhaps. It is about him," he added, matching her gaze.

Lirien's eyes flicked toward Thane, then to Erynn. Just for a moment. Then back to the bard.

"You've gotta be kidding me," Thane said, shaking his head slightly. "There's no way that's about me. I just got here."

Almost on cue, the bard hit a riff rising into a theatrical crescendo. The bard didn't look at them, didn't seem to notice them at all. His eyes were closed, his hands moving by memory.

And yet, Thane swore the man stole a glance at him during the final verse.

As the strumming of the strings ended, the bard bowed and slipped away, the lute cradled under his arm like something precious.

No applause. No questions. Just the slow return of clinking mugs and murmured conversation.

Thane stared at the stage, his stew forgotten.

The song still echoed. Like a warning. Or a promise.

Then the fire cracked loudly, like punctuation.

Minutes turned to hours, and the fire had burned low, throwing long shadows across the tavern floor. Most of the locals had drifted out with nods and yawns.

Garrus shuffled back into the room with a tray and began clearing away empty mugs. He eyed Kaelir on his way past.

"Don't burn the place down," he muttered. "But if you

do, make sure you take the outhouse with it. Damn thing's cursed."

The group chuckled softly, and Garrus vanished with a final grunt. The tavern door closed behind him, and the room fell into a gentle hush. Just the firelight, the creak of wood settling, and the faint murmur of the river outside.

"So the Test is in the shadowed city of Salile," Erynn said as she reached into her satchel and pulled out a small, weatherworn scroll, unfolding it on the table. A map. The others leaned in.

"To avoid prying eyes, we'll need to move before first light heading north," she said, tracing a path from Comstock toward the mountains at the southern edge of the Wastelands. As her finger moved along the map, she paused, holding it in place. "We'll camp here —it'll be a push, but worth it. And this ridge?" She moved her finger just a bit more. "The Codex says it holds some of the oldest trees in Arbelon."

Lirien leaned closer, brushing her fingers against a trail that cut through the hills. "We'll need to avoid this stretch here—too exposed."

Kaelir nodded. "We'll stick to the wooded paths. This stretch past the ridge will slow us down, but it's safer."

Thane watched them—all clustered around the table, heads together, murmuring like they'd done this a thousand times. Like this world mattered.

"Why do you care so much about this prophecy?" Thane asked, his voice softer than usual. "About me? I mean, you just risked your lives with those Riders."

Erynn blinked, surprised by the question. She straightened slightly. "Because you might be the one who can save us. And because… I believe in what the Codex says."

"And I believe in what I've seen," Lirien added quietly, briefly looking away from the map in his direction.

No one spoke for a moment. The fire crackled, throwing flickers of light across their faces.

Cael leaned back slightly, voice calm and steady. "Belief isn't just about prophecies, Thane. It's about what we choose to fight for."

Thane stood slowly, walking a few steps closer to the hearth, eyes fixed on the flames. They danced and twirled like something alive. The bard's melody still pulsed within him, but something darker stirred beneath it—coiled and waiting.

He ran through the whispers he'd heard in his head since loading into this place—each one relentlessly prodding him forward. Even the one from his bedroom.

But how was that even possible?

Memory or madness, he wasn't sure. But the words in the song and the ones in his head—they were too close. Too aligned.

There were no whispers now. But he couldn't shake the feeling that something was watching.

"I've been hearing something," he said quietly. "A voice, in my head. It speaks to me. It says things. But it's... not normal."

Chairs scraped softly as heads turned. Cael's brow furrowed, but before he could speak, Erynn perked up, her tone shifting from curiosity to concern.

"A voice, speaking to you? That's not in the Codex." She frowned, thinking. "But sometimes I hear things too, so it's not that strange."

"I wish we could dismiss it that easily," Cael said. His voice had gone grave, all warmth gone. "But if it is what I think it is, then this voice—it's very old and very dangerous."

Erynn frowned, reaching into her satchel, pulling out her copy of the Codex. She set it on the table with a thump, fingers jumping to various pages before she looked up again. "I swear there's no mention of the Chosen One hearing voices, but that doesn't mean it's meaningless. It could be a sign."

Thane turned, arms crossed. "Oh, great. More signs. Should I add hearing creepy whispers to my résumé as your savior?"

"Mock it if you want," Cael said flatly. "But be careful. If this is what I think it is... *Echo* may already have its eye on you."

The name landed like a weight.

Erynn stiffened. "Echo? As in... the old stories? The Echo of the Rending?"

Cael nodded. "Older than stories. It was a force even the Architects feared. Something that twists magic and memory. If it's stirring again—"

"Then we're already behind," Kaelir said quietly.

Silence fell. The map still lay open, the lines and paths glowing faintly in the firelight.

Lirien stood first, brushing dust from her cloak. "We need to rest." Her eyes lingered on Thane a moment, unreadable, then she turned and headed for the stairs.

Erynn hesitated before following. Then Kaelir rose. "We leave early," he said, then gave Thane a look that was hard to place—part concern, part challenge—and disappeared upstairs.

Cael stood last, his hand briefly touching Thane's shoulder. "Whatever's whispering to you... don't listen too closely." Then he followed the others.

Thane stayed by the hearth.

He listened.

No whispers came. But the silence felt worse.

As he rose to head to bed, Thane paused. A weight at

his wrist caught his attention—a dull pressure, familiar and out of place.

The watch. His dad's watch. Somehow he hadn't noticed it before, not since loading back into Arbelon. But there it was, worn and scuffed, the second hand still ticking away.

He stared at it for a long moment. It didn't make sense. Nothing else he wore on Earth had come with him. And yet... here it was.

A chill ran through him. He tugged his sleeve down over it and said nothing. It's best to keep this to himself. At least until he understood it better.

And then, for just a moment, he let himself believe that maybe—just maybe—Arbelon was actually real.

Then he buried it deep. There's no way it could be.

13

BACKROADS AND BYPASSES

THE FIRST LIGHT of dawn hadn't yet crested the eastern hills as the group made their way out of the inn. A ghostly mist masked the river and clung to the village with a stillness carrying a kind of unspoken warning. Their footfalls were hushed, words few. Garrus stood in the doorway of the inn, arms crossed, his usually gruff demeanor softened by something more reserved.

"Stay off the roads," he muttered to Kaelir as he passed. "And stick to the trail out of town that I showed you."

Kaelir offered a curt nod. No goodbyes. Just necessity.

As they moved into the narrow alleys between houses, Thane heard something behind them—a faint scuff, a cough stifled too late. He looked back and spotted a handful of villagers lurking in the gloom, watching them go. None spoke. Their faces were unreadable, shadowed by the early morning haze, but their presence alone sent a chill up his spine. He filed it away. Another layer of paranoia to chew on.

The group left the town behind, stepping into the

embrace of the Arbelonian wilds. The trees loomed close, damp leaves brushing against Thane's shoulders. The dirt path was narrow and winding, half-swallowed by the underbrush.

Thane broke the silence first. "Would it have killed us to keep the horses? This isn't exactly a speed-run."

Kaelir didn't slow. "Horses would only get in the way. We'll be using trails even they wouldn't dare traverse. We stay remote. Hidden. Safer."

He gestured toward the dense forest ahead, a thicket of shadowed trees and creeping vines. The air shifted, a cool dampness laden with the smell of decomposing leaves. More alive, but more dead at the same time.

"Great," Thane muttered. "So we're hiking away from these Riders—on foot."

Lirien glanced back at him with a faint smile. "You'll manage."

Her tone was warm—genuine even—but it needled Thane, scraping against something tender. The assumption that he was stronger than he felt. That he'd make it, just because he had before. But she didn't really know him, that his days were already cut short. He bristled, muttering under his breath as he adjusted his pack more roughly than necessary.

With the forest swallowing their path and only the sounds of distant birds and rustling branches to guide them, the group disappeared into the shadows of Arbelon. The valley ahead held secrets, and Salile awaited.

The forest thickened as they climbed, and darkness turned to light. Towering trunks wrapped in moss flanked the trail, their canopies high and tangled, weaving a greenish gloom that swallowed the light. The path turned narrow and uneven, forcing the group to walk single file.

At times, there was no clear trail at all—just stone and roots and Kaelir's quiet confidence leading them forward.

Birdsong flitted above them, strange and echoing, as though it came from nowhere and everywhere at once. Even Thane felt the pulse of something deeper here, beneath the surface of things—a sense of age, of reverence.

Carvings marked the occasional stone along their way. Weathered sigils—not quite language, but not random either. Erynn noticed them first, tracing one lightly with her fingers as they paused to catch their breath.

"The Architects left traces," she said, her voice low. "Not just in cities. They walked this world. They shaped it. Sometimes you find signs where you least expect them."

"Elinath Stones," Cael said, glancing over. "Some say they marked these stones to guide the way. Others say they were meant to ward off danger."

"Either one will serve us well," Erynn said, giving Cael a small smile. "But it's good to have someone along who actually believes in the old ways," she said, smirking as she bumped shoulders with Kaelir, hinting at something more.

"Alright, alright," Kaelir said, exhaling a half-laugh. "You know me—I'll leave the past to your dusty pages. What matters to me is what's in front of us."

Thane didn't comment, but he looked a little closer at the next boulder they passed, reaching out to touch one of the sigils.

The path crested a final hill—and the trees fell away.

Thane stepped into the light… and stopped.

Before him stretched a vast valley, unlike anything he'd ever seen. He recalled seeing it on the map the night before—the Hallowed Vale. The light sketches on the map didn't really reveal its true grandeur.

In the distance, cliffs rose like titans on both sides of

the valley, sheer and ancient, as if cleaved by the hand of something divine. Sunlight flooded the basin below, catching on the river that wound like polished thread, on fields of gold-green brush. From the cliff walls, magnificent waterfalls crashed out over jagged outcroppings, sparkling the air as if dusted with powdered crystal. Even from this distance, it was breathtaking—a place so impossibly vast and pure, it felt like a dream carved into the bones of the world.

And nestled within that dream, spanning from cliff wall to cliff wall… was Salile.

It didn't shimmer with sunlight. It absorbed it. The city lay veiled in a slow-drifting shroud, as if the world had exhaled some ancient fog to keep it hidden. Here and there, towers pierced the gloom, reaching skyward—sharp, glinting peaks like the spines of some sleeping beast. Light caught only the edges—a sliver of glass, the curve of an arched window, a slanted rooftop. The city beneath laid in shadow like a black opal in an abalone shell—dark, iridescent, and strange.

It was beautiful. And wrong. An enigma.

His eyes continued to trail downward. Near the valley's far edge as it approached Salile, dark shapes jutted upward —monolithic, stair-like ridges half-lost in distance and haze. The scrawled words on the map had just read "The Steepes". Something about them unsettled him. But he didn't know why. He blinked and turned his eyes back up toward the city itself, pulled into its mystery.

No one spoke.

He heard his own breathing. The soft rustle of leaves.

A faded memory sparked and Thane swallowed hard, his eyes growing misty. For a moment, he was standing with his mother at the edge of Glacier Peak in Yosemite Valley, watching the world unfold below them. She'd said she wanted him to see everything—every wonder, every wild thing the world could offer.

This was one of those places. But his time was running out. He'd never be able to show her this place or see any of the things they used to talk about.

That truth struck deeper than he was ready for. A weight settled in his chest that he didn't know how to displace. There was no escaping his reality. Not here. Not anywhere.

He blinked again and wiped his eyes, pretending it was the wind. When he turned his head, Lirien's eyes were on him. She didn't say anything. Just gave him a moment—and then looked away, letting him have it to himself.

That meant more than words ever could.

They made camp beneath a twisted canopy of bone-pale trees, not far from a rise overlooking the Hallowed Vale. The sun had dipped behind the western cliffs, and the light had gone strange—duller, more muted, as if the world was holding its breath. Even the fire Kaelir built seemed to burn lower than it should've, like it too understood where they were headed.

Kaelir emerged from the brush, dragging a thick, uneven log behind him. He tried to muscle it toward the fire, but his foot caught a root, and he pitched forward, the log bouncing and rolling uselessly aside as he barely caught himself before tumbling with it.

"Very dignified," Erynn said, trying not to laugh. "Reminds me of the time you tried to wrangle a goat that got loose in the high pastures above Drenhold."

Kaelir looked up sharply. "No, it doesn't."

"Oh, it absolutely does," she grinned. "Same energy. Wild terrain, impossible odds, and you falling flat on your face while yelling at an animal that couldn't care less."

"I didn't fall. I... slipped."

"You tripped over your own sword," she said, and Thane could hear the delight in her voice. "Twice."

Kaelir muttered something unintelligible and returned to the mossy log, dragging it to the fire, his ears pinking slightly in the firelight.

Thane blinked, caught off guard by the familiarity in their banter. "Wait. You two know each other?"

Erynn smirked. "He's my brother."

Thane paused. "You're serious?"

Kaelir let out a weary sigh. "Unfortunately."

"He's not so bad," Erynn said, throwing a pine cone in Kaelir's direction. "When he's not trying to boss everyone around or brood like a tragic forest spirit."

Kaelir dodged the pine cone without looking. "Says the woman who thinks trees whisper back."

"They do," she shot back, matter-of-fact.

Thane raised both eyebrows. "Wow. Ok. Family road trip. This just got a lot weirder."

The fire crackled between them, laughter fading into something softer. The warmth lingered, drawing the edge off the day's tension. For a moment, it felt like maybe— just maybe—they weren't walking straight into a nightmare.

Thane poked at the fire with a stick, watching embers flit up and vanish.

"So… this place we're headed. Salile. What's the deal with it, anyway?"

And just like that, the weight returned.

Erynn looked up from across the fire. "Salile was the heart of the Architect's empire," she said. "A city unlike any other, built long before even the oldest records."

Thane raised an eyebrow. "So… creepy fog city built by ancient aliens. Got it."

"They weren't aliens," she said, a small smile tugging at

her lips. "They were the Architects. And Salile was their masterpiece."

"You've studied it," Cael said, not quite a question, not quite disbelief.

"I've done more than study it," she said. "My mother had a copy of the Codex—one of the few surviving outside the Obsidian Athenaeum. It's mine now, but I've been piecing together fragments ever since I could read."

"Correction. She's been obsessed since we were kids," Kaelir added offhandedly as he poured water into a pot to boil.

"Let's hear what you know," Cael said, leaning forward, the doubt in his voice clear.

Erynn met his gaze, steady. "I know what I've read. What I've studied. What I've lived with." Then her voice softened, like she was sharing a secret with the dark.

"Salile was the center of the Architect's empire—built into the bones of the valley itself, guarded by the Steepes. They say it's older than memory. Beautiful, yes… but cursed. It fell during the Rending—when something broke that was never meant to. What happened inside the city that day… no one agrees on. Some say the magic twisted. Others say the city turned on itself."

Thane squinted into the fire. "And what's in there now?"

Erynn hesitated.

"They're called the Unseen," Cael answered stoically.

"No one knows what they are—not exactly," Erynn said, picking up the thread, her voice low. "Some say they are guardians. Others, executioners."

The fire popped, startling Thane, as an awkward silence held the camp.

Cael cleared his throat, his voice still hoarse when he

spoke again. "There are those that believe the Unseen are the Architects themselves, lingering spirits of their kind."

"No," Erynn said, shaking her head. "The Codex does not support that."

"I happen to agree with you," Cael replied. "The truth is not written. Many secrets of Salile remain hidden."

"Perhaps from some," she said now standing and turning away. "But not from me."

She stood, back to the fire for a moment too long, deep in thought.

"What do you mean?" Lirien asked, no longer able to keep her silence.

Erynn turned back, settling quietly in her seat once again. "These Unseen—they don't walk. They don't speak. But if you draw their attention…"

She trailed off.

"Then what?" Thane asked. "They kill you? Or just whisper creepy stuff until you run away?"

Her eyes met his. "They take you. And no one ever sees you again."

"She speaks the truth," Cael said, Lirien and Kaelir nodded in agreement. "None who have entered the city have ever left it."

Thane's face had gone still. "What? Why the hell—"

"But things *have* been written," Erynn said, speaking over him. She turned her eyes to meet Cael's. "The Codex says that you can enter Salile and survive. Silence is the only way through. No spoken word, no name, no song. Speak, and the Unseen wake."

"That can't be right," Cael said slowly. "I've read the Codex too. I've never seen that passage."

"It's not in the public transcriptions. My mother's copy was… less edited. She said the truth was kept hidden to stop people from plundering the city. If everyone knew silence kept them safe, they'd flood in with empty pockets and greedy hands."

Cael leaned forward, his voice cracking. "Why was I not told of this?"

"Like I said," Erynn shrugged. "It was a closely held secret that few know even to this day."

Cael considered that—and then, to Erynn's quiet satisfaction, gave a small nod.

Thane stared into the fire, the crackle of embers now distant beneath the weight of what he'd just heard. "So... this city," he said quietly, "people go in, and they just... don't come back?"

Erynn didn't answer right away. She studied him for a moment, her expression gentler than usual. Then she reached across the space between them and laid a hand on his shoulder—steady, warm.

"If we're careful, we'll make it through," she said. "You're not alone in this."

The contact was brief, but it lingered—enough that Lirien's gaze sharpened from across the fire. She didn't say anything, but the way her jaw tensed was hard to miss.

Thane looked down at Erynn's hand, then up at her, a flicker of something unreadable crossing his face.

"I didn't ask for backup," he muttered, voice lower now. "But... thanks."

She gave him a nod, then withdrew her hand, her eyes returning to the flames.

The fire popped. The silence crept back in.

One by one, the others drifted off—Kaelir doing a final check of the perimeter, Lirien rolling into her blanket without a word, Erynn curled up near her pack, the Codex at her side. The fire had burned low, more glow than flame now.

Thane remained where he was, poking absently at the

embers. Cael settled beside him with a quiet grunt, not looking at him at first.

"I know you think all of this is just a waste of time," Cael said, his voice low, meant only for the space between them. "That it's some story you're caught up in."

Thane stiffened. He didn't respond—eyes fixed on the fire.

"But sometimes, stories are all we have," Cael continued. "They're what keep us going. And maybe, just maybe… they're true enough to matter."

Thane glanced sideways at him, something flickering behind his eyes—not trust, not yet, but the first hints of it. A crack in the wall.

Cael didn't press. He stood, brushing the ash from his hands. "Get some sleep," he said. "Tomorrow won't be easy."

Thane didn't answer. But he didn't look away either.

14

AT THE GATES OF SALILE

THE SUN WAS JUST BREACHING the horizon when the group broke free from the last tangled edge of forest and stepped into open land.

The Silent Reach stretched before them—an endless, golden expanse where grass swayed like it was listening. A low wind swept across the field in long, hushed sighs, creating an almost melodic hum that prickled Thane's skin. There were no trees, no birdsong, just open space and silence that pressed in like a held breath.

In the distance, cliffs carved the sky—dark and unmoving, standing sentinel over a valley lost to time. Somewhere between them lay Salile, though nothing of the city could be seen now. A slow-drifting fog veiled the valley between the cliffs in layers of shifting gray, thick and unnatural, as if the land itself had secrets it refused to share.

Thane couldn't see the city, but he could feel it.

Even from here, the fog radiated a wrongness that settled deep in his chest. A stillness not just of silence, but of something deeper—older. The others felt it too. He could see it in their expressions. Uneasy. Wary. And no one spoke a word.

The Steepes, if they were visible at all, were little more than shadows folded into the terrain, hidden by the low swales and ridges of the Silent Reach. But they were coming. The scale of everything here—the cliffs, the valley, whatever lay beyond—was immense. The kind of scale that made Thane feel small in ways he didn't like.

He swallowed hard, trying not to think of the Test. But the thought came anyway.

A cursed city. A valley scraped clean by hands not human. A trial waiting in silence.

Kaelir's voice was hushed, but sharp. "We'll be exposed here. The Riders' eyes are always watching. Stay close, and move quickly."

No one argued.

They moved at a brisk pace, boots brushing through the knee-high grass. The world felt too wide, too big, too quiet. Thane couldn't shake the feeling that they were being watched—not by people, but by the land itself. The dark city loomed ahead in shadow. The others kept glancing over their shoulders, watching. It made him nervous and soon he followed suit. He kept glancing over his shoulder now, half expecting the trees to be following.

As they approached the subtle ridge of a swale, Lirien slowed beside him, turning back while shielding her eyes against the morning glare. "What is that?"

Thane followed her gaze. A faint dust plume had begun to rise at the far end of the plains—slow at first, but growing, shifting with the breeze.

"Son of a bitch," Kaelir muttered and picked up speed. "They've found us."

No one asked how. There wasn't time.

They sprinted now, weaving through the waving grass,

breath coming fast and short as the plume thickened behind them, spreading like a storm. The calls of ravens screeching overhead. Thane's legs burned, his lungs seared, but the jagged rise of stone ahead gave him focus.

The Steepes emerged from the valley's base like a giant's staircase—monolithic and terrifying. Each step stood at least fifty feet tall, carved from dark, weathered stone. Between the steps, winding ramps—built, it seemed, for carts or beasts of burden—hugged the rock, narrow and with grooves for grip worn smooth by centuries of use.

Even Kaelir hesitated for half a second, staring up.

"They're bigger than I remember," he muttered, then led the charge up the first incline.

As they climbed, the air began to change.

Thane felt it before he saw it—cooler, heavier, touched with moisture that clung to his skin. The sun, still climbing, suddenly seemed weaker, its rays dimmed by the first tendrils of mist curling down from the cliffs above. It drifted in slow spirals, not like natural fog, but like smoke exhaled from ancient lungs. The city's shroud didn't reach this far, but it loomed just ahead.

A few steps later, he saw his own breath fog the air.

And then—he felt it.

A faint vibration, deep in his wrist. He staggered, lifting his arm.

The watch—his father's old, beat-up watch—was vibrating faintly. The hands were spinning, not ticking, whirling around the face in a blur. Just as suddenly, they stopped—snapping into place as the pulse steadied beneath his skin.

Not random. Not wild. Rhythmic. Like a heartbeat.

His breath caught. He stared at his father's watch— now quiet, the hands locked in, ticking steadily—but not like the tick of a clock. His skin still tingled beneath it, the pulse steady. Alive.

This wasn't just nerves. This was something else.

He pulled his sleeve down, hard. Hid it. Whatever this was—he didn't want the others to see it. Not now. Not until he understood it himself.

He'd been ignoring it since the day it showed up with him in Arbelon—too strange to explain, too personal to share. But this? This felt like more than a coincidence. Like the thing had been waiting for this place.

And maybe... so had he.

Then came the voice sliding through his mind like smoke, oily and intimate.

"They're coming to quiet your power. Run to the city. It's your only chance."

The whisper. That voice. It had a name—Echo—whatever the fuck that was.

He hadn't heard the voice since Earth. It always came at the worst times. Like it knew when the cracks were starting to show. And now, here it was again—dripping poison and promise in equal measure, pushing him away from the Riders, pulling him toward the city.

Cael had warned him about the voice—that whatever it was, it wasn't to be trusted. Thane hadn't taken it seriously at the time, but now? With the Riders bearing down and the gates just ahead... it was hard not to listen.

Echo's words were always the same—sharp, seductive, too certain. But Cael's had weight. The kind that stays with you. The kind that made you second-guess, even now.

Still, what choice did he have? If he stayed, the Riders would take him. If he ran—at least then, he'd have a chance.

He shook his head, tried to steady his breathing. But his hands wouldn't stop trembling.

Behind them, the Riders broke from the rise of the Reach—shadowy figures on fast, lean mounts, their formation tight, efficient, terrifying. The ground thundered under their charge. Dust rolled in waves.

"Don't stop!" Kaelir shouted, drawing his blade as he pushed ahead as they finally climbed from the Steepes.

Thane looked up as the gate came into full view—an enormous arch of black stone rising from the plateau of the Steepes like the bones of some forgotten beast. Nothing was visible beyond the shroud. There were no walls. No towers. Just the archway—freestanding, impossible, veiled in the thickening mist.

It was larger than any doorway had a right to be. Fifty feet high, at least. And through it, only shadow.

The shroud spilled outward, curling along the ground in whispering tendrils. It hadn't reached them yet, not fully, but the mist clung to Thane's skin like cold breath. The air shifted—heavy, strange. Even light seemed to bend around the archway.

Above it, symbols had been etched into the stone— delicate, flowing, unreadable. They shimmered faintly, not glowing, but resisting the mist itself, as though their memory refused to be erased.

Erynn stepped closer, her expression unreadable. "This place wants to be hidden," she said softly, almost reverently.

A chill traced Thane's spine. It wasn't fear, exactly. It was reverence. Dread. That quiet certainty you get standing in front of something that has outlived time.

The Riders closed in behind.

The gates loomed before.

And Salile waited—silent, shrouded, eternal.

The Riders mounted the Steepes faster than any expected, spreading out behind them. Bostick's voice rang out across the plateau, sharp and cutting: "Give us the boy, and the rest of you live!"

Thane's pulse exploded in his ears. Echo's words curled again in his skull.

"Run."

They sprinted. The gates loomed ahead. The Riders gave chase—relentless, inhumanly fast.

The plateau stretched wide at the top of the Steepes, a cold, barren shelf—mist coiling along the stone like it had breath of its own. The gates stood ahead, enormous and still, but they felt no closer. Not with the sound behind them.

The drumbeat of hooves.

The gates remained out of reach. And Kaelir turned, sword drawn, lips pressed into a grim line. "They're upon us."

They all stopped, turning with Kaelir. The time for running was over.

From the crest of the rise, shadows broke into sharp fidelity—Riders, a dozen strong, their dark forms like splinters against the morning sky. They dismounted in unison, steel flashing as they dropped low and spread into formation. Their boots struck stone like hammers. One step after another.

Thane's gaze snapped to them. Their armor was scarred, ill-fitting in places—patchwork remnants from their last encounter. One Rider dragged a leg behind him. Another's dark crimson cloak was shredded at the shoulder. While several wore bloody scars, haphazardly bandaged.

Something in him hardened. He didn't know if it was the magic, the mist, or just the end of running—but he was done hiding.

If the game wanted a fight, then a fight it would get.

A smug grin spread. "You look worse than you did

when we left you bleeding in the trees," Thane said, his voice sharp, biting. "Didn't think you'd come back for seconds."

Kaelir shot him a look that could've curdled fire. "Shut your damned mouth—they outnumber us."

Bostick stepped forward, clipping up the visor of his helm. His expression was cold, eyes locked on Thane like a blade unsheathed.

"You have a smart mouth, outlander," he said. "Let's see if you're still smiling when this is over."

Kaelir stepped forward in front of Thane, steel in hand, voice low and unyielding. "You're not touching him."

Bostick gave a humorless chuckle. "Still trying to be a hero, huh, Kaelir? You've always had a knack for dying on the wrong hill."

Kaelir didn't flinch. "This is the right hill."

The words echoed louder than they should have, swallowed quickly by the shroud's encroaching silence.

And then, with a flick of Bostick's wrist, the Riders charged.

Their boots struck stone in tandem, blades drawn, crimson cloaks flaring behind them like blood in the wind.

Kaelir barked, "Stay close!" just as he stepped into the first blow. Cael moved beside him, quarterstaff at the ready, turning aside a strike meant for Erynn. The two men moved as one—different weapons, different rhythms, but united by necessity.

The whispers came first—just out of reach. Then the subtle cracks alighted on his skin. Dim but forming. Thane could feel it brushing against the edge of his mind— threads he could almost grasp. Almost. But each time he reached, they slipped away.

Come on, you came before. Why not now?

Nothing. Only silence and the heat of his own frustration.

Then—

A pulse.

His wrist.

The watch.

It throbbed beneath his sleeve—first soft, then insistent. It felt alive, in synch with the beat of his heart. And the beat of something else.

He stared at it, stunned. Whatever it was doing, it wasn't random.

From the side, Cael turned slightly as he deflected a blow, his eyes flicking to Thane for just a breath—registering something. But the fight pulled him back immediately.

Then chaos reigned.

A Rider lunged at Lirien. The blade arced high, catching what little light the mist hadn't stolen.

She dodged just in time, spinning and slashing with her gleaming white blade—drawing a streak of red across the Rider's arm. The man snarled, turning immediately on her again.

Thane didn't think. Weaponless, he did the only thing he could. He surged forward, shoulder slamming into the Rider's chest. The man staggered back, unbalanced, and Thane stood protectively in front of Lirien. She shot him a glance—equal parts gratitude and disbelief—before steeling herself for the next threat.

Nearby, Erynn moved like a shadow given purpose—impossibly fluid, every motion precise. She dropped low beneath a Rider's swing, her momentum carrying her into a sweeping arc that knocked his feet from under him. Before he hit the ground, she struck twice—an open palm to the throat, then snapped her knuckles into the joint of his sword wrist. The weapon clattered free as he dropped, choking.

She pivoted, flicking a small, etched disk from her belt. It spun through the air and clipped another Rider's cheek, just enough to turn his head and break his focus. By the time he looked back, her heel was already rising toward his chin.

Thane blinked, watching her move. *Where the hell did that come from?*

It wasn't just skill. It was something else. She didn't fight like Kaelir or Lirien or Cael. No wasted motion. No brute force. Just control. Balance. Lethality honed down to an art.

A mere paces away, Kaelir and Bostick met in the center. Their blades clashed in a flurry of steel and sparks.

"Still clinging to that honor of yours?" Bostick sneered between strikes.

"Better than selling my soul," Kaelir growled, and pushed forward with a brutal, three-strike combo that forced Bostick to retreat.

Then came the moment. Similar to the fight from Trosten.

A single Rider slipped through the crowd, blade raised high, charging straight at Thane.

Everything froze.

The voice came, not shouted from the battlefield, but welling up from inside.

"Let it out. Do not fear it."

It was Echo. Again.

Thane's muscles locked. His blood surged hot, not with fear—but with something sharper. Wilder. The threads of magic that had evaded him moments before now drifted close again... but different. Not clawing. Not chaotic.

Inviting.

They shimmered just at the edges of thought, brushing his mind like fingers on glass. He didn't reach this time. He didn't have to. The Wild Magic just pooled —quiet and vast, like it had always been there beneath the surface, and he'd only just now remembered how to see it.

Then a pulse at his wrist—the watch.

It thrummed like a second heart, each beat in perfect synch with the rhythm of something deep inside him. Whatever this was, it wasn't panic. It wasn't rage. It was something older. Larger.

His skin cracked open with light—thin glowing fractures racing across his arms like veins of power beneath the surface. Not violent. Not painful. Just… ready. The world warped around him, edges softening, sounds distant.

He didn't know how he did it. Maybe he didn't do it at all.

But he took hold of it. And the Wild Magic answered, rising to meet the moment—as the Rider closed in, step by step, heartbeat by heartbeat, tick by tick.

It erupted, wild and vicious, but focused. Whether formed by some thought in his mind or a feral desire to live, a blade of pure energy flared from his outstretched hand—crackling, chaotic, and wicked. With a flash of his hand, it swept through the air and severed the Rider's sword arm at the elbow. The blade and limb dropped to the stone with a wet clatter, blood spraying in an arc across the gray stone.

The Rider's scream tore through the quiet.

And then—

Silence.

Everyone froze.

Even the mist paused, like it had to witness the moment.

"It responds to you because it remembers," Echo said, filling the void. *"Just as you will."*

Thane stared at his hand, the magic still humming through him, matched beat for beat, tick for tick. For once, the Wild Magic hadn't thrown him to the ground. For once, it didn't tear him back to Earth.

But it didn't feel like it belonged to him either.

Kaelir's voice broke the spell. "To the gates! Now!"

They moved as one—dragging, stumbling toward the archway. Lirien just behind Thane, her blade ready, her eyes fixed on him.

They reached the edge of the gate. Then—

A cry.

Lirien. A Rider had grabbed her, dragging her back toward Bostick. She fought, twisting, but the Rider had her arms pinned. Bostick approached calmly, sword at his side.

"Trade yourself for her, boy," he called. "It's a fair deal."

Something snapped in Thane.

He stepped forward.

The magic surged again—violent, unrelenting. Another blade, brighter this time, born from instinct and fury, lashed out across the battlefield.

The blade cut clean.

And the Rider's head hit the stone with a wet thud. Then his body.

Thane rushed forward and grabbed Lirien's wrist, dragging her free.

The other Riders faltered, horror etched across their faces.

"Good," came Echo's whisper, curling in Thane's mind like smoke. *"Now they're beginning to see."*

Bostick's mouth twisted—not in fury, but in something

close to fear. "You don't know what you're playing with, boy," he said, backing a step.

Thane turned toward him, the magic still humming in his bones. The watch on his wrist throbbed harder now. Blood trailed from his nose.

He was swaying on his feet—but still standing, still in Arbelon.

Lirien caught him, steadying him as they moved toward the mist.

"Stay back," Thane warned, his voice low, layered with something unnatural.

The Riders didn't follow.

They didn't dare.

They slowed near the arch, mist curling thicker now, slicking their skin, dragging the warmth from their bones. The shroud spilled from the city gate in twisting tendrils, swallowing color, sound, distance. The archway rose before them—black stone, open, and silent.

No wall. No gate. No Doors.

Just an impossible void.

Thane stared into it, breath catching. He couldn't see what lay beyond. Not really. Just fragments. Shapes that flickered and changed the longer he looked. Buildings that weren't there. Cobbled streets that weren't flat. He blinked and they were gone.

His voice was low. "Are we sure about this?"

Cael didn't hesitate. "No. But we've come here for a reason."

That was enough.

Together, they stepped forward.

Into Salile. Into silence.

But just before Thane passed into the mist, Echo's whisper found him once more—sharp and soft and close.

"Not a word."

15

———

NOT A WORD

THE CITY SWALLOWED them whole the moment they passed through the archway. One step in, and the light didn't vanish, not exactly—it dulled. Muted. As though the mist itself drank it in, leaving only a twilight hush. Shapes and buildings loomed, visible but shrouded in gloom, like the city wore a veil of half-shadow and silence.

Fog slithered around their feet, curling up their legs like something with weight and intention. The sounds of the world outside—the rustling of the wind, birdsong—were gone, devoured by the hush.

It wasn't just silence. It was a *stillness* that felt unnatural. Like the city wasn't abandoned, but paused—held in place by something too boundless to name.

No wind, no echo, no life. The only sounds came from them—their breaths, slow and shallow. Footfalls tapping like drumbeats against the cobbled streets, far too loud in this abandoned place.

They gathered just inside the city walls as Cael raised a finger to his lips, motioning for silence. A reminder.

No one spoke.

142

No one dared.

Kaelir motioned and they pressed on. Deeper into the city.

Stone buildings lined either side of the narrow avenue, worn by time but still sturdy. Some had intricate carvings etched across their facades—tales of forgotten figures and mythic symbols—but the fog blurred the details. Others were more functional, squat and windowless, built to endure.

All were empty. No banners. No fires. No decay.

Just… abandonment.

Up ahead, the mist thickened, curling between alleyways and doorframes. It shifted like it had somewhere to be—slow, purposeful.

Thane froze.

Movement. Human-shaped. Just for a heartbeat. A silhouette in the fog, tall and thin, drifting across the road ahead like someone just passing through.

Kaelir halted beside him, eyes narrowing toward the same direction, his hand hovering near his blade. Erynn widened her stance beside Cael, clutching her dagger so tightly her knuckles had gone pale. And Lirien slid in beside Thane, her shoulder brushing against his, her eyes forward.

For a moment, they all saw it—*or thought they did.*

But then the fog folded inward again, swallowing whatever had been there. Now gone.

Thane blinked, then shook his head, his heart racing. It was probably nothing. But then he looked at the others. Their expressions were clear—it was more than nothing.

Lirien turned to Thane. She didn't speak—couldn't—but her hand touched his as their eyes briefly met in a quiet reassurance. It lingered longer than necessary—grounding him, steadying him—before withdrawing with a shared nod.

Thane hated how much that settled him. He didn't want comfort. Didn't want connection. Not here. Not now. But still—she had steadied him, whether he liked it or not.

After a moment, they pushed on. Thane followed, more slowly and vigilant now, his eyes roaming the alleyways and dark windows like they were full of watching things. This place… it reminded him of something. A feeling from Earth he hadn't thought about in months. The hallway outside his hospital room at night. That emptiness, the lost feeling, the knowledge that nothing good waited for him.

His jaw clenched.

Why was he even here, doing this? Helping these people. Risking himself. He didn't owe them anything.

Hell, this wasn't even real. It was just a game. He could've logged off.

And yet, he didn't. He'd come back.

He'd killed for them. Not like in Asmenson—this time he'd *chosen* it. The second Rider hadn't even seen the strike coming. And it was brutal.

He told himself it was to protect Lirien.

She hadn't flinched at the savagery of it. Hadn't looked at him with fear. Just that same quiet trust that now walked beside him.

Was that what it meant to believe in something?

He thought of Lirien's fingers brushing his. The way Erynn had looked at him in the late hours at the Hog's Breath Inn. The way Cael, despite everything, pressed the Elders to test him.

And under it all… something else was changing. Something inside him. He didn't want to admit it. But part of him wasn't sure anymore—if it was all just a simulation, or something more. Something that mattered.

His footsteps slowed.

Ahead, the fog shifted again, revealing more of the road, more buildings rising like teeth out of the gloom. His watch pulsed on his wrist, tucked safely away up his sleeve. Ticking in time with his heartbeat. Ticking in time with something more, something deeper.

He let out a shaky breath, watching his mist spiral in the cold air. This was supposed to be a distraction. Something to fill the time before he died. But he'd killed someone back there. Not a monster. Not a glitch. A man. And Lirien had looked at him like he'd done the right thing.

The silence wasn't just quiet—it was deafening.

It demanded reflection.

Maybe that was the scariest thing about Salile. It made him listen to his own thoughts—good and bad. There was nowhere to hide.

The street narrowed. The buildings leaned inward, crowding tighter as the group pressed deeper into Salile. The fog thickened, swirling low across the stone. It pooled in gutters and spilled from darkened doorways, twisting with the slow, deliberate motion of something alive.

Kaelir raised a hand, halting them at a three-way fork.

Each path ahead vanished into haze. No signs. No markings. Just silence, stone, and the curl of mist around their boots.

Erynn stepped forward slowly, peering down one path, then the next. Then she pointed upward.

Above the leftmost path, the stonework bore faint carvings—swirls half-erased by time. The others were blank. But the air down that leftward way felt... looser. The fog drifted there instead of clinging.

Thane took a step forward—then stopped.

Something stirred. Not sound. Not thought. A rhythm behind his ribs, like a plucked string.

Then it came—three notes. Not in his ears, but inside him, clear and unmistakable.

He knew the tune before he knew why.

The song from the Hog's Breath Inn. The one the bard had played. The one he hadn't been able to shake for reasons he hadn't understood until now. It was ancient. And it called to him.

The notes returned, faint but insistent, like breadcrumbs laid in air.

Thane stepped slowly between the paths, testing the space around him. The melody sharpened near the left. Faded near the others.

He turned back to the group and tapped his ear. Cael furrowed his brow. Erynn tilted her head.

They didn't hear it.

Thane pointed down the left path and moved, his steps slow and deliberate.

The others exchanged wary glances—then followed.

The song returned at every split, rising faintly in one direction, falling silent in others. Thane followed it by instinct. Not logic. Not faith. Just a rhythm that lived in his chest now.

They moved quietly, the fog thickening again around their feet. Kaelir's eyes darted through the gloom. Erynn glanced at Thane, confused but trusting. And Lirien stayed close—always close—her shoulder brushing his sleeve more often than not.

Then came another fork. Three paths again.

But this time… no sound.

Thane waited. Focused. Nothing.

The left path looked clearer, somehow more inviting.

The mist thinner that way, more open. Like something had prepared it.

Kaelir stepped forward and pointed firmly down the path to the right.

Thane shook his head. Raised a hand. Telling them to wait.

But Kaelir had made up his mind—and moved. The others followed.

The cold hit instantly—a sharp breath of winter cutting through the gloom.

Thane felt it crawl into his chest. His breath caught, and his skin burned where the mist touched it.

The fog surged, twisting with sudden purpose.

Distorted figures stirred in the mist.

Shadows. Human-shaped, but wrong. Twisted. Jerked forward in stuttering mimicry of their movements.

Erynn stumbled, her face pale. Cael caught her arm before she fell. Kaelir cursed under his breath, drawing steel that meant nothing here.

The shadows began to move toward them, their presence suffocating.

Thane turned to run, motioning sharply for the others to follow.

Erynn stumbled again, her breath ragged—bumping into Lirien and sending her tumbling. Thane saw Lirien's lips part. She was about to speak—he saw it in her eyes. One sound, and they were dead.

Without thinking, he leapt forward, pressing his hand to her face. No sound came. Not even a whisper. Their eyes locked. Hers full of gratitude, his full of fear.

Kaelir and Cael scooped them up, pressing them forward.

From behind, one of the shadows reached toward Cael. Its arm blurred and stretched in the mist—passing through Cael's shoulder. Cael jerked back with a silent hiss, grabbing at his shoulder like something had struck him. No blood. No wound. But Cael's eyes said enough—waving them back the way they'd come.

The fog drew back behind them, slow and reluctant. As if it had almost had them—and wasn't ready to let go.

Back at the previous fork, the melody returned this time. Soft. Familiar. Clear.

Thane bent forward, catching his breath. The others caught up behind him, silent and pale. Erynn pressed a hand to her chest.

No one looked back.

They looked at him. Waiting.

He pointed—and turned toward the left path. No one questioned him this time.

The corridor twisted. The buildings changed—older, heavier, their stones etched with patterns nearly lost to time. Every step forward matched a note in the melody—building, climbing, resolving.

Then the fog parted.

They emerged into a small square, surrounded by resolute towers. At its center stood a domed building of grey stone, its walls covered with ancient murals. Above the doorway, carved deep into the stone—the broken circle. Again.

Thane saw it pulse. Just once.

A faint blue glow—just like his VR headset—then gone.

He stepped forward, pausing at the doorway. The melody faded as his hand met the stone, and the door creaked beneath his touch. The fog behind them didn't follow. It just hung there, still and waiting.

His heart beat fast. Not from fear. From something else.

Recognition.

This place knew him—somehow.

He thought again of Lirien's touch. The figures in the fog. The Rider he'd killed without hesitation—no glitch to blame this time. No second thought.

He wasn't just here to complete a quest. He wasn't even sure it was a quest anymore.

This world had weight. Consequences. People who looked at him like he mattered.

And that weight was starting to change him.

He wasn't sure about their Codex and its prophecies, or if what he was feeling was real.

Ahead, the door was cracked—and behind, they all stood watching him like he was the answer.

Whatever this Test was and what it would ask of him— he had no idea.

But apparently, dying worlds had a thing for dying kids.

16

UNREALITY

THANE STEPPED FORWARD and pressed against the stone door. It didn't budge—until Kaelir and Cael stepped up beside him, adding their weight.

Slowly, the door opened with the sound of stone remembering how to move.

It wasn't loud—but in the silence of Salile, it felt seismic.

As Thane stepped across the threshold, a faint sound stirred—like a breath caught in stone. One by one, ethereal blue torches flared to life around the perimeter of the chamber, their flames hovering just above iron sconces without touching them. Each lit in a slow progression, circling the room until the last ignited on the far wall— casting pale light over the pedestal at the center.

In the torchlight, the chamber didn't so much unfold as awaken—walls rounding into view, shadows shrinking back to reveal age-worn stone.

No golden altars. No gleaming thrones. Just a wide, circular space built entirely from stone. The ceiling domed high overhead, traced with crumbling frescoes that curved like constellations. Dust drifted in the stillness like the chamber had been holding its breath for centuries, waiting for someone to disturb it.

And now they had.

Thane moved further in. Each step echoing as if marking time—like he was late to something that had already begun.

Behind him, the others stepped in one by one, eyes scanning the walls, boots whispering against stone.

None of them spoke. They all knew better.

The frescoes curved down from the dome, bleeding into the chamber walls—paint faded by time, but not lost. Scenes worn thin, edges blurred, yet the stories endured. A figure with light in their chest, reaching into something vast and dark. Another cradling something broken—curved like the crescent of a dying moon. Another walking into fire, alone.

Erynn and Cael moved along opposite sides of the chamber, studying the frescoes in silence. Their hands never touched the walls, but they traced above them, gesturing to symbols, pointing at motifs. The Broken Circle appeared more than once—subtle in some places, overt in others. The entire chamber seemed built around these painted stories.

At the center stood a pedestal, carved from the same cold stone as the floor. Its surface was smooth and feature-less—except for two small, dark openings carved into the flat surface of the pedestal, one on each side. Nothing marked them. No symbols. Austere. At its base, the symbol appeared again—the Broken Circle, carved deep into the stone, its edges shadowed by the torchlight.

Erynn circled slowly along the curved wall, her fingers tracing the air just above the faded paint. She paused near one panel—tilted her head, studying a shape barely visible in the torchlight—and motioned for Cael.

He joined her, eyes narrowing. They exchanged a few subtle gestures, silent but precise. Cael nodded once, his expression tightening like something had clicked into place.

Whatever they were reading in the frescoes, it wasn't random. They clearly saw something they felt was the key. At the same time, they both turned to Thane, then pointed toward the pedestal—specifically, the dark openings carved into its surface.

Thane glanced between them and the pedestal, frowning. What were they expecting him to do? He literally had no idea—only that all eyes were now on him.

Cael exhaled, then stepped past him. With deliberate slowness, he raised both hands and hovered them just above the openings—then eased them toward the stone as if demonstrating what was required. He didn't complete the motion. Just let them hang there, glancing back for Thane's reaction.

Thane stepped back half a pace. His gaze bounced from the openings, then to Erynn and Cael.

Did they want him to put his hands in those holes?

No fucking way! For all he knew, they were full of spiders, snakes, or worse. This place had been abandoned for ages —anything could be living in there now. *Did they think he'd just do it because of some ancient fresco?*

But before he could properly protest, Erynn stepped forward, pulling a scrap of parchment from her cloak. She knelt near the pedestal and scribbled quickly, her brow tight. When she stood and handed it to him, her expression was grave.

You must leave your hands in until it ends—no matter what.
If you pull them out early...

The rest wasn't written.

But Thane didn't need the rest—he already knew.

This was it, then. The Test—waiting in the dark, just like everything else in Salile.

He took a breath, but it didn't help. The pedestal now looked distinctly like a trap, perfectly placed to draw him in. Every part of him screamed to step back. To log out. This was their future, not his.

He turned, already halfway to saying something—to mock the rules of this city, to mock the prophecies of Arbelon. Their demands for silence and reverence were ridiculous. He was over it.

But Lirien was there.

She hadn't moved from the doorway, but now she stepped forward—slow, steady, like the moment might break if she rushed it. Her fingers found his hand. Warm. Certain.

She didn't speak. This place wouldn't allow it.

As the others watched from the edges of the room, she mouthed the words: *I believe in you.*

He hated how easily she cut through his armor.

Hated that part of him needed to hear it.

Thane looked back at the pedestal. No glowing glyphs. No dramatic fanfare. Just two openings. One for each hand. The broken circle etched into its base—calling to him.

He didn't know what would happen. Didn't know what it would ask of him. But he was done pretending he didn't belong here.

The others had made their move.

Now it was his.

He stepped forward. And reached in.

The stone was cold.

Not biting. Not sharp. Just still—*too still.*

Thane slid his hands deeper into the openings.

He expected cobwebs. Roughness. The gritty feel of age and decay.

But the inside was too smooth. Wrongly smooth. Like something had sanded the stone from the inside. Prepared it for him.

Then it moved.

Not the stone. Something inside it.

Fingers.

Too long. Too many. Human-shaped, but not. Like they'd been carved from darkness.

They wrapped around his wrists—not yanking, not violent. Just… enclosing. Like they'd been waiting for him. Or maybe he imagined them.

Panic rose fast. He tried to pull back—instinct, nothing more.

But the hands inside wouldn't let go. As if the Test had decided for him.

A hiss of breath caught in his throat.

And the world fell away.

He was back in the hospital.

Fluorescent lights humming overhead, the antiseptic sting of bleach in his nose. The hallway stretched too far in both directions, impossibly long. He knew this place. Knew it down to the ache in his bones.

Except it wasn't right.

The lights glitched—flickering into torchlight, then back again. The walls rippled with carvings he didn't understand that vanished when he blinked.

Something skittered along the ceiling.

He turned—and he was in Arbelon again.

But the chamber was gone, replaced with a garden half in bloom, half in rot. One side bloomed with impossible color. The other—gray, brittle, withering to dust.

A woman stood in the center. Her face obscured by a veil of light. But she radiated something ancient and mournful—the world pausing in her presence.

She raised her hand, and the garden dissolved.

Behind her, Arbelon crumbled. Cities smoldering in ruin. The sky cracked like old glass. And at the center of it all—the Heart of Arbelon. Beating faintly. Weak. A dying thing.

"Only you can heal it," she said.

But her voice…

Her voice was his mother's.

Whispers now. The hospital. The garden. Salile.

They folded in and out of each other like pages in a book written sideways.

Somewhere, someone was sobbing.

He blinked.

Now he stood in the hallway again.

This time a dozen glowing monitors lined the walls. Each flickering.

One showed Cael wounded, crawling. Another, Erynn in prayer. Yet another, Lirien's laugh echoing under stars.

Then one screen changed.

It showed him.

But not him.

A twisted version—skin stained with wild magic. His eyes were sunken, lost.

The Heart of Arbelon shattering behind him.

Then Lirien's voice.

"Only you can stop this."

He turned to her.

But it wasn't her.

Instead, Dr. Hughes stood before him. Calm. Sad. Familiar.

"You've been hallucinating again," the doctor said. "Side effects of your disease. Dissociation. Delusions."

"You're not real," Thane whispered—but he didn't sound sure.

The doctor tilted his head. "So you believe this is real? Arbelon. Wild Magic. Her?"

A pause.

"It's just your brain trying to survive what's already killing it."

"Then why does it feel like it matters?" Thane asked.

The doctor just smiled. Sadly. Like someone watching a mistake unfold.

"Thane, you just need to ask yourself this: Is it more likely that you're really in some magical video game, or that it's your brain trying to cope with the reality of your disease?"

Thane staggered.

He looked down—and the floor was gone.

He was falling through Arbelon. Through fire. Through stone.

Through memory. Dragging every broken thing to the surface.

His father's watch.

No—not just a watch. It pulsed now, faint and strange, as if syncing with the rhythm of the Heart itself.

Thane lifted his wrist, instinctively, but the space around him had changed again. He was no longer falling —just floating in stillness, the watch burning cold against his skin.

What are you?

A symbol appeared on its face—the Broken Circle— glowing briefly. The same symbol that pulsed through Arbelon. Through the Heart. Now through him.

A feeling stirred. Not memory. Not logic.

Recognition.

This mattered.

He didn't know why.

But it mattered.

There was a blinding pulse of blue light from the watch, and he was back in the garden again.

Only this time, Lirien stood in front of him. No veil. Just her.

"I believe in you," she said. Her voice was soft. No urgency. No demand.

Only belief.

"You have to decide what's real," she added. "Me. This world. The Heart."

A beat.

"It doesn't matter what's real, Thane. Only what you choose to fight for."

She reached for him—but didn't touch. Just hovered there, her hand open.

And then she was gone.

Thane stood alone.

The Heart pulsed beneath the ground in time with his father's watch.

The Test wasn't asking him to prove anything.

It wasn't about prophecy. Or fate.

It was about choice.

What do you believe in—even when you don't believe in anything?

The pressure vanished.

The hands—if that's what they were—let go.

Thane gasped and yanked his arms free.

They were clean. No wounds. But he shook. His breath ragged.

For a second, he thought he was still falling.

But the stone was under him.

He was back in the chamber—silent, still.

The blue torchlight flickered.

He stumbled again.

And Lirien caught him.

She said nothing. Only held him, grounding him in the silence, her hand gripping his, her eyes steady.

I'm here, her look said. *I've got you.*

And for the first time in a long time, Thane let someone catch him.

Something inside him had changed.

Thane steadied himself, leaning on the stone pedestal, Lirien's silent touch still grounding him. His arms throbbed from the Test. His chest burned like it still carried echoes of whatever truth had been carved into him.

Kaelir's hand shot up—warning. His eyes darted to the entrance.

A shadow moved beyond the torchlight.

From the far side of the chamber, a figure stepped through the gloom—confident, deliberate.

Bostick. Alone.

He didn't speak. Just walked in with a hunter's patience, sword drawn. His eyes swept the room, pausing only when they landed on Thane.

That pause was long. Measured. And silent—as if he too knew the guarded secret of Salile.

Then—a tap.

The tip end of Bostick's sword struck the stone floor. A slow, rhythmic knock. One. Two. Three.

It echoed louder than it should have in the hush of Salile, like someone drumming on the lid of a sealed tomb.

No one moved. No one spoke.

Because they all knew—words had weight here. And summoning the Unseen took only a whisper.

Thane's heart raced. But his hands didn't shake. Not anymore.

Bostick's head tilted ever so slightly. He didn't smile. Didn't threaten. But the message was clear: *You're not what they say you are. You're just a scared little boy playing a game you don't understand.*

But something had changed.

The watch on Thane's wrist pulsed—once. Then again.

And something in the air shifted.

A low vibration hummed through the floor. The glow of the Broken Circle on the pedestal pulsed like a warning.

The fog thickened—not swirling, not drifting, but creeping inward like it had a mind of its own.

Then the stone walls began to bleed shadow.

Shapes peeled from the surface—figures slouched and wrong, too long in limb and too thin in frame. More rose from cracks in the floor, silent and stretching. Not summoned. Released.

They didn't walk. They emerged. Like the chamber had been holding its breath, holding its secrets until now.

The Unseen were coming.

Even Bostick froze, his sword dipping as the first Unseen turned toward him. Not fast. Just… inevitable. His confidence faded as his eyes darted between Thane and this new emerging threat.

The chamber darkened.

The torchlight shrank.

The Unseen surged forward.

Cael stepped in front of Thane, as if to shield him—until Thane raised his wrist. Because, for some reason, he knew that his father's watch mattered here.

In this place.

To them.

His watch glowed hot against his skin. He lifted it high, and the Unseen froze mid-step. They had no eyes, no faces, but it was clear their attention was on him. Waiting.

His voice wasn't loud. But it didn't need to be.

"Hold," he said, seeing Cael's shocked eyes. "You are mine."

The Unseen paused. Their impossible shapes quivered —but they obeyed.

Bostick backed away, fast now, his blade coming up between him and the nearest creature. His eyes moved away from Thane, fixed on the Unseen. Backing toward the door.

The Unseen quivered in place, like hunting dogs being held back. Bostick swung—fast, efficient, precise. His weapon passed right through the nearest.

No impact. No blood. No scream.

Just a shimmer of cold.

His weapon had no use in this place. Salile and the Unseen had different rules.

Thane raised his watch higher, the light flickering like it was alive. Beating. Ticking. Both at the same time.

"Go," he said, his voice hollow with command. "Make sure he doesn't make it out of this city."

A ripple passed through the Unseen.

And then—they peeled away.

A dozen of them surged after Bostick, who had now turned, desperate, in full sprint out of the door. The fog swallowed them all.

And just like that—Bostick was gone.

But not alone.

The remaining Unseen stayed behind. Still. Watching. Waiting for Thane's next command.

Thane lowered his arm slightly, breath sharp in his chest. His skin was damp. His limbs felt like glass.

He hadn't been sure that would actually work, but now that it did, he knew what needed to be done.

He turned to the remaining Unseen, voice low but tense.

"Lead us out," he said.

The Unseen moved. Not drifting this time—but jerking forward in slow resistance. Each step seemed labored, unwilling. The magic was forcing them. Not guiding them.

Thane stepped in behind them. The others followed, blades drawn, nerves frayed.

Cracks of light spidered along Thane's skin—his wild magic leaking as he held the power steady. The watch pulsed like a heartbeat—too fast, too stressed.

The city's fog shifted at their approach, but not in retreat. In defiance. It *watched*. It pressed. It waited.

Behind them, more Unseen emerged. At every corner, every new path, more joined the slow procession. They weren't leading the group. They were being herded by them. And the pursing shadows were barely held back by whatever Thane was doing.

The space around the group tightened. The air thickened. The silence felt like a scream waiting to break.

Sweat poured from Thane's brow. His steps slowed. His chest rose and fell like he'd run a mile uphill. Still, he said nothing. He pressed on, trying to save them.

Cael broke the silence. "Are you—can you hold them?" he whispered.

Thane nodded. Didn't speak. Couldn't. All of his effort was just on holding them back. Away from the others. Away from Lirien.

The cracks on his arms glowed brighter, spreading out to the rest of his body slowly. The magic holding back the Unseen was beginning to fray at the edges, wavering like heat on stone.

Erynn stumbled. Lirien caught her. Kaelir's hand twitched on his blade.

And then—they saw it.

The archway.

Stone. Tall. Just like the one they'd entered on the Steepes. But through this one—sunlight. A road. The way out.

But the Unseen pressed closer. The bubble of Thane's magic was shrinking.

Kaelir reached in, throwing Thane over his shoulder, and shouted—"Run!"

The group broke into a sprint.

The last yards stretched like a dream. The Unseen surged. Thane's magic flared—wild, burning—then vanished.

They tumbled through the archway—into sun, into warmth, into sound.

Behind them, the Unseen slammed into the archway like a wave. Faces formed now—twisted with fury. Bodies crashed against the threshold, unable to pass.

They screamed. Not with sound. But with motion. With fury. With *denial*.

The group collapsed onto the sunbaked ground. Gasping, but alive.

Cael dropped to a crouch, face pale. Kaelir stared at the sky like he didn't believe it was real.

Thane sat, hands on his knees, staring back at Salile.

The city pulsed like it hated them for leaving.

"It's not just a game," he muttered.

Lirien touched his shoulder, kneeling beside him.

"Whatever you think it is," she said slowly, gently. "You're part of it now. We all are."

Thane didn't answer. But he didn't argue either.

They stood there a long time, catching their breath.

Then Cael turned to Thane.

"What did you see in there?" he asked quietly. "What did you learn?"

The others turned too. Not with suspicion, but with belief that he had to be the one.

Thane hesitated. His mouth opened. Closed.

He thought back to the Test. What he'd seen, or thought he'd seen. It was hard to know what was real, and what wasn't. But he had a choice to make.

"The Heart," he said. "I need to heal it. If I don't, this place falls apart."

Erynn's brow furrowed. She exchanged a glance with Cael.

"That's… tricky," she said. "The Heart is everywhere and nowhere. It's—"

"No," Thane cut in, his voice firm. "It does have a home. I've seen it. We need to find it."

The faces that looked back at him were full of skepticism, like he'd said something blasphemous.

Erynn glanced at Cael, and him at her, their expressions conflicted. A moment later, she leaned toward Cael, whispering, "He speaks the words of the Oracle. We need to go to Veydris."

Cael shook his head, his lips pursed.

"Absolutely not," he whispered back. "That place is a graveyard for fools chasing illusion and fantasy."

"We don't have any other options," Erynn shot back, her whispers sharp but measured. "If anyone can help us, it's Aelith," Erynn insisted. "Her followers swear she can see the Heart."

Cael let out a long breath, then looked at Thane.

"Fine," he muttered, resigned. "We go to Veydris. But don't say I didn't warn you."

Thane nodded. "If that's where we need to go, then let's go."

Without another word, they turned from Salile—no more debate, no more delay.

He didn't know where Veydris was. Or what waited for them there.

But for the first time, Thane wasn't running away.

He was walking toward something.

17

INTO THE WASTELANDS

THANE DIDN'T LOOK BACK. He didn't want to.

Neither did the others.

Salile lingered behind them, shrouded in darkness. Hidden and forgotten to time. But dangerous and protected.

Though the sun blazed ahead, its warmth did little to thaw the chill Salile left behind. The streets and alleyways they'd walked only moments ago were already slipping into memory—vanished behind its eternal veil.

If Salile was a city suspended in time, what lay ahead had been devoured by it.

It felt like stepping off the map—into the forgotten. Into the abandoned.

The Wastelands.

The cliffs that bookended the city continued northward into the sun—but here, they were different. Bleached. Bone-dry. Dead.

They tapered off in the distance, giving way to the endless expanse of desert—barren flats interrupted by jagged buttes, wind-worn arches, and dry ancient riverbeds choked with thorn and wind-scoured bone. It was beautiful in the way a blade is beautiful—stark, sharp, and uncaring. At the edge of sight to the north, barely visible through the heat shimmer, the snowcapped Velspire Mountains stood like a broken crown, sentinels to the barren ice-choked northlands beyond.

The early morning light burned rust-orange against the cracked red stone, the sky a cruel, cloudless stretch that offered no comfort and even less shade. And then the heat struck them—oppressive and unrelenting.

Nobody spoke for the first hour. The silence was not camaraderie—it was fatigue, the kind that sits behind the eyes and tightens the throat. Even Kaelir, always vigilant, looked worn.

They'd stripped down to their lightest layers—jackets tied around waists, sleeves rolled high, collars open to the scorching air. Even then, sweat clung to them like oil. The sun had no mercy.

Lirien moved ahead of Thane, her tunic clinging to her frame, her skin slick with heat and dust. Her arms—scarred, sun-darkened, strong—moved like she'd done this before. There was grace in her efficiency. Power in how she endured without complaint.

Thane wasn't sure why he noticed. But he did.

The heat pressed against him from every side. His shirt stuck to his back, damp and useless. Each step dragged. His temper edged up, brittle and sharp. But then he looked down at his wrist. The watch.

It ticked softly, a sound impossibly clear in this wide, dead place. And with each tick, he could feel a pulse—not just in the gears, but in himself. A mirrored echo that rippled beneath his skin.

He flexed his fingers. The faintest shimmer of Wild Magic danced across his knuckles, and the cracks—those pale blue veins of energy that had first appeared in Asmenson—briefly flashed across his skin, pulsing in time with the watch's beat.

Cael's voice cut into the quiet.

"That thing you wear—where did you get it?"

That's when the voice returned.

Let him ask. They fear what they can't control. But you? You were never meant to be controlled.

Thane didn't flinch. He didn't speak. But Echo— its voice, its presence—whatever it was, it was louder now. Clearer. More confident. It no longer felt like a symptom to him. It felt like a companion.

Thane glanced up, eyes narrowing. "It's my father's."

Cael's eyes stayed locked on the timepiece. "It's not your father's anymore."

"Leave it," Thane muttered, his anger rising. "It doesn't matter."

"It does," Erynn said behind him, her voice quieter, but firm.

He knew it as well as they did. There was something about that watch—it might as well have been shouting.

But they didn't have a chance to press further.

"Why the hell are we walking through a desert?" Thane blurted, the heat biting at his neck. "There has to be another way."

Kaelir glanced over his shoulder, sweat dripping from his jawline. "There is. It's called the Emerald Pass. Out of the Silent Reach. On the other side of Salile." He gave a dry, humorless smile. "Would you like to head back that way?"

Thane exhaled sharply and turned away. The sweat felt like it was boiling under his skin. He hated this place. The light. The silence. The heat that clung to everything like a second skin.

"That's enough," Lirien said, not unkindly. "We need to find cover before the sun gets higher. If we don't stop soon, we'll burn or end up killing each other."

There were various nods and grunts of agreement.

"There," Kaelir said, pointing to the lee of a broken stone ridge, where a jagged overhang offered a sliver of shade. The Wasteland's heat was a living thing—dry, blistering, metallic on the tongue. Sweat dried the instant it formed. Every breath tasted like it had passed through fire.

The sun fell behind the ridge-line, but the heat lingered, pulsing off the stones.

As the others settled into the shade, Cael crouched low, brushing his hand along the sand until his fingers struck something buried—smooth and cold. He scraped the surface clean to reveal the edge of a half-buried Elinath Stone, like they'd seen in the woods on the way to Salile. But this one had a deep crack across its surface, though the carvings on it were whole and intact.

From the inner pocket of his cloak, he pulled a sliver of bone—shaved smooth and notched at one end.

"No, don't," Erynn said, grabbing his arm, her eyes soft with concern. "It's cracked."

He paused, looking her in the eyes. "We've got days ahead. If we don't make it out of here, it's all for nothing."

They both shared a breath, eyes connected, and then she released her grip.

He crouched again, brushing away more of the sand. The crack in the stone pulsed faintly—as if the magic was leaking.

He exhaled once, then placed the bone to its surface and began tracing sigils carved into the cracked face, muttering words that were low and foreign, syllables that seemed to twist the air itself.

A low hum bloomed beneath their feet. Then, a shimmer—thin at first, like heat rising from the sand—expanded outward in a rush of blue light.

The temperature dropped instantly. Cool, crisp air swept over them like a wave. The dome held, faintly glowing around them.

Lirien sighed, collapsing against the rock wall. "Best thing I've felt in weeks."

"Whoa, a little AC… nice pops," Thane said, laying on the ground, wiping the sweat from his brow.

Cael said nothing. A thin line of blood trickled from his ear and pattered onto the stone. He wiped it away with the side of his hand.

"This place isn't stable anymore," he muttered.

"The Rending did many things to this world," Erynn added, handing him a square of cloth.

Behind her, Kaelir leaned against the rock of the overhang. "At least the old ones left us something useful for once."

"Says the eternal skeptic," Erynn smirked. "But the old ones left us more than just stones, didn't they?"

She turned, her gaze landing squarely on Thane. "Isn't that right?"

Thane tensed. The question slid under his skin.

"What do you mean?" he asked, already knowing.

"That watch," she said gently. "It's not just a keepsake."

Thane looked down at it, the metal catching a faint shimmer of sunlight as it pulsed against his wrist.

"It was my father's," he said, quieter this time.

He didn't want to think about the hospital room. About his father's hand going still. About the way the watch had kept ticking.

"That's all it is."

"You sure about that?" Cael asked. "Because I saw it back there in Salile. It's more than a mere timepiece. I think we all know that."

Thane's hand closed over the watch. "I don't want to talk about it."

He tugged his sleeve down over the watch, but the thing still pulsed against his skin—steady, unrelenting.

Erynn didn't press. Not yet. She reached into her satchel and drew out the Codex, its leather binding dulled by years of use. She knelt in the sand, flipping through the weathered pages with slow precision until she stopped at one.

She turned the book toward Thane. "It's already been drawn."

Thane hesitated, then leaned forward.

There it was.

The sketch was precise. The same spiral face, the same flared edge, the same block numbers. Even the little nick near the edge.

He swallowed hard. Something twisted in his chest. How could a drawing of his dad's watch be in this book, in this place? It made no sense.

Cael knelt beside Erynn, studying the page. "It's called a Foccil," he murmured. "I remember seeing the name once. Nothing more than a footnote in a closed archive."

"It was forgotten," Erynn added. "Disappeared to time. Until now. It was said to allow one to harness the power of the Wild Magic… wielded only by someone from beyond."

She looked at Thane. "The Chosen One."

He didn't respond. Couldn't. His throat tightened, eyes still on the page. Trying to make sense of it all, but failing.

"I'm not him," he muttered finally, almost to himself. "You're putting too much faith in that book. In me."

Erynn closed the Codex softly. Dust settled between them.

"Maybe," she said. "But even the Codex doesn't say who he'd be. Just that he'd come."

Cael didn't argue. He took the Codex from her and opened it again, slower this time, reading in silence as if he were seeing it all anew.

No one said anything more.

And in the quiet, the watch ticked—steady, unyielding.

Later, as the dome of cool air shimmered around them and the stars began to bloom above the horizon, they sat in uneasy companionship.

Lirien pointed skyward. "That's the Ox-Sisters," she said. "They say they carry the heavens on their horns."

Erynn added softly, "And that one—Tir'Elin. The Traveler's Eye. Long ago, people named the Elinath Stones named after it. Said to watch over those who wander. Some even say it sees the roads we don't yet know we'll walk, guiding us."

Kaelir snorted. "Or maybe someone strung those stars together centuries ago to tell you what to believe."

Cael chuckled, but there was no humor in it. "Just like Aelith. Stories sold to the desperate."

Erynn stiffened. "That's not fair. You don't know her."

"I know more about her than you can imagine," Cael replied. "And her type. Mystics, prophets—they all claim to see the truth, and they'll all take coin to tell you what you want to hear."

Lirien shifted, uneasy. "But she helps a lot of people. She gave us a warning—about you. And tried to undo the damage."

Kaelir stepped in, his hands raised in quiet protest. "We're not doing this. Not here. The desert doesn't care who said what to whom years ago."

But Cael pressed forward, heat rising in his voice. "That's not what happened. We all know it. And yet people keep twisting it to make her look like some savior and me the villain."

He turned away sharply, muttering, "I took the fall for the good of Arbelon. But that still doesn't make her right."

Erynn let out a quiet breath, gaze flicking back to the stars. "Maybe not. But sometimes it's not about being right. It's about needing hope. And she gives that to people."

"Just be careful," Cael said, quieter now. "She let me down. She might do the same to you."

A heavy silence circled the group. Brief. Fragile. Then Kaelir laid a hand on Cael's shoulder. "For what it's worth, I never believed those things about you. If I did, you wouldn't be here."

Cael nodded, meeting Kaelir's gaze, and let out a deep sigh.

That was enough to settle things. For now.

The conversation shifted—softer, unfocused. Stories of the Wasteland. Snatches of dry humor. Talk for the sake of talk.

Thane let their voices drift into the background as he lay back in the sand, arms folded behind his head.

The stars stared back—indifferent, ancient, familiar.

They looked no different from the ones back home. Just different shapes. Different names. And yet, the same sharp ache bloomed in his chest. One more thing to leave behind.

He was about to close his eyes when something about the stars changed. Some moved wrong. One constellation rotated. Another blinked, too rhythmically.

He blinked. They went still again.

In the silence, something flickered at the edge of vision

—a shimmer, like heat rising, but colder somehow. A glitched mirage of the group walking ahead of themselves… but they looked wrong. Dimmer. Faded. Like echoes more than people. They moved with urgency, glancing over their shoulders.

A shadow passed through the illusion. Dark and too fast. Then—nothing.

A flicker of unease slid through his chest.

Was it a trick of the heat? A glitch in the world itself?

Or something deeper—something inside?

A voice sprouted in his mind. Calm. Clinical. The white hum of hospital fluorescents.

"The line between reality and delusion grows thinner with time," said Dr. Hughes—his voice echoing from the depths of memory, as crisp and unshakable as if he stood in sand.

For a second, Thane lay motionless.

Maybe his sickness didn't care which world it took first.

He closed his eyes, wishing it all away. But his wishes never came true. Not anymore.

He should've told them. But he didn't know how. He was tired. Holding himself together. Holding his mother together. It was too much.

Almost on cue, Echo's whispers came from the darkness.

You are more than their beliefs. They will survive if you survive.

He hated that it made sense. Hated more that part of him wanted to believe it.

He didn't tell them this, either.

It seemed the desert was a place that kept its secrets.

"We move out," Kaelir said, breaking the silence as he slung his pack over one shoulder.

The shimmer of cold air vanished as Cael pressed his hand to the cracked Elinath Stone. The carvings flickered once, then died. Heat spilled back into the space like a tide returning. Oppressive. Heavy. Real.

No one said a word. They just stood, adjusted gear, fell into line.

Ahead, the path dipped into a narrow pass flanked by two crumbling spires of stone. The moon hung between them, pale and perfect—a dream framed in dust.

18

DUSTWALKERS

Moonlight washed the broken flats in ghost-light—harsh, colorless, surreal. The Wastelands whispered just beyond the edge of sight.

Heat returned with a vengeance and pressed in on all sides—dry and metallic. Even in the darkness, the air shimmered, bending the horizon.

They walked in silence, heads low, each breath gritty with dust.

Kaelir stopped first.

He knelt beside a patch of discolored grit and brushed it with the back of his hand. Bone. Fingers curled skyward. A shredded tunic still clung to the wrist, sun-bleached and tattered.

No one spoke.

Cael crouched beside Kaelir, brushing the brittle bone with the back of his hand. It disintegrated under his touch.

"Wind doesn't do that," he muttered—low and grim, more to himself than anyone else.

Then his eyes shifted. Past the bones. Up the canyon wall.

Thane followed his gaze. Deep gouges—etched into the stone, sharp and deliberate.

"What does?" Lirien asked, her voice quiet.

"Something else," Cael said.

Thane's skin prickled. The rhythm of his watch ticked harder against his wrist.

They moved on. A little faster now.

For the next few days, they slipped between dusk and dawn, walking through the dark, resting in the day anywhere they could find shadow deep enough to dull the sun. Their water-skins ran dry, with no sign of respite.

The Wastelands stretched endless before them. Cracked red stone. Black glass. Dead riverbeds choked with salt. Their skin burned. Their throats dried. And the heat—always the heat.

They passed the shattered remnants of a desert town. Half-buried walls. Arches collapsed in on themselves. Cael called it Brugla, a waypoint lost during the Rending. Once an oasis. Now only whispers—skeletal shadows in the moonlight.

Thane thought he saw movement in the ruins. A flicker. A shimmer.

At first, he chalked it up to glitching—fragments of stone misaligned, as if torn code had been stitched to failing hardware. The kind of artifacting he'd seen a hundred times in VR.

But the longer he looked, the less certain he became. The shimmer held... wrong. Not like a rendering error. More like something broken.

The Rending, they kept calling it. He'd thought it a myth, or narrative dressing. But now...

What if this wasn't a glitch in a system? What if it was a scar in the world itself?

He looked to Cael, about to point it out, but the shimmer was gone. Just broken ruins again.

He paused, waiting for it to return.

It didn't. So he said nothing. But something in him kept watching.

It was in the early morning hours of the fourth night, they happened upon them.

A crescent-shaped ridge broke the line of the horizon. Just beneath it, orange fires burned low. Shapes moved in the blooming light of dawn—tall figures wrapped in dirt-brown robes, their hoods drawn tight. Iridescent embroidery shimmered faintly across their sleeves.

They paused on the rise, staring down at the faint glow of firelight.

"Wayfen," Erynn murmured, her voice low with something like awe.

"Are you sure?" Kaelir asked.

"The robes. The spirals. I've read about them," Erynn said. "Plus, who else would be trekking across the Wastelands heading to Veydris."

"She's right," Lirien said, stepping beside her. "They're from Wayfe—the city on the coast at the far western edge of the Wastelands. I've spent some time in Wayfe before. With my parents. A strange people. Some call them pilgrims. Others gypsies. But either way, one thing is clear. They follow Aelith—and believe she sees beyond the veil."

"Not just followers. Religious fanatics, bordering on lunacy," Cael added with a sneer. "Most of them are high on desert root, hoping that Aelith will solve all their problems."

"Well, in all fairness, she's done some good," Erynn said. "That's why they still cross the Wastelands seeking her counsel."

"She gives them the desert root and takes their coin." Cael's jaw clenched. "It's all calculated. All manipulation. Believe me, you don't know the half of it. We're best to steer clear of that lot. Nothing good comes from Wayfe."

"But we're out of water," Lirien said, her voice calm but firm. "They know this land. If anyone can help us survive the stretch to Veydris, it's them."

"Assuming they don't try to convert us or drug us into a trance first," Cael said.

Kaelir cut in. "We don't have a choice. We've got half a skin left, and they've found good shade for the day ahead. If they're dangerous, we'll know soon enough."

Cael didn't respond, but his silence was a reluctant agreement.

"I'll go first," Lirien said. "I've spent time with the Wayfen. I know their ways."

They descended the ridge slowly, deliberately—blades sheathed but hands never far from hilts.

As they neared the camp, the Wayfen turned from their firelight. Their eyes caught the glow, but no weapons were drawn. Only silence.

At first, Thane thought it was reflection. But then he saw it clearly.

The whites of their eyes weren't white at all. They were rust-colored. Clouded. Like clay-water dried to the inside of a bowl. Not just one. All of them.

Lirien stepped forward, drawing her hood back. She raised one hand, palm to the sky, and laid the other over her chest.

"May the sun carry your truths, and the stars keep your path," she said in a soft, remembered dialect.

There was a murmur among the Wayfen. One woman crossed a spiral over her chest. A young girl echoed the gesture.

An elder stepped forward—movements slow, his eyes carrying the same rust-hazed pallor Thane had already seen. Now, up close, it was unmistakable. Not firelight. Not illusion. Just something else the desert had done to them.

"And yours," he answered, bowing his head.

Lirien lowered her hands. "We come without blades drawn. We walk as you walk."

Another pause. Glances passed between several Wayfen.

"That is the way," the elder said. "What is it you seek?"

"Shade, water, and safe passage east," Lirien answered.

Erynn stepped forward by Lirien's side. "Can you help?"

The elder looked across the group, his eyes holding on Cael for a beat too long.

"You bring danger to our camp."

Cael moved, a half-step forward, but Erynn was quicker—slipping ahead of him.

"We are no different than you," Erynn said, her tone steady. "We cross the Wastelands to seek the guidance of Aelith. Her vision will light our path forward."

Silence held a moment longer—then the elder glanced toward his kin. A few nodded.

That day, they shared the shade.

The Wayfen moved like cogs—quiet, deliberate, shaped by ritual. Their camp was a simple ring of woven mats and sandstone ovens, the smoke thin and fragrant, laced with the scent of drying herbs and burned root. Their dirt-brown robes seemed to melt into the rock, only the shimmer of embroidered spirals catching the eye when they shifted in the light.

The elder who had spoken to them introduced himself simply as Tomael, and then said no more for hours.

Another Wayfen, a wiry and sun-scorched man named Jeyin, showed Lirien and Kaelir how they trapped moisture beneath flat stones and pulled water from sandbanks—techniques older than cities, handed down by dustwalkers before the Wastelands ever had a name.

That afternoon, as the heat reached its worst, the fire was extinguished and low chants began. Harmonic. Steady. And in a language Thane couldn't fully understand. A woman traced symbols in the sand with her thumb as she hummed. A child danced barefoot between mats, her hair blowing in the breeze. She stopped in front of Thane, tilted her head, and puckered her lips as if deep in thought.

"I saw you in a dream," the girl said softly, her eyes locked on him. "You came through the veil. Just like she said."

Thane froze.

The girl moved on, already laughing at something Lirien said. But her words lingered.

Subtle as smoke, Echo's voice seeped into the silence.

They see what you deny.

Its whisper was there one second, gone the next.

Thane looked toward Cael—ready to say something. But Cael was speaking quietly with Erynn.

"They worship shadows," Cael muttered, his gaze on the chanting Wayfen.

"Or they remember more than we do," Erynn replied, not looking at him.

Cael paced a few steps away, then turned back. "You see their eyes? That rust haze? It's not from the heat. It's the root. It eats at them from the inside. Aelith has them so deep in a trance they think her hallucinations are holy."

"She hasn't hurt them," Erynn said. "They go to her by choice."

Cael didn't laugh. Just shook his head. "They're drugged. She sells visions wrapped in dreams and desert flowers—it's a racket. She whispers just enough to make them feel special, and they follow her across the sands until they drop dead with her name in their mouths."

"Enough," Lirien snapped. Her voice was low, but final. "She gives them hope. Maybe that's all they've ever wanted."

Cael didn't answer. He turned away, jaw set, not ready for any more discussion.

Thane retreated, staying on the fringe, but slowly he found himself drawing closer. The Wayfen whispered when they thought he wasn't listening, their chants shifting just slightly when he passed.

He didn't understand the words.

But he knew the tone.

Reverence.

He caught Lirien watching him once, standing just outside the firelight. Her arms were crossed, her face unreadable. He looked away.

He closed his eyes for just a moment.

A breeze passed—warmer than the desert wind. When he opened them again, the sun was gone, replaced by soft twilight. He sat on a wooden bench beneath a wide, open sky. Trimmed hedges bordered the courtyard. Lavender drifted in the air.

It was the hospital garden.

His mother sat beside him.

"I always liked this place," she said, a twinkle of warmth in her eyes. "You used to bring your books out here while I was working. You'd sit for hours, just reading."

He nodded. "I remember."

The memory wrapped around him like a blanket. She felt solid, steady—like she used to be, before everything broke. But she looked tired—somehow older and worn.

She smiled faintly, her hand settling gently over his.

"You've come so far," she said. "And you've done so much. I'm so proud of you."

He didn't answer. Just sat in silence, letting the moment fill him. The sky above pulsed faintly—red, then blue, then still again.

Her fingers tightened slightly.

"You don't have to come back," she said, still gentle.

Thane turned. "What?"

"I mean it." Her eyes glistened, but her smile didn't fade. "This world… the one you're in now… maybe that's where you were always meant to be."

He stared at her. Something about her voice was off somehow—like a recording wearing thin.

"All I'm saying," she said, turning to him. "Don't carry guilt, sweetheart. Do what you have to do. I'll survive."

Her hand was cool now. Not cold—just cooling. Like heat draining from a dream.

"You can stay," she said softly. "You have my blessing. It's okay."

The sky flickered again.

Then the bench was empty.

"Thane."

His eyes flew open with a gasp. The colors of the twilight garden dissolved back into harsh desert light.

In the blink of an eye, the phantom of his mother was gone—replaced by Lirien's concerned face hovering over him in the Wasteland heat.

"It's time to go," Lirien said gently.

Around them, the Wayfen camp was bustling in quiet preparation to move. Afternoon had given way to evening —he must have drifted.

Lirien's hand was on his shoulder, steady and anchoring.

Thane sat forward, swallowing hard. His skin was clammy, and his heart thudded against his ribs as if trying to shake off the dream. He forced a nod.

"Okay," he managed in a rough voice.

Lirien studied him for a second, concern knitting her brow, but she didn't press. She offered him a water-skin, and Thane took it with a trembling hand, trying to mask the shake as exhaustion.

As he rose to his feet to follow Lirien, Thane cast one last glance at the spot beside him.

Empty.

Of course it was empty.

There was no comforting embrace here, no mother's voice—only the fading echo of a dream. He rubbed his hand unconsciously, where his mother's fingers had touched him moments before.

The ache that remained felt all too real.

The next thing he knew, they were breaking camp, traveling with the Wayfen beneath a starry sky. The rhythm of the desert had taken hold—quiet feet on sand and cracked stone, breath timed with the wind. For the first time in days, their steps felt guided. Purposeful.

They seemed to be walking forever in a trailing line through the darkened sands. As the horizon bloomed toward dawn, the Wayfen slowed. Another group approached from the east—thin, dust-caked figures moving like ghosts through the dark.

These were not pilgrims.

These were returners.

Faces gaunt. Robes caked with red dust. Eyes colored with rust.

They had already been to Veydris.

They filled the space below a large outcropping carved into the sandstone over centuries. The walls were painted with abstract images, swirling and broken.

The two groups of Wayfen shared quiet greetings, folding into one another like old pages of the same book. No smiles. No embraces. Just bowed heads and murmured names, the desert way. Ash was passed from palm to palm and rubbed beneath eyes. The fire was relit. A ring was formed.

Tomael introduced the leader of the returners as Kessef, an older Wayfen woman with darkened skin cracked by wind. She walked with a staff carved from petrified bone. The others in her group deferred to her without question.

They sat in a wide circle—Wayfen and outsiders alike. A long tapered pipe packed with desert root was passed. No pressure, just ritual. Simply passed around the circle, left to right.

Kaelir was the first to refuse, then Lirien.

Erynn gracefully declined. While Cael waved it away with a sneer.

Thane took it, examined it. It smelled oddly comforting to him, stirring something just beyond memory. He sniffed its sweet plume and—after a beat too long—brought it to his lips, taking a deep drag. He immediately started coughing, trying to spit out the smoke, as the Wayfen to his right gently took the root from him with a deep smile.

Kessef watched from across the circle without judgment.

"Many look down on Aelith's gifts," she said softly. "Fewer understand them."

Thane didn't respond, but he didn't look away either.

Later, as the sun spun above them, the returners spoke. Of Veydris. Of the spires. Of Aelith.

"She is… not as she was," said Kessef, her voice thin. "Older. Brittle, perhaps. But her visions are clearer than ever."

They spoke of their experience with Aelith and of news from the south. Fractured images. A figure walking through fire. The name *Asmenson* passed through their lips many times.

"The village burned," another said. "While the sky cracked blue."

This news sent whispers through the Wayfen. An unease settled upon them.

Erynn stiffened. "You've already heard about Asmenson?"

"The world speaks through Aelith," Kessef replied. "And we listen."

Cael folded his arms. "And what exactly did she tell you?"

"She said one has come from beyond. Carrying death. Walking toward the place where all ends must begin."

A chill spread up Thane's spine, setting goosebumps on his skin. He didn't know what that meant. *Was he the one from beyond? Was he carrying death?* Neither one sounded great, and whatever that last part meant was beyond him. Something Kaelir apparently shared.

"That's comforting," Kaelir muttered under his breath.

The Wayfen turned their gazes to the group.

"What do you seek from Aelith?" Kessef asked.

There was a pause. Then another. Followed by empty glances.

Cael stepped in.

"We seek clarity," he said, his tone cool. "A riddle solved. Nothing more."

The Wayfen exchanged glances. Someone snorted. Another frowned.

"Seems a long way to travel for a riddle," Kessef said.

The silence stretched. Long enough to settle.

No one said more. Not Cael. Not Erynn. Not even Lirien.

They were willing to let it lie. Let the half-truth hang there.

But Thane couldn't. Not after hearing the sky cracked blue and someone had come from beyond carrying death.

He glanced around the circle. Watched Cael's arms stay folded, his mouth pressed into that familiar, unreadable line. Watched Lirien shift her weight, like even she didn't want to challenge the Wayfen's belief too directly.

So that's it? We're just pretending none of this sounds familiar?

He opened his mouth, closed it. Then opened it again.

A half-laugh escaped—tight and bitter.

"Well," he said, "it's not like one of us is the Chosen One or anything."

The Wayfen didn't smile.

But their eyes lingered. Too long. Too still.

A few shifted where they sat.

One of the children whispered, "He's lying like they do in dreams."

Thane blinked.

He turned slowly toward the girl, but she was already looking elsewhere, humming to herself as if she hadn't just peeled him open with a sentence.

He looked back to the fire, jaw tight.

"Yeah," he muttered. "Well… sometimes there's no point in having dreams."

No one responded. Not the Wayfen. Not his companions.

But their silence felt different now.

No one said it aloud, but something had shifted.

That day, as the desert heated and their circle of fire dimmed, no one slept easily.

They rose before the sunset. Quiet goodbyes passed between the two Wayfen groups—bows, murmured blessings, a final pass of ash across the cheeks. Packs were gathered. The fires extinguished.

The returners turned west. The pilgrims to Veydris turned east.

Lirien adjusted her pack, the fabric stiff with dust. Kaelir and the others readying themselves for the night of travel.

Thane stood apart, watching the dunes shift in the wind, still thinking about the girl's voice, about dreams that lied.

Then came the sound.

A low, steady thumping. Faint at first. Then louder.

Hoofbeats.

The Wayfen froze.

"Hide," one whispered. "Riders come."

Kaelir was already moving, stepping between the dunes, eyes scanning the horizon.

Cael's hand locked on his quarterstaff. "No," he muttered. "Not them. Not here."

"You think it's—" Erynn started, voice tight.

"It can't be," Kaelir cut in. But even he didn't sound sure.

Even Lirien's fingers went to the hilt at her side.

Dust plumed on the ridge—too fast. Too many.

Thane's blood surged. He felt it coming, the Wild Magic curling inside his chest like a coil pulled tight, his skin crackling with a faint blue light. This time, he didn't resist it. He was ready.

And then—

They came.

Red-armored figures burst over a dune—marauders on lizard-like beasts, bone-armor clattering. Weapons drawn.

The lizard-beasts shrieked as they barreled down the ridge, red armor catching flame in the waning light of dusk. Dust swirled. Bone blades flashed.

Wayfen screamed—real, guttural fear. Some ran for the rocks. Others dropped to their knees, heads pressed to the earth.

Kaelir drew his blade, eyes narrowing. "Not Riders," he muttered. "Armor's wrong. Beasts too."

Cael stepped up beside him, staff in hand. "Desert marauders," he said. "But they're not supposed to ride this far east."

"Doesn't matter," Kaelir said. "They're armed, and they're coming fast."

The world turned frantic. Voices. Dust. Shouting.

Thane stood frozen as one of the younger Wayfen stumbled past him, eyes wide with terror. The fear was contagious.

His breath caught—and the magic surged.

A pulse. Like a second heartbeat. Blue light flickered at his fingertips, then his chest, then rising in faint lines across his arms like veins on fire.

He didn't know what he was doing. Only that he was *doing it*.

A voice rose—high and cracked. Then another. Then dozens.

"Celes'tio… Celes'tio…"

The word laced through the camp like wildfire.

The marauders slowed. One pulled his beast up hard. Another lowered his blade. A third turned and vanished into the haze.

Thane stepped forward, instinct pulling him between

the Wayfen and the riders. The air crackled around him, wind drawn into a tight funnel.

Then—one of the marauders dropped to a knee.

Another followed.

Their leader stood silent. Then knelt as well.

Thane's hands were still glowing. Blue light crackled through his veins, humming just beneath the skin. He felt weightless—like he could breathe the magic, *become* it.

And in that moment, he didn't want to stop.

The Wayfen were still kneeling. The marauders too.

He could speak. Command them. Make them worship. Or end them. At his whim.

A single word either way.

The pulse of his watch grew louder—clicking in rhythm with his heart, faster now, like it knew.

He didn't move. Couldn't.

Then Lirien stepped in, her hand closing gently over his wrist. Not forceful. Just *there*.

"Thane," she said, softly but firmly. "That's enough."

Her voice cut through it. Not power. Not prophecy. Just presence.

He looked at her, saw no fear in her eyes—just concern.

Slowly, the glow faded. The air calmed. The magic receded like a tide withdrawing from shore.

Cael's voice came next, rough and hollow.

"Celes'tio. It means... Chosen One in the old language."

The Wayfen didn't cheer. They bowed lower. Whispered the name.

Celes'tio... Celes'tio...

Thane didn't feel powerful.

He felt *seen*.

Then, from the calm that followed chaos, Echo whispered—silky, slow, undeniable.

They bow to you now.

They will follow you forever.

Thane's breath caught. The words curled in his mind, seductive and soft.

Not a threat. Not a lie.

A truth carried in the sunlight. His path set in the stars.

And that scared him more than the magic ever had.

19

WELCOME TO VEYDRIS

NIGHT HADN'T YET BROKEN, but the camp stirred with quiet purpose. Fires reduced to ash. Packs cinched tight. The Wayfen moved like shadows—soft steps, no voices, only farewells traced in soot across cheeks in spirals of parting.

But the air held something else now. A tension. Not fear—reverence.

Wherever Thane stepped, whispers followed. Murmured prayers. Eyes dipped low—not out of shame, but something near worship.

He didn't know what to make of it. Part of him still wanted to write it off—just some mechanic, some programmed behavior, NPCs looping on a script.

But no one bowed to him back home. No one sang when he passed. No one touched his arm like he was real. Most people had already written him off. Forgotten about him. Here, he wasn't forgotten. He was remembered. Revered.

That unsettled him more than he wanted to admit.

Tomael approached last, robes whispering against the sand. His rust-hazed gaze lingered on Thane, deeper now, the kind of look meant for prophecy—not people.

"Walk true through the veil," the elder said.

Thane meant to answer. Meant to offer some response. But his throat closed. A nod was all he could manage.

One Wayfen placed a bone-carved charm in his hand—a spiral etched in red. Another bowed so low his forehead brushed the stone.

No one said his name.

They didn't need to.

Even the marauders were changed. They moved quieter now, eyes lowered, their armor dulled by dust and something like humility. One offered the reins to Thane without a word. Just a nod.

The rest of the group mounted up with other riders. By the time they turned their mounts toward the east, the Wayfen had already faded into the dunes behind them—*but they never turned their backs.*

The journey toward Veydris passed in soft rhythm.

The Wastelands faded behind them, but not gradually—*suddenly.* One moment they rode over cracked shale and sun-bleached stone. The next, the world changed.

Green. Everywhere. Vines curling through fractured earth. Trees wide and gnarled, their bark pale as bone, moss climbing like veins. The air shifted—cool and damp and humming with life. It stretched the horizon as far as the eye could see.

They had crossed into the Great Forest.

No border. No warning. Just a line, invisible and absolute. Cael said it was but another imprint of the Rending. Leaving the Wastelands in devastation.

Behind them, the desert still baked. Ahead, the forest dripped.

A breeze threaded through the trees, cool and wet against Thane's skin. He pulled his cloak tighter. After days of blistering heat, the chill felt like a lie.

Finally, the forest swallowed the last glimpse of the desert behind them.

When the marauders pulled their steeds to a stop, it was without a word. Just a low whistle, and the bone-armored lizards knelt. Their eyes blinked sideways, tongues flicking as if tasting the air.

The group dismounted in silence, boots crunching soft underfoot.

One rider nodded to Kaelir, then turned away. Another glanced at Thane—not in fear, not in reverence, just a kind of recognition, like he was recording this moment. Preparing his memories for the firelight stories to come.

The lizard-beasts hissed once, then darted off with surprising speed, their massive tails slicing ferns aside like oars through water. Then they were gone, swallowed back into the green.

Thane watched them vanish.

"Okay," he said. "I know no one's gonna say it, so I will. That was weird. Right?"

Kaelir smirked. "You weren't on the one that kept trying to bite Cael."

"It had judgment in its eyes," Cael muttered. "Deep, biting judgment."

Lirien just shook her head. "Let's move."

They didn't make it far. Ahead, just off the trail, a statue rose from the earth like a forgotten tooth—stone dark with age, half-swallowed by moss and roots. It leaned, weathered and cracked through the middle, as if the forest had tried to reclaim it, pulling it back into the dirt.

As they drew closer, its shape resolved. Not just any

statue—a shrine. Once sacred, now collapsed into memory. Its face had been mostly worn away, features eroded by time. Still, what remained was… familiar. Not specific, not detailed. But something in the shape of the brow. The tilt of the chin. The way the mouth had once held a line.

Thane stepped closer, hand brushing the stone. He didn't mean to. It just happened.

A memory tugged at him. Not sharp. Not recent. But deep. It wasn't him the statue looked like. That's what unsettled him most.

Erynn knelt beside the base, her hand hovering over the inscription. She traced the runes carved in jagged lines, barely legible through the grime.

The Chosen Comes to Unmake What Was Made.

Her voice was quiet, but it cut through the silence.

Cael crouched beside her, his expression unreadable. "This isn't in the Codex," he said flatly.

"That," Erynn said, rising to circle the statue, "we can agree on."

Lirien had been watching. She saw the way Thane's fingers lingered along the statue's chin. How his shoulders had drawn tight.

"Does it mean something to you?" she asked softly.

Thane turned—too fast, like he'd been caught in something.

"No," he said, sharper than intended. He looked away.

Lirien's gaze lingered. Not pushing. Just watching. As if she didn't quite believe him—but chose not to press.

What exactly he saw, he wasn't ready to say. Couldn't. Not here. Not with the others so close, with that face half-lost to time staring back—echoing of something lost long ago. The grief came sudden, uninvited—choking tight in his throat. Not fresh, but still sharp in the quiet places. The ones he never let anyone see.

He stepped back, hand falling from the stone like it burned.

They regrouped in a clearing just beyond the shrine. No one said much. The forest had its own pressure, its own rhythm—slow and deep and old. Even Kaelir stopped scanning the trees after a while, as if it were pointless.

They worked their way down the path to a rise above a valley below.

That's when the towers came into view.

Veydris.

But they weren't towers. Not exactly. They were spires —black glass, impossibly thin, impossibly tall, like needles driven into the world. Too smooth to be carved. Too seamless to belong. The spires didn't feel built—they felt left behind. The forest parted around them with eerie precision. The trunks closest to them bent away—as if pushed.

Thane stepped closer, and something inside him tightened. A recognition, subtle and knowing.

Cael shifted beside him, grimacing.

Lirien noticed. "You know this place?" she asked.

Cael hesitated. "You could say that," he said crisply before turning away.

She didn't ask more. He didn't offer.

The path narrowed, framed by root and stone, until the spires loomed like blades through the canopy.

The forest deepened. Shadows stretched, drawn long by the rising sun behind them. Morning light filtered through the canopy like fractured glass—cutting the mist into slivers. The air was cooler here, wetter, humming faintly with birdsong and insect clicks, but the silence beneath it all still held.

Then the path rose, curling around a ridge of black-veined stone. Just beyond it, the trees began to thin.

They had arrived. Not by grand gate or guarded road. Veydris didn't announce itself. It simply… appeared. And then, from the heart of the city, came the welcome.

Three figures approached in silence—two cloaked in white, faces veiled, quarterstaves of amberwood gleaming with inlaid spirals and crescent glyphs. Their steps were soundless, purposeful. Guards, clearly, though there was nothing threatening in their manner.

Between them walked a woman dressed not in white, but in slate blue. Her veil was sheer, revealing a face marked with fine lines and rust-hazed eyes that shimmered in the morning light.

She stopped before them, her gaze sweeping the group.

Erynn moved forward about to speak, but the woman moved past her, her eyes softening as they settled on Cael.

"It's been a long time," she said, voice light, almost fond. "You're late, you know."

Cael blinked, caught off guard. "Late?"

"She expected you years ago. Not that she'd admit it."

Cael's mouth twitched, not quite a smile. "She always did have poor judgment."

The woman chuckled. "You're just saying that because she chose me over you in sparring."

"Once."

"Twice," she corrected. "And you've never let it go."

There was a brief, warm silence between them. Then the woman's tone shifted—softer, more careful.

"She'll want to know you're here. I told her to keep your room… just in case."

"You would," Cael murmured, and this time his voice had no edge. "Always the optimist."

"Someone had to be." Her smile lingered, but her eyes

said more. "And she… well. Let's just say she never stopped watching the road."

Cael looked away.

"It's not a social visit," he said finally. "We have urgent business."

"I can see that," she said glancing to the others. "But don't pretend urgency can erase the past. Not here."

Cael started to speak—then stopped. "Some things are not so easily forgotten, Vesha. You of all people should know that."

"Yes, well, maybe some things should be forgiven."

They stood for a bit too long holding each other's gaze. Something knowing passing between them.

Vesha finally turned to the others with a broad smile. "Welcome to Veydris. Please come with me. There's food. Rest. And shade—though I imagine the desert left little of your strength to spare."

She turned and led them deeper into the city, the white-cloaked guards flanking her without a word. The spires of Veydris looming high above them, black and silent.

The city itself did not rise so much as ascend. What seemed like a clearing became a staircase. What looked like a grove became a plaza. Veydris revealed itself slowly, like layers peeled from the world.

Vesha led them through winding paths of dark stone and overgrown moss, the sounds of the city growing only slightly with each turn—a whisper of water here, a chime of metal there. It didn't bustle like Trosten or hum like Salile. It *breathed*. Alive in its forest melody.

As they passed through a stone archway, the two guards remained behind. Unlike the other places they visited, this place had no curious onlookers. Only the spires—rising impossibly high and strangely quiet. The kind of quiet that made Thane's skin itch.

They crossed a stone bridge suspended over nothing, the void beneath it veiled in mist so thick it seemed to breathe. Thane kept his eyes forward, unwilling to guess how far the drop went.

At the far end, a tall structure rose—a mix of sculpted archways and glasslike black spires, softened at the edges by ivy and carved sigils that reflected the rising sun.

Vesha stopped before an arched entryway carved with spirals and inlaid with pale stone. She rested her hand against a wooden door, and it opened with a soft click.

"Still the largest in this wing. And still… as you left it," she said gently.

She glanced back at Cael. He gave a quiet nod.

"I'll inform Aelith… she'll want to see you." With that, she dipped her head and disappeared down the corridor, her footsteps lost to the hush of the spires.

The room inside was vast—larger than any of them could've imagined. The floor was polished obsidian veined with silver. High arches framed windows that let the dawn spill across thick rugs and worn, velvet-lined furniture. A desk stood on the far wall. A table in the center held a bowl of fruit and fresh water. Folded tunics and robes lay neatly on a side table, untouched.

The place didn't feel empty.

It felt *tended to*.

As if Aelith had preserved it like a memory she couldn't let go. Not just a room. A sanctuary. A hope.

Silence lingered as they walked into the room until Lirien broke it.

"So," she said, arms folded. "Care to explain what all *this* was about?"

Cael didn't answer. He moved to the desk by the far wall, opening a drawer.

Erynn turned to follow. "Wait—so you two were a thing?"

"We all make mistakes," he answered tersely. "Anyway, it was years ago."

"And so this is this *your* room?" Erynn asked rhetorically. "She just kept it like some sort of a shrine?"

"She's sentimental," Cael muttered.

"Sentimental is a photo or a locket of hair," Lirien said. "Not extra linens and fruit platters."

"She obviously still holds feelings for you," Kaelir added, unable to hide his grin. "You must have had her in your trance."

The others chuckled, unable to hold it in any longer.

"I'm going to pretend I didn't hear that," Cael said, still acting as if he were looking for something in the drawers.

"Why didn't you say something? Anything?" Erynn said. "Now this is a little awkward."

"Did you kiss her?" Lirien asked in a hushed tone, delight creeping into her voice.

Kaelir laughed. Thane and Erynn joined in.

Cael stopped what he was doing and looked up, exhaled slowly, without saying a word.

"You *did*," Lirien added, louder this time. No longer able to hold back her own laughter.

Erynn arched a brow. "This explains so much."

Lirien folded her arms. "It really does, doesn't it?"

"Enough," Cael said, voice firm but not harsh. "It's been a long walk. Perhaps we rest before someone says something *deeply* regrettable."

He didn't turn—but Thane caught the flush at the back of his neck.

The others laughed quietly, drifting into the space. But Thane lingered near a window, letting the chatter fade behind him.

The forest spread out before him—the sun cresting above the upper boughs.

The air inside the quarters held something else. Something that felt out of place or wrong.

And he wasn't sure he liked that.

20

THE VEIL AND THE VOICE

THEY'D BEEN SUMMONED NOT long after Vesha left.

Cael walked ahead of them, saying nothing. But his pace didn't falter.

He knew the way.

Turning a corner, a long hallway ended with an open door and a waiting stillness.

No guards. No sentinels. No herald to announce them.

The chamber was quiet when they entered.

Inside, the walls curved like the inside of a great shell, tiled with fractured mosaics that shimmered in layered gold and deep umber. Swirls of stars and strange symbols looped overhead in patterns Thane couldn't follow. Constellations bent inward. Glyphs spiraled into themselves.

It didn't look designed. It looked… remembered. Like the room was holding on to something long-lost. And beneath it all, a pulse—soft and steady, like a breath drawn and held. Thane could feel it behind his bones.

The light didn't come from torches. There were no candles, no chandeliers. It came from the stone itself—a soft golden glow that rose from unseen seams in the floor and shimmered faintly through the air like dust motes caught in the room's luminosity.

They stood there for a moment, uncertain.

Then she entered.

She didn't sweep in or descend from some high stair. She just appeared—moving from shadow to light as though she'd always been there.

Her robes hung like smoke, dark gray laced with silver thread that caught the glow of the floor. Her hair was dark, streaked with pale wisps like faded starlight, coiled into a knot held by a pin of ambered glass. She moved like someone who had nothing to prove—each step precise, quiet, and absolute.

Her presence didn't demand attention.

It drew it.

Her eyes were the strangest part—neither young nor old, but something between, as if time had bent differently for her. Not rust-hazed like the Wayfen, but clear, piercing. Eyes that had seen too much and still chose not to look away.

She stopped before them and studied the group, gaze passing over Kaelir, Lirien, Erynn, and Thane—before finally landing on Cael.

She smiled.

"You've grown harder," she said, her voice warm and haunting. "But I see the man you were still flickering beneath it all. The one who used to believe. The one so full of hope."

She paused. "And I think he's still in there. Even if you don't."

Cael shifted. Not just uncomfortable—guarded. His jaw clenched, but his voice was steady.

"You always knew how to pick your words," he said. "But let's not pretend we left on good terms."

Aelith didn't flinch. But her smile faded.

"No," she said softly. "We didn't. And I carry that, Cael."

There was a pause—just long enough for something to pass between them. Not anger. Not blame. Something soft. Something known.

She stepped closer, reaching out. Her fingers brushing lightly against his wrist. A breath of contact—no more. Her voice dropped, quiet enough that the others couldn't hear it clearly.

Cael didn't pull away.

His eyes meeting hers.

"You used to smile more," she said. "Before the council. Before we both broke what we were."

Cael looked away. His shoulders tensed, and his breath caught for half a second—too brief for anyone but her to notice.

"You were always meant to come back," she added—barely a whisper. "Even if you never believed it."

Cael met her eyes again—just for a moment.

"Perhaps," he said, his tone matching hers. "But not today."

And in that moment, something unspoken passed between them. Not healing. But the memory of what it felt like.

Then he looked away.

Her smile stayed, small and sad. But she didn't press further. She turned, and her gaze shifted again—landing on Thane.

The temperature in the room dropped. Or seemed to. The breath behind the silence thickened.

She didn't speak right away. She didn't blink. Just

watched him, quiet and intent—as if trying to place him in a memory not her own. As if she were reading a ripple in time that hadn't reached the surface yet.

Thane held her gaze, but something in him pulled tight.

Then she spoke.

"You carry death with you."

Her voice was calm. Not a warning. Not a curse.

A fact.

She stepped forward. Slowly. Deliberately.

Her hand rose, not in threat, but in wonder. She touched his cheek—not a caress, not quite. Just the back of her fingers brushing skin, like testing if something so doomed could still be alive.

"A sickness beyond Arbelon's making," she murmured. "And yet, it has shaped you… tied you to us. Bound you in ways even I cannot see."

Thane flinched. A shiver raced down his spine. His hand moved instinctively to the inside of his coat, brushing against the place where the watch sat.

It didn't tick. But it pulsed. He could feel it. Like a second heartbeat. Slower. Deeper.

Inside him.

The others tensed.

Erynn's stared, wide-eyed. Lirien took a step closer to Thane, wary. Kaelir moved subtly, placing his weight forward, one hand near his weapon. Even Cael's brows pulled low—not in doubt, but in dawning concern.

Thane's throat tightened.

"I—" he started, but the word stuck.

He didn't know what he'd meant to say. Deny it? Confirm it? Joke it away?

The fear wasn't in her words. It was in how much truth they held.

Aelith's eyes softened—not with pity, but recognition. Then she stepped back, her hand falling slowly, as if reluctant to break the connection.

"The veil is thin with him," she whispered. "Too thin."

Her head bowed. Silence followed—thick and still.

Thane felt the chill in her words settle into his bones. He didn't fully understand what she meant. Yet something in him did. Something hidden. Something unraveling.

"Why have you come?" she asked, though the answer was already written in the dust of things long set in motion.

Cael stepped forward, voice steady but restrained. "We came for answers."

Erynn's voice cut through. "No. We came for the Heart."

The words rang, sharper than she meant—but true.

"You seek what has no place," Aelith said, her voice low. "What was not meant to be found." She turned to Cael. "You must have told them that."

"We seek it because we must," Erynn said. "Because it's breaking everything. And you—"

"Have certain gifts," Cael said, stepping forward beside her, more contrite now. "The boy passed the Test. In Salile."

That gave Aelith pause.

She turned away, walking slowly to the room's center. The light around her shifted, dimming without dimming. Her outline blurred—just a breath—and then came the words.

"So you came seeking answers?" she asked, still facing away.

"No," Cael said. "We came seeking your guidance."

She slowly turned, eyes landing on Cael. "You once called me a liar. A crazy lunatic. A danger to Arbelon."

She paused, the pain clear in her eyes, the way her voice wavered on the edge. "And now you come seeking my help? After all these years?"

"Many things were said that should not have been," Cael murmured. "And I was not the only one who said them."

"No," she said. "You weren't. But yours hurt the most. And, still, here I am."

Erynn stepped forward. "I don't know what happened with you two. But, right now, we need your help. You've seen further than any of us. The world brought us here. If anyone can help lead us to the Heart—it's you."

The silence resumed it hold on the chamber.

"For the sake of Arbelon," Erynn added quietly.

Aelith turned to Erynn, nodding.

"For the sake of Arbelon."

"We will let the spires guide us…" she added, turning away.

Thane took a step back. Just one. But enough to feel it. That pull again. That voice—like something ancient had taken notice.

Echo's whisper curled in his mind.

"Smiles hide the sharpest blades."

Across the room, Aelith froze.

Her smile faltered—just for a breath.

Then her eyes snapped to Thane, sharp as a blade drawn from a sheath. But she looked past him. Just for a second, like she saw something standing behind him that no one else could see.

Her eyes lingered, searching the shadows—then, wordless, she turned away. She stepped back into the center of the room and lowered herself slowly to her knees.

Her breath deepened. Her shoulders softened. She closed her eyes—and when they opened again, the pupils had rolled back, white and unfocused, seeing something far beyond them all. Her arms rose outward, palms to the sky. The very air seemed to hold its breath. To the spires.

Then her voice came—not loud, but rhythmic. Like the beginning of a song no one remembered how to sing.

She didn't speak to them. She spoke to the stone beneath them. To the spires above. To the dark memory of the room itself.

Thane's watch stirred against his chest. A faint tick. Then another. The rhythm matched her words. Matched his breath. Matched his pulse.

The light dimmed without darkening. A shimmer passed through the floor, like heat bending in reverse.

The chamber held them all—silent, still—waiting. And then—she spoke. Her voice not her own. It echoed through the chamber—not louder, but deeper, dissonant, like it didn't belong to a single voice at all. More than one. Each syllable blended from the many.

The air itself recoiled with the sound. Even the light seemed to withdraw.

> *"He is the wound. And the weaver."*
> *"The threads twist around his soul."*
> *"He may mend what was torn… or unravel what remains."*
> *"The Heart called to him through the veil.*
> *But his answer remains unspoken."*

Then silence again.

A long, awful silence.

Aelith's eyes fluttered open.

Her shoulders sagged. Then she pitched forward, catching herself with both hands against the floor. Not weak. Just worn thin—like something had passed through her and not all of it had left.

She stayed like that for a breath. Then exhaled, slow and hollow. One hand lifted to her brow. She wiped the sweat away like it had meaning.

No one spoke.

The silence didn't just linger—it pressed in. Dense and trembling. Heavy with what she'd said. Heavy with what it didn't explain.

Thane felt it like a weight against his ribs.

He is the wound. And the weaver.

What the fuck did that even mean?

It bent them all, that silence—each trapped in their own thoughts. Until Erynn stepped forward. Her voice cut through like a thread pulled taut.

"We need more than riddles, Aelith," she said—not unkindly, but with weight. "Everything led us here. To you. The Heart—where is it? If he is to heal it, we need to know."

Aelith turned to Erynn, her expression unreadable. "The Heart is everywhere and nowhere. Its pulse echoes in the stones, the stars, the void. Through the veil itself." As she spoke, she rose slowly to her feet—composure returning like a mask being drawn into place.

Erynn's brows furrowed. "That is not helpful either."

Aelith gave a faint, knowing smile. "It can be found. You need to have faith in the ways of the spires."

Erynn pressed, undeterred. "But the Codex—"

"The Codex," Aelith said, gently interrupting, "is an imperfect record. Not a key. It tells you how things *were*. Not what they've become."

Erynn's jaw clenched. "Then help us understand. We don't have time for spirals and symbolism."

Cael stepped forward, his voice sharp, disappointment flickering behind his words. "She's already told you what she always tells everyone—half-truths wrapped in mist. That's her way."

Aelith's eyes flicked to him. She didn't bristle. She didn't rise to defend. She simply sighed. "And yet, you returned," she said, quiet. "Seeking my guidance again. Didn't you, Cael?"

He looked away, jaw tight. He didn't answer. But the silence between them said enough.

Then Aelith turned back to Erynn. She raised her hand, palm open, as if feeling the weight of something only she could sense.

"The Heart has anchors," she said. "Focal points. Wounds in the world where its pulse can be heard. And felt."

She paused.

Then looked to Cael. Her disappointment matching his.

"The Henges. One of them lies to the west. In Skyreach."

She said the words to him—but her eyes told a different story. One of memory. One of sorrow.

"Skyreach Henge?" Kaelir repeated under his breath, glancing at Lirien.

"But the Codex says nothing of these Henges," Erynn muttered. "There's no mention of them as a focal point."

"And maybe that's the problem," Cael snapped. "You're treating the Codex like it's scripture—but even you know it's been altered, filtered through hands that feared what it might reveal."

Erynn narrowed her eyes. "And you treat anything unexplained like it's dangerous. Not all mystery is corruption, Cael."

"No," he said. "But you do believe her. Just like I do."

"Yes," Erynn breathed. "I do."

The silence cracked sharp between them.

Lirien shifted. Kaelir's arms crossed tighter. The room felt on edge.

"Enough," Kaelir said, stepping between them. His voice wasn't loud, but it carried. "We're not here to debate scripture or spirit. We're here because Arbelon demands it."

He looked at Cael. Then to Erynn.

"We follow the threads we've got. All of them. No matter how tangled they are."

The tension didn't vanish—but it thinned. At least enough to breathe.

Aelith watched quietly, her eyes dimmer now—tired in a way Thane couldn't name.

"You're weary," she said finally. "Cael can take you to the dining hall. Food has been prepared."

She hesitated. Just a flicker—barely more than a breath.

"But if the road still calls you…" Her voice softened. "I won't keep you here."

Thane felt something shift behind those words. Not a threat. A quiet kind of grief. Perhaps the reunion with Cael finally proving too much.

"No," Kaelir said, his voice measured. "It was a long trek through the Wastelands. Food and rest will serve us well."

Aelith nodded once, her head lowered. "Don't let me keep you then. I will join you shortly."

She turned and walked into the shadows.

She didn't look back.

21

HONEY AND BARBS

THE DINING HALL shimmered with quiet opulence.

A low, elongated table stretched beneath an arched ceiling of dark wood inlaid with silver. Embroidered cushions lined the sides, each dyed in deep tones of crimson and green. Incense curled in the corners, fragrant and heady—cardamom, roasted clove, something sharp and floral Thane couldn't place.

They were already seated when the servers began moving through the room.

Not guards. Not veiled in white or slate or blue like the others in Veydris.

These wore robes of amber and deep ochre. Their faces hidden behind translucent veils, their movements too fluid to track easily. Silent. Coordinated. Like a dance meant to distract.

Vesha sat near the head of the table, speaking in quiet tones to a woman Thane hadn't met, her rust-hazed eyes flickering toward Cael every so often.

A few Wayfen were seated among the guests, their robes brushing against the same embroidered cushions, their voices carrying soft laughter between bites. They spoke freely, without formality—comfortable, even.

The meal itself was something out of a dream.

Dishes were placed one after another—steamed rice perfumed with saffron, slow-roasted meats coated in sweet spices, fruits marinated in honey and herbs. Flatbreads warmed in earthen bowls. Sauces glimmered in small carved basins, thick and rich and red as fire. And flagons upon flagons of different colored wines poured freely.

No one mentioned that Aelith had not yet arrived.

But her place at the head of the table was unmistakable—marked by a single, violet-glass cup and a braided ring of silver vines atop the cushion where she would sit.

Thane leaned back on the embroidered cushion, letting the smells of spice and roasted meat settle into his skin. He let his eyes wander lazily across the murals adorning the walls of the room—ancient scenes flowing and overlapping like stories too old to remember. Here and there, he glimpsed strange figures and ancient cities painted with care. Beautiful. But strange—like Veydris itself.

The conversation drifted around him—low, unhurried. The hum of the feast, soft as bees on a blooming bush.

He looked at the others. Cael and Erynn were deep in conversation. Kaelir smiling, talking to a Wayfen seated next to him, almost relaxed. Lirien sat next to Thane, leaning forward to refill their glasses as a subtle chime sounded, and a hush passed through the dining hall—not loud or sudden, but absolute. Even the clinking of bowls and shifting of cushions stilled.

Aelith had arrived.

She entered without fanfare, her robes the same dark smoke threaded with silver, though now she wore a narrow circlet across her brow, etched with glyphs that shimmered faintly under the hall's amber glow. Her presence silenced the room more thoroughly than any command could.

The veiled servers parted without being signaled.

She didn't acknowledge them. She didn't speak. Just walked slowly, purposefully, past the rows of seated guests, her eyes gliding over them like shadows across a sundial. She paused only once—when her gaze passed over Thane. A flicker of something unreadable crossed her face, then it was gone.

She sat without ceremony.

The violet-glass cup was filled before she touched it. But she didn't drink.

"I thank you for coming," she said, her voice quiet but carrying easily. "And for your patience."

Her tone was calm. But not warm. Not like before. There was distance now. Like a veil drawn not over her face, but behind her eyes.

Across from her, Cael didn't speak. He watched her closely, one hand resting flat on the low table.

Kaelir cleared his throat lightly. "This is quite gracious… more than we expected."

"Much is unexpected," Aelith replied. Her gaze still hadn't touched Cael's.

Erynn leaned forward. "We were told you would join us sooner," she said. "I hope everything is alright."

"Things are always as they must be," Aelith said softly. "The road bends where it must."

Something about the words, the way they were delivered. It sat uneasy with Thane, like something had just been wound tighter. The scent of saffron and smoke now mingled with something beyond his grasp, something colder. A sharp edge that didn't belong in this place.

Aelith broke the silence once more, her eyes finally meeting Cael's. For a breath, she seemed almost to falter.

"You brought him to me," she said, and for the first time, her voice was not entirely steady. "And the Heart revealed its will."

Cael nodded once. "We only hope that will is for salvation."

Aelith lowered her gaze. When she smiled, it was a brittle thing, shivering at the edges. It didn't reach her eyes.

"We do what we must," she murmured. "Whether we wish it or not."

She reached for her cup. Her fingers curled around the stem. Still, she didn't drink.

Her gaze lifted, drifting once more across the table—but now, it lingered.

First on Cael.

Then Thane.

And then the door behind them.

Her voice, when it came, was quieter than before. Measured. As if every syllable had been counted in advance.

"I wished it could have been different," she said.

Cael's eyes narrowed. Old memories resurfacing.

"Aelith… what have you done?"

But her gaze had already dropped.

The outer doors opened with a soft grind of stone on stone.

And the Riders stepped through.

Six of them. Clad in black and dark crimson. Armor worn but polished, each bearing the sigil of a pyramid of three broken circles, stitched in silver on the cloaks that trailed behind them. Their footsteps fell in unison, boots silent against the stone.

The servers vanished.

Not fled. Not screamed.

Vanished.

As if they'd never been there at all.

The cushions made their positioning awkward. Kaelir rose first, his blade drawn with cool efficiency. Lirien followed, moving instinctively toward Thane. Erynn's breath caught—her fingers twitching toward the small pouch at her side. Even the Wayfen stood, confused, unsure of the Rider's intent.

And at the head of the table, Aelith remained seated. She hadn't moved. Hadn't looked back.

"I did what I had to," she said softly. "For Veydris."

Cael stood.

The betrayal was written on his face—etched in the lines around his mouth, in the hollow behind his eyes.

"You brought them here," he said. "To this sacred place."

Aelith didn't answer. She didn't need to.

Because now Bostick entered.

He walked like he'd been here before. Like the place belonged to him. His armor clean and crisp, his blade sheathed but his hand resting casually on its hilt. Behind him, more Riders—spreading wide, fanning to the exits, sealing the room in quiet efficiency.

Thane's watch ticked once. Only once. And then fell silent.

Bostick came to a stop across from Aelith. His eyes swept the group. Cold. Predatory. Amused.

"You always did set a fine table," he said to Aelith, a voice like worn leather.

She looked at him, but didn't speak. Didn't rise. She only said, to no one in particular, "I asked them to go. They chose to stay."

Bostick didn't rush. He simply stood there, surveying them like a man choosing cuts of meat.

"You've come far," he said, glancing toward Cael, then to Thane. "But it ends here."

Kaelir slid forward, his blade catching the hall's light.

"Careful," he nodded toward Thane. "You remember what happens when you crowd him."

Bostick's smile didn't waver.

"This time we took precautions," he said lightly.

He moved to the side table, plucked a glass of wine without hurry. He lifted it, studying the slow swirl of magenta, then lowered it casually to his side.

"You'd be surprised what people will give up," he mused. "Just for a bit of free food. A simple drink."

He set the glass down with a soft clink, then took a step forward.

Across the room, Lirien in front of Thane, the pommel of her ethereal blade in hand, ready.

Cael hadn't drawn his weapon. But his eyes never left Aelith.

"You did this," he said to her.

Her expression didn't change. But the flicker of pain was there—in the way her fingers curled into her robes, the way her eyes didn't quite meet his.

"I tried to give you an out," she said.

The words landed cruelly.

"We need to move," Lirien hissed, her eyes darting to the exits. "Now."

Erynn's eyes scanned the room. She reached for her satchel, only to find it missing. Taken at some point during the meal. She hadn't even noticed.

"How? We're surrounded," she muttered.

They were. And the Riders weren't posturing.

They were waiting.

It had all been planned. Prepared.

Thane stepped forward, drawing in a breath. He didn't

speak. Didn't yell. He just reached inward, searching for the threads of that chaotic flame he'd commanded so easily in Salile. The one that had saved them.

But it didn't come.

Nothing came. Just a dull ache behind his eyes. A flicker of cold in his blood.

He tried again, gritting his teeth.

Still nothing.

Thane's eyes widened. He looked down at his hands, palms trembling.

"I—I can't feel it," he said, voice barely audible.

Erynn turned toward him. "What do you mean?"

He stumbled, catching himself against the table.

"Something's wrong," Thane muttered.

Kaelir snapped his head toward the servers—gone now. Vanished.

"The food," he said. "It was laced."

Bostick smiled. A slow, knowing smile.

"Just a pinch," he said, lifting two fingers. "Enough to keep the fire dim. We couldn't have him lashing out again, could we?"

Thane's mouth went dry. He looked at Aelith. She still hadn't risen. But she was watching him now. Her eyes unreadable. Her voice even softer.

"I didn't know," she whispered.

But even she didn't sound like she believed it.

The silence swelled again. And that's when the Riders moved. Swords drawn, encircling the table. Every escape blocked.

And Thane—their Chosen One—stood powerless in the center of it all.

22

VEILBORN

THE DOOR SLAMMED SHUT behind them, and heavy bolts slid into place.

Cael's old quarters had become their prison.

Outside, the muffled shuffle of boots and low voices told them the Riders stood guard.

Inside, the windows were sealed. No weapons. No way out. Only the cold silence of betrayal.

The room felt smaller now. Stripped of its warmth. The fruit bowls cleared. The light dimmed to a shallow haze.

They were alone. Entombed.

"They drugged him," Lirien said, pacing.

Kaelir leaned against the far wall, arms folded, every muscle drawn tight. "And we walked right into it. Like children."

No one responded.

Thane sat near the window, head low, the weight of failure heavy in his chest. He could still feel the dull ache behind his ribs where the magic wouldn't rise.

"They took my blades," Lirien said again, sharper this time. "I let them take my blades."

"It's not your fault," Erynn muttered. "None of us saw it coming."

Cael said nothing. He stood near the door, unmoving. His back to them. His silence louder than the rest.

Finally, Thane spoke.

"She knew," he said quietly. "Didn't she?"

Cael didn't turn. "Of course she did."

Lirien stopped pacing. "You think she's with them?"

"I think," Cael said, "that she made a choice. Like she's done before."

"The Council?" Kaelir asked.

Cael's jaw tightened. "She betrayed me then, too. Said it was to protect the Order. That she was saving me from myself."

"And now?" Thane asked.

Cael finally turned. "Now? I think she believes she's doing what she must to protect Veydris."

Kaelir stood by the door, jaw tight. "We were fools."

"No," Thane said, his voice distant. "Just hungry. And tired."

That earned a sharp glance from Cael.

The silence stretched—taut and splintering—until the first shouts shattered it. Steel rang against steel. A cry—sharp, panicked—then silence.

The group froze.

A heavy thud. A gurgled rasp. And finally, the unmistakable clang of a body hitting stone.

Thane stood, backing instinctively toward the center of the room.

Kaelir mirrored the move.

Cael stepped forward just as the door burst open.

Bostick barreled in, dragging two limp Riders—

bloodied and broken—by the collars of their armor. His hands slick with blood as he kicked the bodies aside and slammed the door behind him, bolting it.

He turned and faced them.

"Quickly," he said, his voice low, urgent. "We don't have much time."

No one moved.

Kaelir's hand twitched like it still remembered holding a weapon.

"You," he snarled. "You did this. You led them."

Bostick didn't flinch.

"I led no one," he said, pulling the crimson cloak from his shoulder and tossing it onto one of the corpses. "Not truly."

Lirien took a step forward, her hand absently brushing the empty place where her pommel would have been. "Then explain yourself."

Bostick looked around, measured the fear in their eyes, the anger in Cael's. Then he nodded. As if a choice had been made long ago, and he was only now allowed to speak it aloud.

"I'm Veilborn," he said. "Like my father before me, and his before him. I've always served the Heart. I never stopped believing. Joining the Riders was my way to ensure what the Veilborn have been doing for centuries wasn't for naught."

Kaelir's eyes narrowed. "You're lying. Infiltrating the Riders is near impossible."

"*Near* impossible," Bostick said. "But not impossible. You know me," he said, pleading to Kaelir. "We trained together as middlings. You know who I was. I never forgot."

The silence loomed again.

Kaelir stepped forward, voice tight. "Prove it."

Bostick nodded, his hands closing in upon one another in rapid succession. A thin spiral of amber light bloomed across his palms, sharp and deliberate.

Erynn stood wide-eyed, watching, as did Cael.

"Proof enough?" Bostick asked, looking at Kaelir.

Kaelir nodded, turning to the others.

"He's one of us. He serves the same purpose."

"Maybe," Cael said low. "But he's still something else entirely."

Bostick turned to Thane.

"Everything I've done," he said, "everything you think was a betrayal—it was to protect you. To ensure you made it this far. To get you to the Heart."

Thane didn't speak. The watch at his wrist thrummed —faint, but insistent, like a heartbeat reawakened.

"I believe him," Thane said quietly. He didn't know why exactly. He just felt it.

"And now?" Kaelir asked. "What's the plan?"

Bostick's gaze darkened.

"Now," he said, "we run."

They unbolted the door and moved fast through the corridors, led by Bostick, Kaelir at his side. Thane followed, the blood rushing in his ears louder than his boots on the stone. Behind him, Cael stalked in silence, every muscle tight.

The spires of Veydris were not quiet now.

Shouting rose in waves. Metal clashed somewhere above. Smoke—faint, acrid—curled down one of the side halls. The city was waking to chaos.

"Why now?" Cael called to Bostick.

"I needed her help," Bostick said. "And she played her part beautifully."

Aelith.

They turned a corner—and found her waiting.

She stood at the edge of the courtyard, silhouetted by torchlight, a curved dagger in one hand, her cloak torn and singed. Her eyes snapped to Cael.

"We're holding them off as long as we can," she said, breathing hard. "The guards will not be able to keep them for long. You need to go. Now."

Cael stared at her. "You planned this?"

"They arrived shortly after you. Bostick came to me, asking about my visions regarding the boy," she said, her eyes briefly flicking to Thane. "Upon hearing them, he told me he was Veilborn."

"There's no time for this," Bostick interrupted. "Her guards are no match for the Riders. We need to go. Now."

"He is right," she said tersely. "The boy has to survive. You must get him to the henge."

She motioned to a stone bench where a bundle waited —their weapons.

She turned to Thane. "Your magic… it will resurface soon. The dose of Witchwight can only quiet your power for so long."

The others grabbed their weapons from the bundle. Bostick scanning the passage behind them. Time was short, and their flight was like threading a needle in the dark.

"Go," she said, pointing down a corridor. "The back gate's open. The Wayfen will cover you through the lower paths out of the city."

"Why are you doing this?" Erynn asked, stunned.

Aelith looked at her.

"Because I believe in him," she said. "And I believe in you. All of you," she said, turning to Cael. "This is my choice."

He stepped closer, something raw and unfinished in his eyes. She took his hand. A pause. Then she leaned in, pressing her forehead to his, just briefly. Her lips brushed his—not hunger, not longing. Just loss.

"I never stopped watching the road," she whispered. "Even when you were gone."

Cael closed his eyes.

"I know."

Then she was gone, back toward the rising noise and smoke.

And they ran.

Pounding down the final garden path, breath ragged, boots skidding on loose stones.

Ahead, the arch of the eastern gate loomed—dark stone hidden in the night—beyond it, the streets of Veydris, still thick with the final dregs of evening trade.

Bostick slowed, scanning the square beyond the gate.

Among the bustle of robed figures, a flash of rust-colored eyes caught Thane's attention—a Wayfen from the feast. The man met Bostick's gaze—and gave a sharp, shrill cry.

The streets came alive.

Wayfen, merchants, and robed citizens surged forward in a living tide, flooding into the square, their bodies pressing against one another. All it took was a man's cry, and the whole city moved like they'd been waiting their whole lives for a savior. Maybe they had. Or maybe it was easier than the thought of giving up, losing hope. That seemed to be why they all journeyed to Veydris.

From the garden path behind them, Riders appeared, blades drawn, pressing forward.

"Traitor," one of the Riders barked. "You've betrayed your oath to Devendor."

"My oath was given before you were born," Bostick clapped back. "It is you who betray Arbelon."

Kaelir stepped to his side, blade in hand.

Thane turned, reaching for the threads of magic, sweat beading on his brow. But each time he grasped at them, they slipped away—limp and useless.

Was it the Witchwight still holding him? Or something else?

The others hesitated, torn between the Riders and the surge of bodies filling the square.

Bostick cursed under his breath.

"Go," he said, without turning, his hand flexing on the pommel of his blade. "I'll hold them."

Kaelir hesitated. "You can't face them alone."

"I can," Bostick said, pushing Kaelir away. His eyes dark with resolve. "I am doing what I was always meant to do. Now you do your part."

He raised his sword, the spiral mark on his palm flaring once again before he closed his grip around the hilt. The air rippled around him, the ancient power of the Veilborn in his blood.

"Get him to the Heart. That's the only thing that matters."

Then Bostick gave Kaelir a final nod. Not a farewell. A command.

"Go."

They turned and plunged into the crowd.

Hands grabbed at cloaks. Voices shouted blessings. The press of bodies became a tide, pulling them forward, pulling them away.

Wayfen figures closed around them—not attacking, but shielding—guiding them through the throng with simple gestures. Down side alleys. Through clanging gates. Past darkened merchant stalls.

And behind them, Bostick met the Riders head-on. The ring of clashing swords fading away, swallowed by the living city.

Thane stumbled once, nearly losing sight of Kaelir

ahead of him, but a strong hand caught his arm—another Wayfen, masked by the hood of a common trader. Wordless, determined.

They pushed deeper into the maze of streets, away from the main thoroughfares. Past walls painted with timeless murals, artisan built archways, candles burning at shrines to things to be remembered.

Every turn seemed random, yet deliberate and certain —like someone had mapped this path long ago. The Wayfen effortlessly guiding them, and they followed without hesitation.

Finally, at the edge of the city's eastern edge, a small iron gate stood open. Beyond it, broken fields plunged into the forest, its trees masked in shadow, the moon and stars hidden behind dark clouds.

Two Wayfen stood waiting.

There was a sudden crack of thunder, followed by a flash of lightning that arced above them, close enough that Thane's hair stood on end.

The Wayfen met at the gate.

One of the waiting Wayfen pressed a small bundle into Cael's hands — sacks of dried food, water skins sloshing faintly.

"Supplies for the road," he said. "From Aelith."

"May the spires guide your way," another said.

Then, almost on cue, the Wayfen bowed low to Thane, pressing a hand to the ground before slipping back into the city.

"Aelith," Lirien breathed.

Cael's head lowered.

"There is nothing left for us here," he said, his voice cracking. "What we seek lies ahead."

Then he turned, heading through the gate.

Kaelir motioned for the others to follow, but he

lingered a moment at the open gate, his hand tightening around the sword hilt. He watched for a moment, and then another, before finally turning to join the others.

They ran until time blurred and breath burned.

Only when they climbed a steep rise and dropped into a dense watershed did they stop. Thane's breath was ragged in his lungs, his head throbbing. They finally collapsed into a small clearing, ringed by towering trees, the sky crackling with lightning. And then rain fell hard—a cleansing downpour, like the heavens wept for them.

Kaelir scanned behind them. "We're clear. For now."

No one cheered.

The silence pressed heavier than before.

Thane sat with his back against a moss-covered tree, pressing the watch to his chest. It was ticking again—subtle, steady. Not like in Salile. But there. A rhythm he could hold on to.

Erynn dropped down beside Cael, staring into the trees.

"She's a good person," she said quietly.

"Yes," Cael answered quietly. His voice restrained. "She just couldn't stand against the Riders—the power of Devendor."

Lirien pulled a flask from her side pouch and passed it around.

"We survived," she said. "With her help. That's what matters."

"No," Thane muttered. "That's not what matters."

The others looked at him.

Thane's eyes stayed fixed on the dark trees beyond the clearing, ruined stone markers, pointing to the endless road ahead.

"We don't know if the Riders were stopped," he said.

"And what about this henge? How do we know it is safe? Nowhere you've taken me has been safe."

Erynn opened her mouth, then closed it again.

Kaelir looked away, mired in his own thoughts.

They all felt it — the dread, gnawing low and constant. He'd spoken the truth. At every corner, the hunters found the hunted. They'd barely rested since the Wastelands. And now they were on the run again—weary, soaked, heading into the darkness.

Thane leaned back against the tree, rain spilling down from the branches above, his heartbeat slowing in his chest.

With eerie purpose—from somewhere deep inside— that whisper came again.

Soft. Coiled. Inevitable.

"They see a savior."

"You see a lie."

"But either way—you walk the same road."

Thane didn't flinch. He didn't know if Echo was friend, foe... or something worse. But it was getting harder to tell the difference. He gritted his teeth, shutting his eyes. Pushing the whispers away. Maybe this was just part of his disease. The part where his mind finally failed him—just like Dr. Hughes had said it would.

Why would his disease be contained to Earth? Different world. Same broken me.

He let out a deep sigh.

The rain deepened, drenching him to the bone. Thunder rolled in the distance, and somewhere beyond the black line of trees, a thin crack of sunrise split the horizon.

East. To the Skyreach Henge.

Whatever waited for them there—salvation, betrayal, or something worse—they would meet it.

There was no turning back.

Not anymore.

23

THE PATH LESS TRAVELED

The rain hadn't stopped for hours.

It came soft and steady, soaking cloaks, pooling in boots, dripping from hooded brows. It blurred the trail behind them and smeared the horizon in gray. No one spoke of Veydris. No one spoke much at all. The forest swallowed sound too easily.

They moved eastward, deeper into the Great Forest—past the known paths and old ruins, into places barely named or long forgotten. There were easier ways to travel than going through the Great Forest—rivers and other waterways—but those were easily watched. The same could not be said for these ancient footpaths.

It was a forest that had been spared from the Rending for reasons unknown. And the deeper they walked, the more faint the paths became.

But the rain finally stopped. Maybe a sign their luck was finally turning.

The trees grew taller, straighter. The undergrowth fell away. There were no dead limbs. No fallen trees. The forest floor was smooth, almost cleared, as though something unseen swept it. It looked like something from a memory Thane couldn't place.

From above, the sunlight—despite the thick canopy—was crisp and golden, like a perpetual afternoon. A cool breeze swept through, just strong enough to dry their cloaks—but it carried no scent, and came from no direction.

"It's beautiful," Erynn whispered, running her hand along the bark of a tall pine. "Like it's been preserved."

To Thane, something felt… off. He couldn't say why. It just did.

Cael motioned them all forward. "Come on. We're making good time. There's a Sanctum at the far edge of the forest—a couple days travel from here."

That's when Thane saw it. And suddenly, the feeling of unease made sense.

A leaf drifted from a branch above and spiraled to the ground. Then it did it again. The same leaf. The same spiral. He blinked.

"Did anyone else see that?" Thane asked.

Lirien glanced back. "What?"

"That leaf. It fell twice. Exactly the same."

Erynn frowned. "I didn't see it."

Kaelir said nothing, but his eyes lingered on Thane for a long moment before turning away.

Thane kept walking, but the feeling stayed with him. He kept glancing up—at the leaves, the canopy, the path ahead—waiting for something to repeat. But nothing did. No loops. No flickers. Maybe it hadn't happened. Though he was almost sure it had.

Later, Thane paused as the trail widened ahead. The forest opened, revealing the long stretch ahead. But it shouldn't have looked like this. Not here.

The trees. The way they framed the landscape ahead.

The giant granite boulders peppered along the trail. He had seen this before. Not in Arbelon. On Earth.

He didn't say it out loud, but the name burned behind his teeth.

Yosemite. Again.

The resemblance was uncanny. As if someone had copied it from memory and pasted it into this world, smoothing over the imperfections. He swallowed hard and turned away.

The deeper they went, the more the forest opened around them. Birds flitted between the branches. Small creatures rustled through the brush. Even the air seemed lighter. As dusk settled in, lightning bugs appeared—first a few, then dozens, weaving through the trees in lazy spirals. It was beautiful. Too beautiful.

Thane said nothing. But the stillness beneath it all gnawed at him, quiet and sharp.

They camped beneath a tree so large its roots had lifted the earth into soft ridges. Its branches curved overhead like sculpted stone, forming a canopy untouched by wind or time. Firelight flickered over the bark, warm and slow, smoke mixing with the boughs above.

The group was quieter than usual. Weary. Worn thin by days of wet travel and tense escapes. For the first time in what felt like forever, the air didn't carry danger. The stillness of the forest seemed to offer something like peace.

Erynn stirred the fire with a stick, eyes distant. "We should talk about what comes next," she said. "About Aelith and her vision."

Cael didn't look up. "Not tonight."

Erynn hesitated, but said nothing more.

A silence followed, until someone asked Kaelir about Bostick—how they'd come to know each other. Kaelir didn't answer. He simply rose and walked to the edge of the firelight.

The tension only deepened.

Lirien shifted closer to the fire. "We can talk later," she said softly, glancing at each of them in turn. "We should rest. While we can."

One by one, the others settled down.

Thane lay back, staring through the branches above. His eyes burned from exhaustion, but sleep didn't come.

The fire cracked. The trees swayed.

Then something flickered.

For a split second, the fire stuttered—not the way flames naturally move, but like a stalling frame in a video. The branches above glitched, doubling, then resetting.

Thane blinked. The world was still again.

He watched for a long time, waiting for it to happen again. But it didn't.

And none of the others noticed.

Morning came soft and golden. The forest greeted them with birdsong and a clean breeze, as if the tense words from the night before had not been uttered.

Thane didn't mention the fire. Or the flickering branches. Or the feeling that maybe—just maybe—the world had blinked.

They wouldn't believe it. They never saw these things like he did.

Around the camp, the mood had shifted. Lirien hummed softly while she rolled up her blanket. Erynn offered Kaelir a cup of tea without a word, and he took it with a smile. Cael stood by the trail's edge, arms crossed, quietly confident.

Their clothes had dried by the fire, and the promise of progress pulled them to their feet.

"We should be to the Sanctum by sundown," Cael said, his voice lighter than it had been in days.

No one argued as they fell in line, pushing eastward again.

Thane followed, but he didn't feel lighter. Not like they did.

Maybe the glitch had been nothing.

Maybe it meant everything.

But if this world was going to use him, he'd find a way to use it first.

GRAYWOOD BULWARKS

THE TREES THINNED as the trail bent eastward, rising gradually toward the foothills of the Skyreach Divide. Dusk had settled over the forest, softening the light and deepening the hush. Up ahead, past the shifting shadows, something glowed faintly like a sliver of moon caught beneath the boughs.

They stepped through a break in the trees and onto the banks of a small lake so still it looked like glass. In the deepening twilight, the surface shimmered—not from any reflection, but from the water itself, its depths casting a soft, bluish-green luminescence. Tiny silver insects skimmed across it, their trails catching the light like thread.

Lirien stepped closer to the lake's edge and looked out across its glowing surface. "I've never seen anything like this."

"Loch Larnnan," Cael murmured. "Old as the Divide itself, they say."

"And by *they*," Erynn said softly, "he means the Alumata. I read once, they came here during the turning seasons—not just to reflect, but to leave something behind.

Some believe the lake's glow isn't natural at all, but memories, seeded by the Alumata themselves over the years—pieces of themselves, stored in the water. But like most things with the Alumata, few know how to read what's left. Not anymore."

"There's more truth to that than you know," Cael said, glancing in her direction.

Thane stared at the lake, wondering if places could really remember. The idea didn't sit well with him. He'd convinced himself that being forgotten was always easier—for everyone. Even here, in Arbelon.

He turned his gaze from the water to the trees beyond.

Around the loch, a forest of squat, massive trees ringed the water. Their trunks were wide as cottages, with bark the color of old stone veined in silver. Low branches reached outward rather than up, creating shaded hollows beneath their wide canopies.

"Graywood bulwarks," Lirien said, almost to herself. "This far east... I thought the only ones left were around Wayfe on the western coast."

Thane tilted his head back to take one in fully. It was like standing beside a cathedral column. The scale was unreal.

Erynn ran her hand along the bark. "These must be centuries old. Maybe older."

Kaelir glanced up at the darkening sky. "Where's this Sanctum, Cael? We should set camp before it gets much darker."

"There," Cael said, pointing toward one of the larger bulwarks near the lake's far edge. Its roots were twisted and moss-covered, but around waist high on the trunk, barely visible beneath a curtain of bark, was a faint rune carved into the wood.

He approached and pressed his hand against the marking, mumbling words that all mixed together.

The bark responded. A seam formed, vertical and smooth, parting just wide enough to reveal a wooden door, inset with silver inlay so fine it looked like thread.

"The Graywood Bulwark Sanctum," Cael announced.

Erynn let out a quiet breath. "I didn't think they built them like this."

"They did," Cael replied. "Not often as grand as this one. But, as you've noted, this is a special place to them."

Inside, the Sanctum was astonishing. The interior had been carved into the hollow trunk with impossible care. At ground level was a round, warmly lit chamber with a low fire already crackling in a stone hearth. A table had been set with fresh bread, soft fruit, and a pitcher of clear water. Cushioned benches curved along the edges of the room, and small lanterns hung from the inner bark, glowing with soft amber light.

Above them, spiraling stairs wound up along the interior of the trunk, leading to several sleeping lofts nestled in alcoves formed by thick limbs. Each loft had a low bed, woven blankets, and a plush down pillows with finely embroidered covers.

Erynn turned slowly in place. "It's... amazing."

"And they still tend this one too?" Lirien asked, turning to Cael.

"They do," he said, nodding, as he propped his quarterstaff against the wall by the door.

Thane didn't share their excitement. On the surface, it looked warm. Inviting. But to him, it was too polished. Too curated. Like his mother's living room back home—cleaned twice over, cushions fluffed, glass wiped down again and again. Not because it mattered, but because it was the only thing she could control. The only way to hide the truth that loomed beneath it all. He hated that kind of lie. He hated this place for making him feel the same.

But the others were already smiling. Laying down packs. Stretching beside the hearth.

Thane moved to a bench near the fire and sat in silence.

Kaelir crouched near the fire, elbows on his knees, eyes lost in the flames.

"Are you ok?" Erynn asked her brother.

"I had thought he'd lost his way," Kaelir said quietly, not looking at her. "When Bostick joined the Riders, I told myself that he'd fooled me, hidden his true intentions. It turns out he had. But a Veilborn… I did not see that. His spent his life in service to Arbelon." He paused, eyes still on the flames. "Who was I to doubt him?"

No one spoke right away. The fire crackled.

Erynn sat down across from him, but didn't press. The silence stretched, heavy but not uncomfortable.

Then someone mentioned Aelith—maybe Lirien, maybe Erynn—and Cael, still standing near the wall, turned toward them.

"I too have misjudged someone today," he said simply, his voice flat. It seemed he had more to say, but instead he looked toward the sleeping lofts. "We've been on the run since Trosten. Let's rest. We can talk more of things at sunrise."

The others nodded, quietly rising, climbing the spiral stairs one by one.

Outside, the glow of Loch Larnnan shimmered against the bark of the Graywoods. Fireflies drifted low to the water, their movements slow and rhythmic, like breath.

Inside, the Sanctum was quiet. Packs were stowed, boots set aside, blankets pulled loose. The last of the firelight played across the woodgrain walls.

Night closed around them, as they drifted off to sleep.

The next morning, the sun rose warm and golden.

Birdsong filled the branches, the kind that somehow sounded closer than it should. The air was sweet, the loch shimmered with its soft bluish light, and a thin mist drifted above the water in perfect curls.

Thane stepped outside and breathed in deeply. It should have felt calming. But there was something too clean about it. The way the breeze came from no particular direction. The way the loch's surface didn't ripple—even when a gust rustled the grasses.

He shouldered his pack and turned as the others emerged from the Sanctum behind him.

"Sleep well?" Lirien asked, stretching.

Cael nodded, adjusting the strap of his pack. "Best night in weeks."

Even Kaelir looked rested. His eyes, always scanning, weren't this morning.

"I feel… reset," Erynn said, staring at the treetops.

Thane didn't answer. His gaze drifted back to the loch. He saw his own reflection staring back at him. When he shifted his stance, the reflection didn't move right away. It lagged, then snapped to catch up.

He blinked.

"Did you see that?" he asked.

"See what?" Lirien asked, distracted as she laced her boots.

Thane hesitated, but the moment had passed. The reflection now mirrored him exactly. The loch's surface now rippling in with the wind.

"Nothing," he muttered.

They gathered their things and began along the trail that wrapped around the eastern edge of the loch, headed toward the foothills of the Skyreach Divide.

Erynn walked next to Cael, adjusting the strap on her pack. "Aelith said the henges were keys. That they could awaken something in the Heart."

Cael didn't slow his pace. "She said a lot of things. Half of them riddles."

"But this one stuck," Erynn insisted. "What if the henges resonate with the Heart somehow? Like tuning forks spread across Arbelon."

Cael gave a faint shake of his head. "Or like seals. Meant to hold something in."

They continued their discussion as the path curved gently beneath the Graywoods. Thane noticed the sunlight dappled the ground in perfect geometric shapes—triangles and diamonds that didn't shift, even as the trees swayed above.

A few minutes later, he saw the same bird pass overhead. Same flight path. Same call. Same flick of its tail feathers.

This isn't right. The patterns. The way the world moves like a looped recording.

He started walking faster. "Guys," he said, louder than he intended, "do any of you see these glitches?"

Kaelir glanced back. "Glitches? What is that?"

"I mean this place. Something's off. The reflections. The light. Even the birds—they're looping."

Erynn frowned. "Looping?"

"Repeating," Thane said, growing frustrated. "That bird," he said pointing behind them, "I've seen it fly by the same way and make the same call. Four times—in the exact same rhythm."

Lirien slowed. "It's a forest. Birds repeat themselves."

"Maybe. But it's just weird," Thane snapped.

Erynn slowed now as well. "You've been edgy since we left the Sanctum."

Thane stopped. "I'm not edgy. I'm just paying attention."

The wind stirred faintly. The treetops moved—but the shadows on the ground didn't in the same way.

"That. You don't see that?"

Cael gave him a level look. "You think shadows misbehaving means something?"

Thane didn't answer right away. His mouth opened, then closed again.

They don't see it. The world's breaking and they don't see it. Or maybe it's not the world. But why am I the only one to see it? Why me? Why here? Why now?

There was only one thing that made sense to Thane.

"You ever stop and wonder," he finally said, quieter now. "Where the hell I came from? Why I'm even here?"

That got their attention. But no one had any answers.

"Just settle down," Kaelir said, his voice tense.

"Settle down?" Thane repeated, not mocking, just tired. He looked at Kaelir. "You spend every waking moment looking over your shoulder... but you've never once questioned me?"

His gaze shifted to Erynn. "And you—you act like I'm some kind of savior. But what if I'm not? What if I'm the thing tearing this place apart? Causing these glitches."

"The Heart acts in mysterious ways," Lirien said, stepping in. "You may be an outlander, but we all live here. We should all want to see it healed."

Thane turned away, running his hands through his hair, then faced them again. "You all talk about healing this place, fixing it like I'm from here. But that's it."

He hesitated, "I'm not from here. Arbelon. I'm from a place called Earth."

"Earth?" Cael repeated, his brow tightening. "That's

not a name from any tongue I know. Is it beyond the Veilspires?"

"Wait," Erynn said, frowning as she flipped open the Codex. "I think I've heard of it—it's across the Thessian Sea, right?" she asked.

"No," Thane said, letting out a long breath. "You're not going to find it in your books. Or your maps. Or anywhere that makes sense."

"What are you talking about?" Erynn asked, more cautious now.

Kaelir stepped forward, his eyes narrowed. "You speak like a man trying to explain a fever dream—or a lie he's told too many times to keep straight."

"Not now, Kaelir," Erynn said, her voice sharp. "Let him answer."

Kaelir held her gaze a moment too long, then turned away, brooding in silence.

"I don't know," Thane snapped. "I feel like I'm losing my mind. None of this should be real. But I can taste the food. Feel the wind on my skin. And this cut—" he traced the line on his cheek "—that hurt."

The group fell quiet, staring at him with unease.

"The longer I'm here, the more real it feels," he continued.

"Why wouldn't it feel real?" Lirien asked softly.

Thane turned to her, expression almost pleading. "Because it's not *supposed* to be. You don't understand— none of you do. You're all just… code. This place—" he gestured around them "—all of it, it's a game. It's made up. And was just supposed to be a place for me to get away."

They stared at him as the silence stretched on.

Erynn was the first to speak. "I don't know what you're talking about. But we *are* real, and we *are* where we think

we are, Thane. We're in Arbelon—together. You're just…
tired."

"This isn't just me being tired," Thane said, turning to
them. "It's more than that."

Cael shifted uncomfortably. "What do you mean more?
Like what?"

"Things," Thane said with a sigh. "I keep seeing things
I can't explain. Things none of you see. I hear things you
can't hear. Like the world's trying to hold itself together—
but failing." He paused, letting the silence stretch. "Maybe
it's not the world that's broken. Maybe it's me."

He looked around, searching for something—anything
—to ground him. But there was nothing.

"So you're saying this is all… fake?" Cael asked, his
tone laced with disbelief.

"I don't know anymore," Thane answered. "Maybe it's
real. Maybe it's not."

Lirien shook her head slowly. "I don't understand. Why
would you keep this from us?"

"What? That I'm from another world? Or that I'm
losing my mind?" Thane asked, his voice firmer now.
"Maybe because you'd think I'm crazy. Like you do now."

Erynn looked stunned.

Lirien's brow furrowed, but she said nothing.

"No one thinks you're crazy," Cael answered slowly.
"We're just trying to understand."

"Understand what?" Thane shot back. "That I thought
this world was a game, and I didn't care if I broke it—or
you. But now I don't know what's real anymore. And if
you can't see these things I do, then maybe it's just me.
Maybe I'm the one breaking. Maybe I'm breaking your
world too."

The others fell silent again, eyes fixed on him.

"And if I'm the reason this place is falling apart…"

He shook his head. "Then maybe I shouldn't be here at all."

There was another long silence before Cael finally spoke up.

"The Heart was dying long before you arrived on our shores," Cael said in a controlled voice, stepping closer to Thane and placing a hand on his shoulder. "You had nothing to do with that."

Thane stepped away, his jaw clenched.

He didn't look at the others when he spoke.

"But I'm dying too."

That froze them.

"Back where I'm from—I'm sick. I've got this disease, and it's killing me, piece by piece." His voice stayed low, almost like he didn't want them to hear. "And maybe it's killing this place too. I'm starting to think that I might've brought it with me."

He finally looked up. No one spoke.

"This world shouldn't feel this real," he said, eyes sharp, voice shaking. "It shouldn't matter this much. But it does. You do. And if it's breaking… maybe that's because of me."

Lirien stared at him. "You're really dying?"

He gave a single, bitter nod.

"I know it sounds insane. Because it is," he went on, louder now. "None of this makes sense. But it's always me in the middle of it. Wild magic. Glitches. Things falling apart. Maybe I'm the fracture point."

Cael studied him, his eyes intent. "You think the Heart is dying because *you* are? That a disease from another world is unraveling Arbelon?"

Thane laughed without humor. "Sounds nuts, right? All I know is we're both broken. And for some reason, it feels like if I don't fix this place... we're both probably done for."

Kaelir stepped next to his sister, eyes leveled on Thane. "If you're broken, how do we trust you to fix anything?"

"You can't," Thane answered. "But I'm going to try."

Lirien stepped between them, brushing up against Thane, and turned to the others.

"Enough," she said, quietly, but her voice left no room for argument. "We *need* him. Whatever this is—whatever's happening—we figure it out together. There has to be a reason he was brought to us."

Erynn nodded, reluctantly. Cael gave a slow nod, though his expression stayed unreadable. But Kaelir's silence felt heavier now, like he was weighing every word Thane had spoken against everything he thought he knew.

Thane swallowed hard, but said nothing.

The wind stirred again. But the shadows didn't move. Neither did the sun. And somewhere behind them, the loch pulsed—soft, steady, watching.

WHEN THE MASK SLIPS

THEY WALKED for a while in silence.

No one spoke, not even Erynn, and that was saying something. The trail narrowed as it wound along a ridge that overlooked the loch below—still glowing, still glass-smooth.

Most of the time, the world looked as it should. But now and then, the shadows flickered wrong, or the light held too long in the trees. The breeze stirred the branches, and sometimes the leaves didn't move—or moved twice, like a skipped frame in a film.

Nothing stayed broken. Everything corrected itself. But it was enough to keep Thane's jaw tight and his eyes forward.

Lirien slowed her pace to fall in beside him. They walked together for several minutes, saying nothing. She didn't push, didn't press. Just matched his stride, quiet and steady, until finally.

"You meant all of that," she said.

Thane didn't look at her. "Yeah."

They kept walking.

"You should have said something sooner," she added, gently. "You've been carrying it alone the whole time."

Thane gave a hollow laugh. "What was I supposed to say? 'Hi, I'm dying, and I might be breaking your world by accident'?"

"No," she said. "Just the part where you're scared."

That stopped him.

He turned to her, eyes sharp. "I'm not scared."

Her brow lifted, but she said nothing.

"I'm not," he repeated.

Lirien stepped in front of him, stopping him with a hand lightly pressed to his chest. "Then why does your voice shake when you say you don't belong here?"

Thane didn't answer.

"I don't know what Earth is," she said softly. "But I know what it looks like when someone is trying to push the world away before it can hurt them. You think that if this place isn't real, it won't matter when you lose it."

He looked away. "Maybe it's not."

"I think it is."

He scoffed. "You just said you don't know what Earth is. You've never even—"

"No, I don't," she said. "But I know you."

That brought his gaze back.

She stepped a little closer. "And I know the way you talk about Arbelon—like it's already gone. Like it can't be yours. But maybe that's not the world's fault. Maybe that's you deciding not to let it be."

Thane opened his mouth, but nothing came out.

Lirien didn't wait. She leaned forward and pressed her lips to his.

It wasn't urgent. It wasn't a promise. It was quiet and certain, like she already knew what she felt—even if he didn't.

He didn't understand it. Didn't know if he deserved it. But he didn't pull away.

For the first time in days, he didn't feel like an intruder in someone else's story. For a moment, the weight eased. The noise quieted. It was just her. Just now. And it felt like the world had drawn a breath and was holding it.

Something in him shifted.

Maybe he was meant to be here. Maybe he was meant to fix this place.

But what if he was too late? What if the damage was already done—and he was the one who broke it?

The thought came unbidden, sharp as a blade. He didn't want to face it. Couldn't. Not yet. Not while her hand was still warm against his chest.

But even as the thought formed, something tugged at the edges.

The loch behind them pulsed brighter. A soft sound—almost a chime, almost a crack—rippled through the trees.

She kissed him like he mattered.

And that was the first thing that felt truly wrong.

Why would she kiss me? Now?

His eyes flew open.

The color drained from the trees—washed out like watercolor left too long in the sun. The path beneath their feet jittered, then dropped slightly with a soft jolt, like it had been rendered again a few inches lower.

Lirien pulled back, eyes wide, breath unsteady.

"Did you feel that?" he asked, his voice barely above a whisper.

She nodded slowly. But then her face glitched before snapping back.

Behind them, the loch pulsed again. And the shadows began to move—rewinding, snapping forward, then stilling again—like someone repeatedly hitting rewind and then play.

Thane gasped.

Cold air punched into his lungs.

His eyes snapped open, his heart hammering.

The loch was gone.

The trail, the trees—gone.

He was at the Sanctum's dining table—but it wasn't the same place they'd settled into the night before. This one was dark and wet with rot. Mold crept up the walls like veins. Every surface seemed to reek of decay.

The air was too still—dank and stale. Like the room had been violated.

Across the table, Lirien, Erynn, Cael, and Kaelir were slumped in their chairs—breathing, but unmoving. Like puppets abandoned between acts.

The hearth was long cold. Shadows clung to the ceiling like oil. The door to the Sanctum had been left open. Stars filled the night sky, but the light from the loch was sickly, greenish, and pulsed in rhythm with something deeper— like a heartbeat heard through water, slow and wrong.

He pushed his chair back from the table. The floor beneath him groaned—not polished graywood, but something warped and splintered. He stood slowly, his limbs stiff and unsure.

"Lirien?" he called, his voice ragged.

No answer.

He touched her shoulder. Still warm. Still breathing. But unmoving.

What the hell is going on?

It hadn't been morning. It had never been morning.

It had all been a lie.

Something shifted in the far corner. The shadows

folded and unfolded like murky water, his mind forming patterns where there were none.

He stepped to the side, trying to grasp what he was seeing before glancing again at the others—in hopes they might be waking.

But they weren't.

A shape stirred in the shadows again, but this time it peeled away from the wall. Not entirely visible. Just the absence of light where light should be. It was vaguely humanoid—taller than a man, hunched, its form flickering at the edges like corrupted data.

Thane's pulse kicked up. The shape wasn't just dark—it was wrong. Like the world couldn't quite hold it.

Its face—or the suggestion of one—tilted toward him. And then it spoke.

"You've seen the fractures," it said. The voice came not from its mouth—if it had one—but from everywhere. From the walls. From the table. From the air itself.

Thane backed up slowly, his mind trying to resolve what he was seeing.

"Who are you?"

It drifted closer, peeling from the wall like smoke. It didn't walk—it unfolded, hovered, its form barely contained by the space around it. Tendrils of thick darkness reached out, ebbing and flowing.

A faint hum pressed behind Thane's eyes—like an idling car.

"They can't see it," it said. "Not like you."

Thane stepped protectively in front of the others. "What did you do to them?"

"They're still dreaming," it said.

"Just deeper."

It moved closer, gliding past the dying embers of the fire. The hearthstone cracked beneath its weight—though it floated, weightless. Its shape left ripples in the air, leaving a path of black mold streaking the wood in its wake. Tendrils flicked closer to Thane and the others, tasting the air like static, searching for a signal.

Thane's pulse kicked up. His instincts screamed for distance, for escape—but there was nowhere to run.

You have power, he told himself. *You've used it before. In Salile. You just need to use it again.*

But even as he reached for it, doubt flooded him. Memories of Veydris flooding in.

What if it doesn't come? Or what if it does—and I still fail them?

He took a breath and pushed the fear down. Closed his eyes. Reached deeper.

Nothing.

Then—like heat rising through cracked glass—he felt it.

First in his wrist. The faint hum of his watch.

Then in his chest. A pressure. Building. Demanding.

A sharp pulse cut across his ribs, and his skin lit with faint fractures of light, like something beneath it wanted out.

The shadow pulsed, retracting slightly.

"Careful," it said, its voice oozing like oil forced through stone. "You'll burn a hole where there isn't one yet."

Thane opened his eyes.

The magic answered this time. Volatile and wild. But his.

He gripped it tighter, feeling it swirl through him—hot with rage, sharp with purpose. The burn of helplessness reshaped into something he could wield.

"I'm done with your games," Thane said through gritted teeth. "Let them go."

A tendril coiled lazily across the table. "I only want to help you," the shadow said. "To help *them*."

Thane's laugh cracked with bitterness. "Right. That's what monsters always say."

His power snapped loose.

With a surge of light, magic flared from his hands—a torrent of radiant force lashing across the room toward the creature.

It hit the shadow—

And stopped.

The air *froze*.

Magic suspended mid-strike, frozen in a prism of stillness. Sound died. The light didn't move. Even Thane's heartbeat felt staggered, caught between beats.

Then—the shadow expanded. Dark matter billowed outward like a cloak unfurling. It absorbed Thane's magic without effort, folding it inward like a collapsing star.

He tried again, yelling this time—forcing the magic forward. But it was like screaming into a void. The darkness held everything still. Like someone had hit the pause button.

And then—a tendril lashed forward, coiling tight around Lirien's throat. She gasped for air, still locked in her dream state. Her head jerked back, before her body slumped on the table.

Thane froze. "No—"

"She dies next," the shadow said, calm as winter.

"Why drag her to an early grave with you?"

The words hit like a blade.

How could it know that? The thought nearly shattered his focus, but the shadow continued.

"You brought your sickness here," it whispered. "You fractured the Heart… or what of it still remains."

It circled him now, its form flickering and stretching in impossible ways.

"But," the voice continued, "you can still be of use."

"To *who*?" Thane snarled. "You?"

"To the world you were born to save."

He turned, eyes blazing. "Arbelon? You think I can fix this place?"

"I *know* you can."

"Then why haven't I?"

"Because you haven't chosen to."

Its presence was suddenly inches from him. The air turned ice-cold.

"I offer you a way forward. A way to save your friends. A way to save yourself."

A pause. The tendril around Lirien twitched.

"But if you refuse," it said, "they all stay here. Trapped. Asleep. Until the rot claims them."

It leaned in.

"And she'll be the first to slip."

Lirien whimpered. The tendril tightened.

"Stop," Thane said, reaching out toward her. "Please."

"What is your life, when compared to so many?" the shadow said. "Save them… save *her*."

Thane stood there, trembling with rage, shame, and something else.

"What do I have to do?"

"Accept."

"Accept what?"

The voice was quiet now. Inevitable.

"Stabilize the Heart. Then leave this world. Forever. Return to your land—your Earth. Never come back."

First his disease, and now Earth. It knew.

It's been listening.

Thane looked at Lirien. Her breath was shallow. Her skin pale.

This thing—whatever it was—it was lying. Of course it was lying.

But what if it wasn't?

He was dying anyway.

"Fine," Thane said, letting the magic fall away from his hands.

"I accept."

The shadow drew closer, its shape resolving back into a vague humanoid. The tendril around Lirien's throat loosened slightly but remained coiled like a waiting threat.

"Say it," the voice whispered. "Speak the terms."

Thane's fists clenched, the magic still burning just beneath his skin—hot, urgent, useless. It coiled inside him like a blade with nowhere to land. Whatever this place was, his power didn't matter here.

Maybe nothing did.

He exhaled, jaw tight, and fully gave in.

"I'll stabilize the Heart," he said through gritted teeth. "I'll fix it."

A ripple passed through the shadow, dark and appeased.

"And when it's done," Thane continued, "I'll leave Arbelon. I won't come back."

"You swear it," the voice intoned, a chill settling through the air like frost. "On the spark that binds you. On the wild thread that sings in your blood."

"I swear," Thane said, barely above a whisper.

Another tendril slipped from the shadow, moving with eerie grace. It hovered in front of Thane for a moment— then touched his forehead.

Thane flinched. The contact was brief—but searing. A flash of cold sank into his skull, not like pain, but like something permanent had been etched there. A mark he couldn't see, but would never forget.

The other tendril slid from Lirien's throat.

The shadow began to dissolve, folds of blackness curling in on themselves like smoke drawn back into a bottle.

"You've chosen," the voice echoed from everywhere.

And then it was gone.

The darkness drained from the corners. The rot peeled away from the walls like old paint in reverse. Light bled back into the Sanctum—soft, golden, and strangely warm. The loch's glow brightened again, no longer green but the calm bluish tone they'd seen before.

Thane staggered forward, breathing hard, one hand raised to his forehead where the cold still lingered.

The Sanctum looked like it had when they arrived.

The rot was gone. The walls were smooth. The fire crackled softly, and the scent of herbs hung in the air.

How was that possible? How was any of this possible?

His breath caught as he scanned the room. The same carved chairs. The same deep-green cushions. The table was even set with a fresh bowl of fruit and loaves of bread.

Like nothing had happened.

He pressed his palm to the table, needing to feel something solid.

Was this another layer of dreams? Or had he imagined it all?

But the table didn't ground him. His thoughts blurred, sliding out of reach.

Dr. Hughes had warned something like this might happen.

Then a dull pulse throbbed where the shadow had touched him, colder than the air, colder than the truth. And reality set in.

Around him, the others began to stir.

Erynn groaned, rubbing her temple. "Did I fall asleep at the table?"

Kaelir coughed, sitting up stiffly. "I… don't even remember sitting down."

But Cael was already alert. He stood quickly, eyes scanning the room with narrowed focus. "Something's wrong," he said, mostly to himself.

He crossed to the doorway, then back to the table, frowning deeper, still mumbling to himself. "We were here. Then we were in the forest. But now we're back… this isn't how it ended."

Lirien sat up last. Her gaze flicked around the room, then found Thane. She rose slowly. "Are you all right?"

Thane nodded, too quickly. "Fine."

She stepped closer, noticing the way he braced himself on the table. "You're pale. Are you sure?"

He drew in a slow breath, steadied his voice.

"I will be," he said, softer this time. "Just… something about this place doesn't feel right. Especially now."

There was a pause. No one moved. But all eyes were on Thane.

Then Kaelir asked, "Did anyone else… dream? About traveling to the henge?"

Erynn looked up. "We were still in the forest. Just beyond the loch. But… we never actually left this place, did we?"

"It seems not," Cael said grimly. He placed a hand on the back of his chair, eyes distant. "I've heard of shared dreams before. Rare. Usually guided. But this?" His voice dropped lower. "This was layered. Directed. There was something different about it."

"So we shared the same dream," Erynn said, still rubbing her head. "But I don't understand. Was it caused by the Sanctum? The Alumata?" she asked, turning her eyes to Cael.

"Not as best as I can tell," he answered softly. "I've never heard of anyone experiencing such a shared dream state outside of Veydris. Perhaps the Heart has broken down even more than we've suspected."

As the others were talking of the dream, Lirien's eyes met Thane's again. She opened her mouth, then stopped. Her cheeks flushed.

The kiss.

Thane flushed too, then looked away. It had felt real—too real. But it was something that could never be.

"Thane?"

Erynn's voice cut through the fog in his mind.

He turned, caught off guard.

"That stuff you said in the dream," she continued, her voice softer now. "About Earth. About dying. Was that real?"

Thane didn't meet her eyes. He just gave a bitter nod.

Kaelir folded his arms. "So what happens now?"

Thane exhaled, starting toward the doorway. "We keep moving. Skyreach Henge is waiting."

Cael stepped in. "Wait." His voice was even, but edged with something harder. "What happened after, Thane? You woke before the rest of us."

Thane looked at him. Then at Lirien. Then back to the others.

He hesitated—just long enough to register.

"Nothing worth talking about," he said, casually. "I couldn't figure out how to wake you up. But then you did."

Cael held his gaze a moment longer, frowning slightly. But he didn't press.

They gathered their things quietly. No jokes. No complaints. The loch was still. The Graywoods peaceful.

Thane rolled his shoulders, adjusting his pack. He still felt the cold pulsing faintly in his head. Still felt the shape of the promise he'd made—one he hadn't told them about. Not yet.

As they stepped back onto the trail, no one mentioned the dream again.

But something had changed.

He'd shared too much, and it felt like they were pulling away.

It always ended like this. Even back home.

Except Lirien, who fell in step with him at the back of the group. They walked together for several minutes, saying nothing. She didn't push, didn't press. Just matched his stride—quiet, steady—until finally, she spoke.

"I'm glad I did it," she said. "Even if it was a dream."

Thane didn't look at her. "Yeah, me too."

They kept walking.

But the weight lingered—the dream, the shadow, the promise.

He remembered all of it. Every second.

He'd saved them. Saved her.

Now he had a promise to keep.

SKYREACH HENGE

THE FOREST GAVE way to the foothills by midmorning. The land rose quickly after that—sharp and uneven, as if the world itself had buckled upward to keep something in. The trail narrowed, the trees fell behind, and the mountains of the Skyreach Divide loomed ahead like they'd been waiting.

The day started bright, the sun high and warm above the valley. But as they pressed deeper into the foothills, the light dulled. A low ceiling of clouds crept in from the east, and the air took on a damp edge. The closer they drew to the mountains, the more the weather soured—the wind turning colder, the sky turning steel.

The warmth of the lowlands had long since faded, replaced by a biting chill that crept through the seams of their cloaks. Thane adjusted the strap across his shoulder, fingers stiff with cold.

Of course it was cold. Not just winter-cold—deep, marrow-fucking cold. The kind that crept into your teeth and didn't let go.

He should've guessed the game—or the world, or

whatever the hell this was—would drag him up into the one place he couldn't stand. Like it knew. Like the Heart had gone rooting around in his head, found the exact thing he hated most, and dropped him right in the middle of it just to watch him squirm.

Cold. Numb. Angry.

That's where it wanted him.

That's where he broke easiest.

His breath came in short bursts, fogging the air as the path beneath them continued to narrow, climbing in broken switchbacks.

Behind them, the land unfurled in layers of soft gold and deep green—the rolling foothills fading into the vast canopy of the Great Forest, which swallowed the western horizon like a continent unto itself.

Ahead of them, the Skyreach Divide rose like a god's wall, sheer and unrelenting. Jagged peaks stabbed into low-hanging clouds, their crests vanishing into storm-colored mist. These mountains didn't border Arbelon—they literally split it in half.

Thane had heard it whispered back in Veydris—*nothing crosses the Skyreaches unchanged.* Looking at them now, he believed it.

He swallowed hard, the wind sharpening with each step. Whatever waited up there wasn't offering shade or respite. It was teeth and stone and wind that bit hard—crisp and cruel. A place built to punish.

They moved onward without words. Everyone wrapped tightly in their cloaks.

The trail grew rocky, hemmed in by steep ridges and frost-laced trees that shouldn't have been frosted—not this early, not here. Roots twisted like skeletal hands from the rock, and ice clung stubbornly to the northern slopes. At their backs, the wind howled down the gorge in a voice that seemed to carry warnings they couldn't quite understand.

A jagged outcropping jutted from the rising slope—not the summit, but a windswept promontory that stood alone, like a watchtower built by the land itself. The mountains climbed higher behind it, vast and indifferent, but this place commanded everything below it. A natural fortress—exposed, stark, and impossible to ignore.

The final climb wound around its base, then curled up through broken rock and scraggly brush until the crest revealed itself.

That's when they saw it.

The henge rose from the summit like the ribs of a long-dead giant, half-swallowed by the mist. Towering stones, jagged and weathered, formed a wide circle etched with worn, ancient runes—barely visible in the gloom. The central stone, taller than the rest, stood slightly off-center, its face lined with deep ridges that seemed to drink in the cold light around it. It loomed like a blade left half-drawn, waiting for a colossal hand to lift it.

Cael stopped at the edge of the ring, his breath catching as he scanned the stones.

"This is it," he said quietly—less a statement, more a resignation.

One hand slid down the haft of his quarterstaff, fingers tightening—not in preparation, but in memory.

He glanced around at the monolithic stones, but didn't step any closer.

The others slowed behind Cael, none of them crossing the threshold. He hadn't, and that seemed reason enough.

They drifted along the outer edge, each in their own silence.

Kaelir came to a stop just behind Cael.

Lirien held her arms tight across her chest, not from

the cold this time, but something else—like stepping too close might invite something they couldn't undo.

Erynn stood near one of the outer stones, her gloved fingers brushing a worn glyph with almost ritual care. Her mouth moved slightly—maybe reciting something. Maybe praying.

Thane stopped outside the ring, just shy of the nearest stone.

He didn't move. Didn't speak. The henge pulsed in time with something low in his chest—something that wasn't quite his heartbeat. He felt it humming beneath the soles of his boots, crawling up through his bones like a thread being pulled taut.

His stomach turned. It wasn't fear. It wasn't wonder.

It was familiarity.

He squinted up at the central stone. The runes were dull in the stone—worn, empty, like carvings that hadn't breathed in centuries. One of them—a jagged edge carved deep near the base—reminded him of the glitch he'd seen in the pool's edge back in the Sanctuary in Asmenson. A pattern breaking mid-flow, fracturing into angular dissonance before snapping back again.

Except here, it didn't snap back. It stuttered—like a loop running too slow, out of sync. Then, piece by piece, it reassembled itself… but wrong.

The wind seemed to hesitate too, like it had been caught in the same pattern. Then it shifted—sharp, cold, unnatural.

Something invisible brushed the back of his neck, and the hairs there stood on end. He turned sharply, scanning the broken ridge lines, but saw only stone and mist. Still, the feeling lingered—like eyes on the back of his skull, just beyond reach.

Kaelir stepped forward first, studying the formation

with narrowed eyes. "So… what now? Is it supposed to do something?"

Erynn's voice was quiet. "The Codex mentioned focal points, echoes of the Heart—but nothing like this. Nothing this clear."

She hesitated. "Aelith was the one who pointed us here. Not the text."

Lirien glanced between them. "There are no other scrolls? No fragments? Anything left behind that might tell us something?"

Erynn shook her head. "This is where the record ends. We're past the last page."

Cael paced a slow line along the outside of the ring, eyes never leaving the center. "Then we're standing in front of something none of us understand."

He paced slowly, rubbing his chin. Then he stopped, turning back to face them, something hard in his eyes. "But, maybe that's the point."

Erynn frowned. "What's the point?"

Cael pointed to the henge, his voice low but certain. "I'm saying this isn't a door. It's a lock. And it's waiting for a key."

Several eyes drifted to Thane.

Of course they thought it was him. Of course the broken world would need the broken kid to unlock it. Made perfect sense.

But it wasn't just them.

The pull had grown stronger—subtle at first, but now… now it coiled tight around his spine, humming through his chest like a tuning fork. It wasn't warm or cold. It was *right*. Intoxicating. Like his body recognized the magic before his mind caught up.

And he wanted it.

For the first time, he didn't brace against it. Didn't resist. He *leaned in*. Let it come. Let it fill him.

It felt like power. Like purpose. Like he'd finally stopped pretending it wasn't his.

The others didn't notice. They were still talking. Still speculating. Like he wasn't standing there. But he didn't speak. Just watched them—circling their prophecies and theories like they meant something.

He exhaled sharply, more of a scoff. "Stop wasting time."

That cut through. Heads turned.

Erynn opened her mouth, but nothing came out.

"Cael's right," Thane muttered. "This place knows me."

He took a step forward, boots crunching gravel.

"Let's get on with it."

The moment he crossed into the circle, the runes didn't just glow—they flared, light blooming along the carved lines in a rush, like they'd been starved for centuries and finally found what they needed.

Not bright. Not warm. But alive. Like something ancient had just opened one eye and fixed it on him.

A jagged glyph tore across the central stone in blinding light—the Broken Circle, drawn in the bones of the world like it had always been waiting—pulsing with the same rhythm as the watch.

The symbol he'd seen a hundred times before, now burned itself into the stone like it belonged there. Like he belonged there.

Thane clenched his fists and drew the magic to him— not gently. Not carefully. Like he *owned* it.

The pull was strong now. He didn't question it—just followed the thread and let it unravel through his hands. He was done pretending he didn't want something back.

With a flick of his hands, he hurled the magic into the central stone.

It responded instantly. Lightning cracked out in every direction, arcing from stone to stone.

The ring of stones came alive in his wake—bright and chaotic.

And the henge didn't settle. It pulsed harder—hungry, alive, ravenous.

The runes on the central stone spun faster, syncing to his magic like a heartbeat finding its rhythm. At the center, the Broken Circle glyph bloomed, not like an explosion, but a sunrise—brilliant, expanding, alive. As if the henge had just found what it had been waiting for all along.

And it wanted more.

The Heart's whisper was gone.

Now it roared.

It tore through Thane like a current with no ground, demanding more.

More power. More magic. More of him.

He pulled on the Wild Magic again, hard—greedy now, hungry for the rush. The surge came like fire in his veins, lighting up everything inside him, and he welcomed it. He gave more of himself than before. More than he knew he could.

The watch answered the henge—not just syncing, but amplifying. Its ticking accelerated, pulsing in perfect time with it, like a tuning fork struck too hard. With each beat, the glyph on the stone flared brighter—echoing the power pouring through him. Seeking more.

Then—something cracked open inside him, and the memories poured in.

They struck fast. Sharp. Like someone had shoved memories into him sideways.

His mother's face—tear-streaked, desperate—sitting at his bedside, mouth open in a soundless cry.

Lirien—grief and rage warring in her eyes—as the ruins of Asmenson smoldered behind her.

The images collided. Twisting and overlapping—one bleeding into the next.

A hospital bed. Inside the walls of Salile. Flames licking the edges of white sheets. Hands reached for him from the smoke, from the bed, from the ruins—burned, bloodied, *familiar.*

Lirien's voice calling from somewhere far away—from a hallway that didn't exist.

The words didn't echo—they tangled and layered, like too many memories trying to speak at once.

He tried to separate the images. To keep everything as it was. But everything became the other, and the other became everything.

His mother's eyes became Lirien's, and Lirien's became hers—wide, wounded, and full of blame.

"You did this," they said in unison, voices glitching like a corrupted file.

The world flickered—not with light, but with memory. Like a dream too broken to finish loading.

He saw the moment he turned away. From both of them.

A scream—his or theirs—split the space behind his eyes.

Everything spun.

He staggered, throat dry, the weight of what he'd done pressed against his chest like iron.

The visions kept coming.

The Heart kept pulling.

Somehow, he still held the magic. It screamed through him, begging to break loose. But he clung to it—fighting, straining, refusing to let go.

And he focused.

Then—clarity.

A sudden shift. A sense of pressure easing. The symbols aligned, the pull smoothing into a rhythm.

He felt it.

He really *felt* it.

The rhythm. The power—his, for once.

"I've got it!" he gasped, half-laughing. "Something's happening—I can feel it."

The runes pulsed once—bright, blinding.

Then the world surged again.

Too much.

The wave hit him like a hammer. He staggered, choking on air that felt like water. His hands shook, straining to direct the flow—but it tore loose, wild and thrashing.

His watch blazed like a second sun, amplifying his energy to something feral, raw.

The central stone hummed, swallowing everything he threw at it.

The air warped—bending inward, flexing like an invisible skin stretching too far. The world around him jittered, slipping out of sync.

For a second, the ground dropped out, revealing blackness beneath—as if the world's geometry had failed to load.

A few of the stones in the ring flickered, duplicated themselves, then vanished—like a corrupted game asset phasing in and out.

He saw the henge. Then nothing. Then the henge again—fractured, skewed and broken.

He felt his body stretched. Torn. And snapped back.

Then it happened again.

And again. And again.

Tremors shook the stones, some grinding in protest, others beginning to lean.

Tendrils of energy lashed from the ring, flailing like limbs, carving jagged lines through air and earth.

A voice screamed from behind him.

"Thane!" Erynn's voice, high and panicked. "You have to stop! This is not the way!"

He couldn't answer.

He could barely stand.

Another arc of power shot past him, shattering a smaller stone in a burst of light and dust.

"No!" Cael shouted, stepping forward, arm raised to shield his face. "Don't stop now!"

He took another step—and was hit.

An arc caught him across the chest and hurled him back. He slammed against one of the standing stones and crumpled to the ground, stunned.

The others shouted. Lirien moved to run to him, but stopped, shielding her eyes from the chaos erupting from the circle.

Cael groaned, lifting his head—barely. His eyes locked on Thane, and he called out, voice hoarse, "You're almost there, Thane—focus!"

But their voices meant nothing now. Only the pull remained.

The roar was back—the Heart, the watch, the henge— pulsing together like a second heartbeat. Devouring. Demanding. Taking everything he had.

He tried again to rein it in. Tried to ground it. Channel it.

But it kept taking.

And that's when he knew—he couldn't stop it.

The realization hit like a blade.

He wasn't controlling the magic. It was controlling

him. The Heart's pull, the watch's amplification—it was too much. And it was tearing the henge apart.

And maybe him too.

The roar crested.

The magic flared again—hotter, wilder—erupting from him like a lightning strike in every direction. Tendrils of raw energy lashed outward, arcing between the stones, crackling through the air with a sound like tearing steel.

Thane's body jolted, locked in place by the force of it. His arms outstretched, head thrown back, mouth open in a voiceless scream. The energy held him like wires on a broken marionette—spasming, seizing, burning from the inside out.

Blood trickled from his nose.

His vision fractured.

Light. Color. Then nothing.

Then everything again.

The runes on the central stone flared—red now, angry and alive. A low, grinding vibration surged from the earth beneath them, deep enough to rattle teeth, a growl felt in the bones.

The Heart wasn't just reacting.

It was defending itself.

The ground beneath the circle trembled as the central stone shifted—tilting slightly off axis. The runes along its face twisted into chaotic, fractured patterns. The Broken Circle glyph blazed like a wound, warping with each pulse.

The smaller stones near the edge of the ring were the first to crack—splitting down their centers with sickening snaps. They toppled inward, crumbling into heaps of rubble.

The larger stones groaned, leaning like wounded giants. One buckled completely, slamming to the ground with a thunderous crash that sent a cloud of dust rolling across the plateau.

The sky darkened—not with storm, but with smoke and magic and something older.

Lirien screamed. Erynn shouted something no one could hear.

The watch on Thane's wrist pulsed wildly—once, twice —then flared. Not bright, but deep, like something internal had activated. Its ticking accelerated, not out of control, but purposeful—like it recognized what was happening.

Its face flickered. Then steadied. Still ticking.

And somewhere, deep in the rush of it all, Thane felt it —an understanding. But he didn't know whose.

And then—

Silence.

The arcs vanished.

The energy dropped.

And Thane crumpled like a cut string.

He hit the ground hard, arms limp, eyes unfocused. His chest moved—barely. His fingers twitched. Sparks crackled along his skin, fading.

The spell was broken.

The stones lay shattered or leaning, coated in ash and dust.

No one moved at first.

Then Erynn dropped to her knees beside Thane, trembling. Her eyes wide with shock, voice cracked and small. "This wasn't supposed to happen," she whispered.

She turned sharply to Cael, her face hardening through the dust.

"You never should've pushed him," she snapped. "You already failed once with the Heart—and you've done it again."

Her voice cracked. "The voice inside me was trying to

tell me. Thane was meant to heal it… not like this. Not through force. But no—he chose to listen to you. Someone who already betrayed the Heart once."

Kaelir stepped between them—not blocking, but present. One hand half-raised, as if to settle the words before they escalated.

His voice was low. "Erynn, enough."

It wasn't a rebuke. Just a thread of reason, tugged into the space before things could break further.

Cael stared at Erynn, his jaw wrenched tight—eyes hard, bitter, unmoved.

Then he turned away without a word, the tension in his shoulders palpable.

Lirien stood frozen a few steps away, arms crossed tightly against her chest. Her gaze hovered just above Thane—unable, or unwilling, to look down.

And in that silence, something between them changed.

BEHIND THE RUSTED GATE

THE ONLY SOUND in the room was the quiet whir of cooling fans—serene, steady, like the world had already moved on.

Thane sat slouched in his gaming chair, head tilted unnaturally to the side, arms slack, one hand draped over the edge. The VR headset still clung to his face. On the desk beside him, his gaming rig, its surface littered with tangled cords—snaking outward like veins.

His chest didn't rise. Didn't fall.

His mother stood frozen at his side, fingers trembling against her mouth. She hadn't moved in minutes—not since he went still.

"Thane?" she whispered again. Her voice cracked. "Thane, please."

The room was warm—too warm. Curtains drawn, stale air pressed close. The scent was faint but heavy—unwashed clothes, old sweat, the breath of machines. An energy drink had tipped on its side hours ago, a half-dried ring staining the desk beside the keyboard.

Doctor Hughes knelt by the chair, pale and focused, his

fingers pressed to Thane's neck. "Still no breath," he muttered. "Pulse is faint. Rhythmic, but barely."

She didn't hear him. Or maybe she did, but it didn't register. She just stared at her son—her boy—his body limp, unresponsive, slumped amid the tangle of wires and machines he spent so much time with.

The headset made a crisp static pop.

She jumped, cursing softly—startled by the noise, her patience with the headset long gone.

Dr. Hughes was already moving. "We need to get it off."

He unlatched the headset straps gently, slowly peeling it away from Thane's face. Underneath, his skin was damp. Pale. His lips parted slightly. Eyes rolled back.

She dropped to her knees beside him. "No. No, Thane —baby, please. Please come back. You promised me—"

"I need my bag," Hughes said sharply, voice clipped. "It's by the door."

She moved on instinct, stumbling toward the hall.

The sirens grew louder outside, now just around the corner.

Dr. Hughes tapped Thane's cheek, then pressed fingers to his jaw, adjusting his position, working methodically. "Come on, kid," he muttered under his breath. "Not tonight. Not in your own bedroom."

Footsteps thundered on the porch. The front door swung open.

"Back here!" Jane called out. "At the end of the hallway!"

Two paramedics came in fast. One with a bag, the other with a portable vitals kit. Dr. Hughes gestured them in without looking up. "Confirmed seizure," he said, keeping his voice level. "No trauma. Shallow pulse. Unconscious for—" he checked his watch "—six minutes."

The woman from the ambulance dropped beside Thane with practiced efficiency, already attaching the leads to him. "Vitals are light," she said, eyeing the monitor. "Let's get him fully checked—see what's going on."

His mother was already shaking her head. "But he stopped breathing. He stopped—he just stopped." Her voice cracked on the last word.

"He's stable now," the paramedic said gently. "Let's just give him a moment."

Dr. Hughes exhaled slowly and wiped his forehead with the back of his hand. "We've bought him some time," he said, placing a hand gently on Jane's shoulder, "but that's all."

Thane didn't move.

Not yet.

Then a breath caught in his chest—shallow and sudden.

Jane froze. Dr. Hughes leaned in fast, fingers back at Thane's neck, watching for rhythm. "That a boy," he said quietly.

Thane's eyelids twitched. A flicker of movement passed through his arms—subtle, disjointed, like a marionette tugged too loosely. His mouth opened slightly. Dry lips, cracked. Then came the whisper.

"Lirien…"

The room stilled.

Jane took a half-step forward. "What did he say?"

One of the paramedics glanced up. "Lirien?" she repeated, uncertain.

Jane frowned. "Who is that?"

No one answered. Just a mixture of shrugs and wayward glances.

Thane's eyes opened slowly, unfocused, rimmed in red.

They didn't lock on anyone in the room—just drifted past them, like he wasn't quite seeing them at all.

His gaze wandered to the edge of the room. Then to the chair in the corner.

For a second—only a second—he saw stone. Smooth, weather-worn, pale gray. Not a chair. Not even wood. A rock, carved with faint sigils.

Then it was gone.

His breath hitched. He blinked again, sharp this time, like something had snapped out of place. He glanced toward the other paramedic kneeling by his side—and for a split second, his face shifted. Jawline sharpened. Shadows fell differently. Not him.

Kaelir.

Then gone.

Thane sucked in air too fast and coughed, doubling over slightly. Dr. Hughes steadied him by the shoulder, checking his pupils again. "Thane. Look at me."

His eyes finally focused—barely. "Where…?"

"You're home," his mother said, kneeling beside him. She brushed the damp hair from his forehead. "You're home, baby. It's okay. Just breathe."

Thane looked at her briefly, but there was no recognition in his face. "I was there," he murmured. "But I wasn't. Not all the way."

"Thane." Dr. Hughes's voice was even but tense. "You had another seizure. A strong one. You were unconscious for several minutes. Do you remember what happened?"

"It was chaos," Thane murmured, eyes scanning the ceiling. "Everything spun out… I couldn't control it."

Jane's brow furrowed. Her gaze flicked to the headset still resting on the floor. "What spun out?" she asked softly. "In the game?"

Thane didn't answer. Or couldn't. His eyes drifted toward the ceiling again, unfocused.

Jane's arms folded tight across her chest.

"This can't keep happening," she said. Her voice was low, but strained. "This thing—this game—is tearing him apart."

Dr. Hughes kept his eyes on Thane, but his tone changed. "I'm not disagreeing anymore, Jane."

She snapped her gaze toward him. "I trusted you." Her voice cracked. "You told me it was safe."

Hughes nodded once—tired, restrained. "It wasn't a problem then," he said quietly. "But now…"

"Now he's—he's—" She couldn't finish it.

"Stable," Hughes said, not unkindly. "But barely. And if this keeps up—"

"I told you it wasn't safe," she said, barely above a whisper. It wasn't blame—just exhaustion.

The room went quiet. The paramedics shifted their eyes elsewhere.

Then a breath shuddered out of Thane—deep and clear. He lifted his head, shoulders rolling, and rubbed his eyes.

Something tingled in his fingertips. Not numbness. Not nerves. Something… residual. It buzzed faintly under his skin, like a current that hadn't fully bled off.

The haze peeled away, slow and jagged. The chaos of the henge gone.

The world had reassembled itself. No stone. No sky. Just drywall and wires and a ceiling that didn't breathe.

Not Arbelon.

Thane exhaled through his nose, sharp. His fingers curled slightly at the edge of the chair, and the static sensation faded. He didn't look at his mother, or Dr. Hughes, or the paramedics working beside him.

He was awake now. Really awake.

Thane shifted and tried to sit up straighter. A tremor ran through his limbs.

He winced.

His right leg didn't move.

He tried again—nothing.

Not numb. Not stiff. Just… gone. His breath caught, and he looked down like he expected to see it missing. But it was there. Limp. Uncooperative.

He cursed under his breath and dragged it closer using both hands. Dr. Hughes moved to help him, but Thane shook his head.

"I've got it. I'm fine," he snapped.

"You're not," Dr. Hughes said evenly.

Thane ignored him. The ceiling sharpened into focus —flat, colorless, humming with that same dead buzz. Everything here was pale. Artificial.

He swallowed hard. He knew exactly where he was. But it wasn't where he needed to be.

"I need to go back."

Jane leaned in. "Back where?"

He didn't look at her.

"Back to your game?" she asked, her voice incredulous.

Dr. Hughes stepped close, placing a hand on Jane's shoulder. She leaned into him without a word, turning her face into his coat. Her body trembled as she tried to stifle the sob.

He turned back to Thane and exhaled slowly, like he was organizing thoughts he didn't want to say aloud.

"Your right leg is showing signs of partial paralysis. It's early-stage motor degradation. Caused by failing neural pathways, Thane. It's progressing."

Jane flinched. She buried her head deeper against him, like hearing it again made it more real.

Thane looked away.

Hughes continued. "This seizure wasn't random. The damage is spreading."

"And the game?" she asked, lifting her head. Her voice was raw. "It's making this worse, isn't it?"

He nodded, grim. "Whatever that system is doing—visual input, sensory feedback—it's overloading his brain. It's pushing him toward these seizures. And they're accelerating the damage."

Jane wiped her face. "Then that's it. We shut it down."

"No," Thane snapped. "I'm going back."

"Thane—"

"I have to. They need me. The Heart is failing. I told them I'd fix it. I *promised* Lirien."

Dr. Hughes looked at him gently. "You promised someone who isn't real."

"You're wrong," Thane said, voice cutting. "She's more real than this."

Jane stepped back, hands to her face. Her voice broke. "Thane, listen to yourself."

"I am."

"No, you're chasing something that isn't there." Her voice grew louder, more desperate. "I feel like I'm losing you. You're fading in front of me and all you can think about is some—some *fantasy world* with glowing rocks and dream girls and fake magic."

"It's not fake."

"Well, it's not real!"

"It feels real to me."

She shook her head, tears slipping now, her voice cracking. "You're dying *here*. You're dying, and all you want is to die faster."

There was a heavy pause, enough for her words to land.

"It's not that, Mom," he said, quieter now. "I don't want to die. I just… I made a promise. And I can't walk away from it. That's all."

She grabbed his wrist—not hard, but with everything she had left. "If you go back… you might not come home again."

Thane looked at her. "I know."

His mother lowered her head and sat down on his bed, silent, spent.

Thane didn't look at her. He shifted uncomfortably in the chair, rubbing his thumb along the worn leather strap on his wrist. His father's watch—scratched, older than him. His mother had given it to him just days ago, without speaking the memory neither of them wanted to revisit.

He hadn't taken it off since.

In Arbelon, it had done more than tell time. It had pulsed, amplified, glowed like it was part of him.

He didn't understand why. Maybe it was the emotional charge—grief, memory, something the Heart could feel. Or maybe the fact that it was a timepiece meant something there, in a world that seemed to bend around meaning.

He didn't know. But it wasn't nothing.

Then something on its face caught his eye. The hands moved—the seconds ticked. But wrong.

Slower than they should. Lagging behind.

Tick… Tick… Tick…

He narrowed his eyes. For a moment, he thought it had stopped entirely—until another second crawled forward. The hands trembled, then stilled. His stomach turned.

No one else noticed. Only him.

Not the paramedics rechecking his blood pressure. Not Dr. Hughes, who was quietly consoling Jane on his bed. The lighting buzzed overhead, faint and steady, like the world was pretending nothing had happened.

But something had.

His eyes stayed on the watch, unblinking. A subtle static buzz prickled his fingers, the same residual current that had danced across his skin when he'd first stirred.

Time wasn't right.

Then the ceiling light flickered. Just once. Sharp and quick, like a power surge. The edges of the room rippled faintly, like water disturbed—then stilled.

No one else noticed. Only him.

The low, mechanical click of the VR headset interrupted his thoughts. It came from the floor beside the chair, where the headset had been left—unplugged. Powered down. Or at least it had been.

But the status light was glowing.

Faint. Blue. Pulsing.

Thane's breath caught. He looked at it, heart hammering. He glanced to the others. The paramedics kept talking. But, his mother—for a blink, his mother's shape blurred— her edges pixelated, smeared like a corrupted frame.

Then she was clear again, seated, unmoving.

His breath quickened.

No one else noticed. Only him.

The glow of the headset flickered again. Once. Then again.

And with it—like a voice caught on wind—he swore he heard her.

"Thane…"

It wasn't his mother. It wasn't anyone in the room.

"Thane… please…"

Lirien.

Her voice was barely audible. A whisper tangled in static and memory. But it was hers—he knew it. Even through the haze, even from another world, he knew.

The light blinked again. Soft. Waiting.

"Lirien?" Thane said again.

All heads turned to him.

Jane stood slowly. "There it is again," she whispered, glancing at Dr. Hughes. "He keeps saying that name."

She turned to Thane, voice tight. "Thane… who exactly is this Lirien?"

Thane didn't respond. His eyes stayed locked on the headset, still pulsing faintly.

Dr. Hughes stepped forward. "Is that someone from your game?"

The light on the headset flickered again, and the room's lights seemed to dip—just for a second.

Then Lirien's voice returned. Clearer this time.

"We need you, Thane… I need you…"

Thane flinched.

Jane saw it—the change in his eyes—and something in her finally snapped.

"Thane," she said, her voice shaking. "There's no one there. You understand that, right?"

He didn't answer.

Jane took a halting step toward him. "I know it feels real to you," she said, voice breaking. "I know it does. But Thane…" —she looked around the room like she was trying to make him see it—"this is your life. This is what's real. Me. The people who love you. Right here."

Thane met her eyes, and for a second, the mask dropped. "It's just you, Mom. You're the only one who still sees me."

Jane blinked, stunned by the words. Then she crossed the room and bent over him in the chair—not graceful, not easy. She wrapped her arms around his shoulders as best she could. Held him tight.

She drew a slow, fractured breath, her hands trembling as she held him. "You have no idea how much that hurts to hear," she said quietly. "But I'm here. I always will be."

Thane didn't move. But his eyes closed. Just for a second.

Then, slowly, he hugged her back.

She drew a slow, fractured breath, kneeling beside him. "I watched your father die, Thane. I sat in rooms just like this one, helpless, while he slipped away. Piece by piece. I held his hand when it went cold."

Thane's fingers twitched around the armrest.

"I didn't get to save him. I don't get to save you, either —not from this disease. But I'm trying to hold on to what I can, for as long as I can."

A silence fell across the room.

Then she whispered, "Please don't leave me. Not this way. Not now."

He held her gaze. And for the first time in a long time, his bitterness faltered. He saw the way she looked at him now—like she still believed there was something left to save. A truth he couldn't ignore.

"I'm not trying to leave you," he said. "But my hand is going to go cold too."

Her eyes welled again. "Then promise me…. promise me that you'll spend what time you have left with me."

He swallowed hard, leaning into her. "Okay."

"Say it," she pressed. "Promise me."

"I promise. I won't go back."

A long silence settled between them. Then she stood, moving slowly—like each step cost her something. She reached for the power cord at the base of the gaming rig, fingers pausing there for a moment before she pulled it free.

The faint light from the headset flickered once. Then died.

Thane's shoulders slumped. He didn't argue.

Jane held the cord in both hands, cradling it like something sacred. "I trust you, Thane," she said softly. "But I need to make sure."

He nodded, silent.

The room felt emptier now. As if a torch had just sparked its last flame.

And the last thing he saw before looking away was the headset on the floor, dark and lifeless.

Dr. Hughes stood and quietly motioned to the others. The paramedics packed their gear without a word. One gave Jane a quiet nod before stepping out into the hall.

Jane lingered. Her eyes hadn't left Thane in minutes.

"I'll help him get to bed," she said softly.

Thane shifted in the chair, grimacing as he tried to move. His right leg felt stiff—like it didn't belong to him anymore. He started to rise, but the leg buckled slightly.

Jane reached out instinctively, but he caught himself. His hand found the edge of the desk, then one of the bedposts. Slowly, awkwardly, he pulled himself upright.

"I've got it," he muttered.

He didn't. Not really. But he wouldn't let them carry him.

He limped toward the bed, half-dragging the leg, one hand gripping the edge of the dresser for balance. It wasn't graceful. But it was all him.

Jane watched without speaking. Dr. Hughes said nothing either.

He sank down onto the edge of the bed, exhaling sharply.

"Try to get some sleep," Dr. Hughes said quietly, already stepping toward the door. "I'll come back in the morning to check on you."

Jane hesitated in the doorway, the power cord cradled under her arm. "I'll be right down the hall."

Thane nodded, finally meeting her eyes. Just for a moment.

She left the door cracked open behind her. Then she was gone.

The quiet left behind was absolute.

Thane sat still, staring at nothing. His hands curled into the blanket, slow and tense. Then one shifted, almost unconsciously, to his wrist.

The watch.

He lifted it slightly into view. The face ticked. Still slow. Still wrong.

Tick… Tick… Tick…

He frowned. *Had it always been this slow? Or was it just another glitch—another fracture between here and there?*

He tapped the face once. Nothing changed.

Tick… Tick… Tick…

He sat in the stillness, and already the ache was setting in.

Not in his leg—but somewhere deeper. The weight of not playing, of not being there. Of being trapped here, in this room, without the only place he still felt alive.

He hated it.

And she had the power cord.

He rested his head against the headboard, exhaling deep and heavy. Just trying to push it all down—for a second, for a single breath. The bed creaked softly under him, and the house seemed to settle into itself. Outside, nothing moved. Inside was a dead end.

The headset still lay on the floor, coiled and lifeless.

His computer was powered down. Its glow was gone.

The silence wasn't peace—it was abandonment.

He finally let his eyes shut. Just for a moment. Long enough time for a voice to slip in from the dark.

"Thane…"

Soft. Familiar. A whisper he wanted to believe.

"Please, come back…"

Lirien.

He pushed himself up, blinking hard.

But this time, the voice didn't fade. It lingered, delicate and fragile, like it might break apart if he reached for it.

He closed his eyes tighter.

"The Heart needs you…"

Her voice trembled—whether with distance or desperation, he couldn't tell.

His hands curled into fists at his sides. Helpless. Whatever this was—this pull—it wasn't just Lirien. It was everything. The way the ground pulsed beneath his feet in Arbelon. The way magic crackled through his veins like a memory he didn't want to lose. The way they looked at him there—like he mattered. Like he was whole.

Even now, his fingers tingled faintly. Not numbness. Not the disease.

Magic. Still there. Still alive.

His heart raced, as his eyes flicked to the headset on the floor. It didn't glow. Didn't hum. Didn't move. But he swore he heard her. That she was calling to him. Somehow. From there to here.

"Thane…"

Lirien. Again. Fainter now. Then silence.

He stared into the silence she left behind—shaken, raw, gutted.

The promise to his mother echoed louder now than Lirien's voice ever had. He could still feel his Mom's arms around him, hear her begging, *Please don't leave me. Not this way. Not now.* And he'd said it. *I promise. I won't go back.*

He meant it. He *wanted* to mean it.

But deep down, even as he spoke, something inside him had already begun to split.

He saw himself from the outside—his face pale, jaw clenched, eyes dull with grief—as if watching someone else make a choice he couldn't stop. The weight of that choice settled behind his ribs and pressed hard. *Was this always how it was going to go?* One promise made. Another broken. Every path just looping back to loss.

His breath caught. He pressed his fists into the blanket, knuckles bone-white.

Tears surged—but he swallowed them. He had to. Because if he let go now, it wouldn't be tears. It would be everything.

He sat in that silence, heat rising behind his eyes, the scream rising with it—

and he buried it. Deep.

His chest tightened. Lirien was slipping away.

His mind raced. His eyes flicked to the headset… then to the tower beside it. Still dark. Still dead. Like a gate rusted shut to the only place he belonged.

But then he remembered.

Thane exhaled, slow and steady. He shifted his weight, dragging his leg around, muscles weak but willing.

He reached over the edge of the bed, fingers closing around the edge of the headset. He tossed it onto the desk, slowly pulling his leg across the floor until he sat in his chair again, taking a deep, earned breath.

Leaning down, he yanked a drawer open—and there it was.

An old power cord. From the dead tower he'd gutted months ago, thinking it might come in handy someday.

And now it would.

He fed the cord into the socket at the base of the rig.

The fans spun up—slow at first, then steadier. A faint hum rose from the tower, and the monitor blinked on with a cold flicker.

On the desk, the headset sat still.

Dark. Silent. Waiting.

Thane pulled it into his lap. The plastic was cool against his skin. His thumb brushed the power button.

He hesitated.

His thumb hovered, motionless. This was the line. He knew it.

Thane didn't move for a long time.

He sat with it, staring at the button. The decision weighing on him.

His mother's voice echoed somewhere in his mind. The hug. The promise.

"You have no idea how much that hurts to hear…"

He closed his eyes.

"I'm not trying to leave you…"

He didn't say it out loud. It just replayed in his mind. But he thought it clearly enough to feel it break inside him.

"I'm sorry, Mom," he said, barely a whisper.

Then he pressed it.

The light flickered once, and the Broken Circle logo awoke.

Blue. Subtle. Alive.

And he didn't look away.

FULL CIRCLE

THANE CAME to on his back, the world slow to knit together.

The sky above him swirled with pale gray clouds, stretched thin and static—too still. Ash danced in the air, the acrid bite of spent magic hanging over the stones. Light flickered at the edge of his vision, as if he were still catching up to the world around him. For a moment, he lay there, blinking, trying to place himself. Had it worked? Was he still—

"Thane." A voice. Close. Familiar. Urgent.

He turned his head and saw Lirien, kneeling beside him, her hand pressed lightly to his chest.

"Come on," she whispered. "You have to get up."

Different words, but the same voice he'd heard minutes ago—on Earth. The echo of it then, and now here, hit something raw.

She said it again. "Please, Thane. You have to get up."

His breath caught in his throat.

It wasn't just the voice that stunned him. It was also the fact that he could move. No pain. No tremor in his limbs. No dragging weight behind him. His leg just… worked.

He pushed to his feet, brushing dust from his palms. And his body responded instantly—*stronger, sharper, alive.* It was like waking from a nightmare into something electric.

A strange warmth stirred at the edge of his thoughts— not his own. Like breath against the inside of his skull.

"*Yes,*" came Echo's whisper.

"*Here, you are what you were meant to be.*"

Thane didn't respond—not aloud. But something inside him nodded.

He took in the henge.

It hadn't collapsed, but something had changed. The stones stood at strange angles now—like they'd shifted slightly to defend themselves. The glyphs etched along their surfaces glitched and shimmered, stuttering like a half-finished thought. The air pulsed faintly with tension, thick with the remnants of his magic.

He took a cautious step forward.

And the glyphs—jagged and erratic a moment ago— flared, then smoothed. The broken lines curved back into form, resolving one by one as the subtle warmth stirred beneath his skin. The magic in the stones recognized him. Or maybe it recognized what he carried.

He glanced at the watch. Its screen ticked smoothly now, no stutter, no lag. A faint pulse of light rippled across the surface, steady and slow—as if it were syncing with the henge itself.

"*That's right. It senses you. It knows you,*" Echo whispered.

A hum moved through the stones. The glyphs along the keystone pulsed faintly, faltering—then sparking to life again, slowly stabilizing.

"*You know what must be done,*" the voice breathed again, stronger now.

"Your path awaits."

As Thane moved closer to the keystone, it seemed to answer—the Broken Circle glyph resolving into place with a soft, steady glow. All signs of the chaos from moments ago, now gone.

A subtle charge danced across his skin. The watch on his wrist pulsed—once, twice—then began to glow steadily.

For some reason, it all made sense, like the Heart was speaking to him, guiding him.

Instinctively, he raised his hand and pressed it to the stone.

At his touch, the Broken Circle carved at the keystone's center flared white-hot — the jagged edges sliding together until the gap sealed with a flash of pure light. Light rippled outward from his touch, spiraling around the keystone. The glyphs ignited in sequence, climbing upward like a chain reaction.

Suddenly, the world snapped into perfect clarity. The glyphs spoke—not with sound, but with meaning. A language he couldn't name, but could *feel*. It wasn't under-standing—more like recognition. As if the words had been waiting for him, written long before he arrived.

"You were always meant for this moment," Echo murmured, silk-smooth and certain.

The glyphs flared white-hot, then inverted—glowing with a soft, unreal darkness. A rift of light blossomed outward from the keystone's center—not an explosion, but a controlled peeling away of the world, deliberate and seamless.

It formed a full circle, still at first. Then it began to swirl, slowly, pulling in sound and air. A low hum built beneath his feet, rising through his chest.

A soft pull rippled outward. Light swirled, slow and sure—until a shape resolved in the air. A window. A wound. A doorway into something green and luminous and impossibly beautiful.

The light from the portal spilled across the stones of the henge. Beyond it, the world opened into a realm unlike anything Thane had ever seen. Not a room, but a space without clear edge or boundary—vast, hushed, bathed in warm, golden light that seemed to come from everywhere and nowhere. Crystal-veined trees arched like cathedral spires toward a sky lost in a canopy that shrouded the skies. Silver leaves drifted through the air, slow and weightless, never touching the ground. Beneath them, a pale stone path threaded through the stillness, etched with glyphs that pulsed softly—like breath drawn slow and deep.

And at the center of it all, suspended above a shallow pool of luminescent water, was a shape—a womb of pulsing light. It was cradled in a web of branching energy that fed into the pool below and the roots of the crystalline trees beyond. Veins of light flowed outward from the orb like arteries, pulsing softly beneath the surface.

The entire realm seemed tethered to it—as if this glowing core were not just housed here, but sustaining everything around it. The power thrummed, alive yet fading—even in this place. Not broken, but breaking. Not dead, but dying.

"Step through," Echo whispered.

"Become what they feared you might be."

Thane exhaled. One breath. No hesitation.

He stepped into the light—vanishing as the portal swallowed him whole.

One by one, the others followed him through. The portal flared with each arrival—Lirien first, then Erynn, Kaelir, and Cael—until the swirl of light finally stilled behind them.

They stood in silence at the edge of the path, the soft

pulses of the glyphs beneath their feet echoing like distant heartbeats. The stillness pressed in—not oppressive, but expectant, as if the place itself had noticed them.

Kaelir stepped forward, eyes wide, his voice barely above a whisper. "What is this place?"

"Something old," Cael said beside him, gaze fixed on the glowing shape ahead. "Older than even the records."

Lirien moved to Thane's side, her expression unreadable, but her presence grounding. She didn't speak. She didn't need to.

They followed the pale stone path, the trees around them swaying in a breeze that didn't touch their skin. As they drew closer to the orb, its shape began to shift—*not physically*, but in the way they *perceived* it. The steady glow flickered. The web of light that cradled it now sparked unevenly, like a failing pulse. Faint cracks spidered along the surface of the orb, their edges rimmed with shadow.

Erynn slowed, her breath catching. "It's not just a source," she said. "It's… suffering."

Her words echoed like a bell rung in a cathedral of silence.

She stepped forward again, faster this time, her focus narrowing. "Aelith was right. This is where it begins. This is where the Heart is to be healed."

Cael looked at her sharply but said nothing. The shadows under his eyes seemed deeper here.

The Heart's glow deepened, dimmed, then flared again —faint, rhythmic, failing.

Lirien touched Thane's arm lightly, her voice low. "For Arbelon."

He nodded.

The magic was pulling at him now. Not violently, but steadily. Like the whole realm was reaching toward him— not asking, not demanding, just *needing*.

Thane took a slow step forward, eyes locked on the flickering core.

"What now?" he murmured. "How do I do it?"

Lirien stepped closer. Her voice was soft, but certain. "Let me show you."

She raised a hand toward his face. He flinched—just slightly—but she didn't pull back.

"Trust me," she said.

He did.

Her fingertips brushed the shallow cut along his cheekbone—the one he'd gotten from the Rider's blade back at the gates of Salile. The touch was warm, and brighter than it should've been. A shimmer passed between them, subtle and golden, and the pain was gone.

Thane blinked. He hadn't even realized it was still hurting.

Lirien met his gaze. "Did you feel that?"

He nodded.

"That's what the Heart needs," she said. "Not control. Not force. Healing."

Healing. He wasn't sure he knew how to do that. But something inside him stirred—like the answer was already waiting.

He stepped forward, drawing in a breath that didn't quite fill his lungs. The pull of the realm was stronger now—threaded into his ribs, his bones. The magic here wasn't wild, not like before. It was patient. Wounded. Waiting.

He extended his hand toward the Heart, its form as tall as he was—close, pulsing, waiting.

The glow throbbed faintly in response, as if it recognized him.

He closed his eyes, reaching inward—not with force, but with the memory of what Lirien had shown him. The warmth of her magic. The quiet way it had worked. Not pushing. Just… offering.

Healing, she'd said.

He opened himself, cautiously, and let the magic come.

At first, it worked. A thread of light slipped from his palm, slow and golden. It reached toward the web of energy around the orb and touched it gently—like a whisper against silk.

The glow flared. The cracked lines along the orb's surface pulsed—then dulled. For a moment, he thought it was working.

Then something shifted.

The thread of light thickened. Uncoiled. Brightened into something hotter, more erratic.

Thane's chest tightened. He tried to pull back, to close himself off—but it was too late.

The magic poured out of him, wild and white-hot, no longer golden. The connection had deepened, locked, and now it was *taking* from him. Channeling more than he meant to give.

The watch on his wrist pulsed violently, its face flooding with fractured light—bright, amber, stuttering—as if it were overloading, trying to contain something far too large.

The Heart shuddered. The veins of light feeding the trees began to flicker, then spike. Glyphs along the path stuttered and rewrote themselves in bursts of radiant distortion.

"Thane," Lirien said sharply, but her voice sounded far away.

He tried to let go.

Tried to stop.

But the magic wasn't just flowing out of him—it was reaching into him, tunneling deeper, cracking something loose.

His breath hitched. His vision blurred.

And the Heart—*the womb of light*—began to break.

Hairline fractures webbed across its surface, glowing white at first—then black. Not the absence of light, but light devoured. The hum turned to a whine, sharp and low, crawling through the ground beneath their feet.

The web of energy around the Heart shivered—fighting to hold it together. As the fractures deepened, something began to take shape inside the orb—a silhouette, curled in place, limbs drawn in tight. Not a child. Not an unborn thing. A full-grown figure, suspended within the pulsing core like a body in dreamless sleep.

Then the shape began to unravel—something dark spilling from it like smoke, slow and sinuous, bleeding free of the light. Not cast by the light, but *dragging free* of it—slow and deliberate, thick with the weight of something *once attached*. Something *once whole*.

The light flared behind it, as if trying to pull it back. But even as the shadow spilled free, another figure remained—still curled within the Heart, unmoving, untouched. One left behind. One bleeding out.

The shadow took form and stood tall, still half-bound to the orb, strands of pale energy snapping like cords. It was almost human—broad-shouldered, fluid, unfinished. No eyes. No mouth. Just a presence. The shadow now made flesh.

It turned its faceless head toward Thane.

And it spoke—rising above the fray.

"Foolish boy. Trading the love of a single girl for the fate of a land."

Thane staggered back as the words struck.

He remembered. The sanctum, the shadow—the promise. The voice whispering in the dark. The bargain he'd made.

He'd promised to heal the Heart—to never return.

It all came full circle.

His magic surged again, uncontrolled. The connection between him and the Heart deepened, becoming a tether —and the orb, already cracking, began to splinter.

The watch on his wrist pulsed violently, light fracturing across its face—white, then red, then violet. The casing cracked with a sharp pop, and then it went dark, dead weight against his skin.

Thane cried out, staggered—but the magic didn't stop.

"Thane!" Cael's voice now. Sharp. Desperate. "You have to let go!"

But he couldn't.

The magic had hold of him much more than he had hold of it.

Cael turned toward the Heart, eyes wide. He saw it— saw the fractures deepening, the veins of power unraveling —and within it, the figure still bound in light, breaking with it.

And then he ran.

"No!" Erynn cried, reaching for him.

But Cael was already moving—throwing himself between Thane and the Heart. His body collided with the beam of wild magic, and for a heartbeat, the world froze.

Then Cael let go.

His own magic—calm, ancient, rooted—exploded outward from his chest. A surge of white-gold light, not violent, but purposeful, *healing.* It surged into the Heart like a final breath.

The pulse hit like a shockwave, flooding everything with blinding light.

And in that final flare—right before everything went white—Thane saw into the Heart.

A shape. A face. Familiar. Impossible.

His father's.

Suspended in light, staring back at him.

A rush of silence collapsed in his ears. Blood ran from his nose. His knees buckled.

And then he fell.

What followed was soundless.

He saw them, only in fragments.

Erynn kneeling beside Cael's still form, his chest charred, mouth frozen in a silent scream.

Kaelir standing still, face unreadable, sword drawn but useless.

The Heart pulsed faintly in the distance—dim, fractured, *barely holding.*

The shadow—Echo—whatever it was. Simply gone. Vanished.

And Lirien kneeled by Thane, hand on his chest, eyes closed.

Then—darkness.

ENJOYED NO EXTRA LIVES?

Thanks for joining Thane and his crew on their psychedelic journey to heal the Heart. If you enjoyed the book, a review would be much appreciated as it helps other readers discover the story.

Looking for more writing from me? Please visit my substack, *detect magic*—there you can subscribe, keep tabs on what I'm writing, and read other stories I've published. Let me know what you think and join the community in the comments.

Visit, read and subscribe at:
https://danblakely.substack.com/

And there's more good news! Thane and the gang are back at it in *The Final Save*, book two in the *Broken Circle* duology.

Still hungry for more magic? Check out my other series, beginning with *The Last Gambler*—a fantasy adventure where a cursed magical dice can grant wishes with a simple roll.

Books by Dan Blakely

The Fall of Fate Duology
- The Last Gambler
- Pieces of Eight

The Broken Circle Duology
- No Extra Lives
- The Final Save

ABOUT THE AUTHOR

My journey started in a sleepy Midwestern town in the summer of 1971, pretty much at the dawn of all that was to be awesome in the world. I still remember watching Star Wars erupt on the world and the late nights playing D&D. Like a gaggle of other kids, that's where my love for fantasy stories took root. I grew up on Tolkien and Donaldson and Moorcock and Herbert and more. Sure, I played soccer and hung out with friends, but I was always looking for fantasy stories to devour. It didn't matter if it was a book, comic, movie, magazine or video game (even Zork!). The endless worlds and stories the human mind can imagine remain irresistible. There's nothing quite like strolling through a freshly created world—simply magical.

Before landing in California, I bounced around from coast to coast. Along the way, my love for fantasy never left. I've always kept journals and notes of ideas. Over the past few years, I've been weaving stories using those ideas to create worlds and the people living in them. I want to introduce you to people and worlds that inspire you, perhaps even surprise you. Hopefully, after meeting them and living in their worlds, you'll long for more, always wondering what happens next. Maybe their stories will even change you along the way. Oh, and of course, a little magic in a story is always a good thing.

Since this is my first book, I don't have a list of other books to direct you to. But if you're interested in reading more from me, please visit me at:

www.DanBlakely.com
https://danblakely.substack.com/

And again, if you loved this book and have a moment to spare, I would really appreciate a short review on the page where you bought the book. Your help in spreading the word is gratefully appreciated and reviews make a huge difference to help new readers find their way here.

The last thing that I would ask is whether you could find one person in your life to recommend this book to—referrals are the lifeblood of stories and I be honored if I've earned that from you with this story.

Thank You!

—

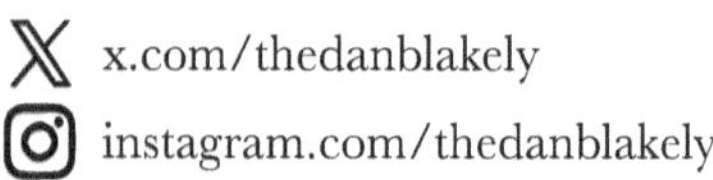

ACKNOWLEDGMENTS

Thanks to my family, friends, and *detect magic* readers. It truly does take a village publish a book after that initial draft. It's been a long process for my first book, but with help of my village we finally made it to the finish line.

I also want to thank you for taking a chance on a new writer and picking up this book. Without you, I'd just be writing into the void. You're the reason why I scratch those words onto paper.